# BIG NICK ENERGY

## MORGAN ELIZABETH

*To everyone who thought the fluffy Hallmark Christmas movies should be a bit dirtier.*

*Merry Christmas, ya filthy animals.*

# FOREWORD

Hello, my friends!

Here we are again, another new book and another chance for me to chat with you all.

Last year, I wrote what quickly became my most popular book, *Tis the Season for Revenge*, and you all gave it *so much love*. I am forever grateful for that. My due date was Christmas and while I was born just before, I think that kind of cemented my love for the holidays and Christmas cheer. You could say I'm more of a Nick than a Shae.

I had the idea of writing this book back in November, when I was down with the flu. As many parents do as soon as Thanksgiving has passed, I was cursing the decision to bring the elf into my house and somehow, my mind went to the idea of a man coming to help a single mom make some holiday magic during Christmas time.

Of course, we're all in our cowboy romance era and I'm *always* in my Taylor era, so what better way to combine them together and make our MMC own a *Christmas tree farm!* The joy! The magic! The ropes!

I would like to note that this book is basically a Hallmark movie with spice. Minimal angst and drama, lots of Christmas cheer. Some-times, you just want something warm and cozy and fluffy (and spicy, don't you worry) this time of year, and I hope you love Nick and Shae and the girls just as much as I do!

A few notes: This book stars Shae, who is the woman (Sharon) leaving an abusive relationship in *Tis the Season for Revenge*. There is conversation about living in a physically and verbally abusive rela-tionship in this story, as it's part of Shae's story. There is no on page abuse.

Remember to always put yourself and your mental health first. Reading is meant to be our happy place.

Other things of note in this book—as always, you'll find sexually explicit content and lots of curse words. One of the spicy scenes includes rope play, but please, please do not use this as a manual. It's meant for inspiration, not instruction.

I love you to the moon and to Saturn.

-Morgan Elizabeth

# NICK

## APRIL

"I'm going on a date tonight," Connor says into the phone. It's propped on my ear as I move along the house, finding and then tugging my boots on. It seems the vet I hired was right when they said Mickey was gonna go into labor soon—I just didn't expect it to be the very same day.

"Yeah? Anyone I know?"

The perk of having your son when you were barely 18 and way too stupid to know better is that we are as close as can be a full 24 years later.

"Nah. Some MILF on Tinder that—"

"Wow, wow, wow, back the fuck up," I say, standing straight and holding the phone to my ear, one boot on and the other halfway there. I have a foal to deliver, but if this is how my son is walking around speaking, said boot is about to be halfway up his ass.

"Chill, Dad, she is a MILF. You gotta see her." I shake my head and stare at the ceiling of my ranch, my home on the Christmas tree farm I worked at for fifteen years before being given the opportunity to purchase it from Old Man Samuels.

"We don't fuckin' talk about women that way, Connor."

"Dad, I—" I cut him off, more information clicking and ratcheting up my irritation with him.

"And what the fuck are you doing going on a date with a woman with fucking kids when you're still one yourself?" I love Connor more than anything on this earth, but he's a bachelor climbing the corporate ladder in New York City. He does not have the fortitude for a woman with *children*.

"I'm not a kid, Dad. I—"

"You bring your laundry to my place every week."

"Because it's too fuckin' expensive in the city to get it done and I don't feel like sitting at a laundromat!"

"And you go on *boys' trips* every other month."

"I can't enjoy myself and date a woman with kids?"

"A woman with kids is more responsibility than you're ready for, Connor. Trust me." He groans like he's regretting calling me, but I know he's taking my words to heart, that I've worked enough to build trust and respect between us that he won't just brush me off. He's a good kid, even if he's apparently about to cross *date a MILF* off some bucket list of his.

"I'm just going on a date!" I finish pulling my boot on and grab a jacket, even though I'm sure within ten minutes, it'll be off in the corner of the barn.

"If I hear you called her a fuckin' MILF, I'm coming there and shoving my boot up your ass."

Silence fills the line, and I take it as a testament to my parenting that even at 24, a threat of that magnitude has him pausing.

"I was just being funny. Of course, I wouldn't say that in front of her," he says, his words low like they used to be when he would defend his dumber actions as a kid.

"Jokes like that become a fuck of a lot less funny when they slip out." I head for the front door, making sure I have my keys on my belt loop.

"God, I was calling to chat, not for a lecture."

"Gotta lecture you at least once a month or they rescind my

license," I say, reaching the coat rack where my worn, dark-brown, almost black hat hangs on one of the pegs.

"Your license?" he asks, confused.

"Dad license. Then I can't tell dad jokes or tuck my tee shirt into jeans for a full six months."

"Maybe they *should* rescind it," he says under his breath. I laugh, placing the cowboy hat on my head.

"Fuck off. Go on your date, let me know how it was after. Gotta go help Mickey have her baby." Then, I'm turning the phone off and walking out the door.

# ONE

## 35 SLEEPS UNTIL CHRISTMAS

### SHAE

It's three days before Thanksgiving and the world is falling apart around me, which unfortunately means I don't have my head on straight enough to lie to my ex when he asks about my Thanksgiving plans.

Okay, okay, so I dated him *one time* before we decided *just friends* would be best, but still.

I met Connor Finch a month after the divorce was finalized, days after my friend Abbie forced a phone into my hands and said, *Swipe on all the hot ones.*

She'd made me a dating profile.

"I'm not ready for that, Abbie," I told her with all the kindness I could muster. She pouted, and I couldn't help it—I laughed at her. "I appreciate you, but no."

"I know you're not ready to find your *forever*, but at the very least, you need a rebound, Shae," she told me, her voice clearly insinuating I was an idiot and she was the one who knew all of the secrets of the universe, including *getting back on the horse, post-divorce.*

Back then, her use of my name still made me smile, still brought a flutter of hope into my chest for a fresh start and a bright future, just me and my girls.

Ditching the full version of my name and moving back to the name everyone called me when I was in high school, before I met Todd, was my first step in reinventing myself after the divorce. When I finally got the nerve to leave, I realized I didn't recognize myself anymore. I decided with this new lease on life, I could be whoever I wanted to be.

I landed on Shae, a name that has always felt comfortable, familiar. My early college years were probably the last time I felt like me, like the independent, spunky, optimistic version of myself. Bringing it back felt like the right decision, the best way to try and emulate the way I was before I met Todd, even if I'm not quite back to spunky and optimistic just yet.

Unfortunately, online dating did not feel like "me," the new *or* the old version, so I had been avoiding it like the plague.

"Abbie . . ."

"No, come on. It'll be fun! I want you to swipe on the ones who are so totally not your type. The young, hot guys." I rolled my eyes at her and sighed.

"Young, hot guys don't want an old, washed-up mom of two." I wasn't being self-deprecating when I said it—I was being realistic. At 35, freshly divorced and with enough baggage to sink the *Titanic*, I was far from the ideal match for a hot, young 24-year-old.

"First off, shut up. Second off. You're a MILF. Young guys *love* MILFS. And we're not looking for a perfect match. We're looking for someone to fuck and move on. A young dude just looking to get off is way less likely to fall in love with you. You don't need people falling in love with you right now." I laughed at her, at the idea of *anyone* falling in love with me right now, and continued to fight, but this was *Abbie* I was arguing with.

A few more fruitless arguments and a glass of wine led me to a dinner with Connor Finch a week later. My hopes weren't high, but as I was getting ready, the excitement of the potential of a first date filling my veins, I saw she was right. It was time. While Todd left us with baggage and fears, I couldn't let him completely strip me of the joy of dating and the hope of falling in love again.

At least, not *completely.*

And it was an amazing first date, if not in the expected way. Instead of a boyfriend, or, as Abbie intended, a boy *toy,* I found a friend. By the end of the meal, we were laughing so hard, I had to wipe tears out of my eyes and we were planning a trip to the zoo with the girls. We both had come to the same conclusion: there was no way us actually *dating* would work.

Instead, we now talk a few times a month, him coming for dinner or taking the girls and me out for a day occasionally, but nothing more. Somehow, this man almost ten years younger than I am has become one of my closest friends.

"Shae?" he asks, interrupting my thoughts.

"Sorry, my head's in the clouds. What did you say?"

"I asked what you and the girls are doing for Thanksgiving?"

I should have seen this coming, considering he's always so worried about us, but I'm so lost in everything, I don't even think before answering.

A few days ago, I came home to find a note from the owners of the townhouse I rent, telling me they are retiring in February and the sale of the building will be completed on January 31st. Unfortunately for me, the new owners aren't interested in renting and plan to fully renovate the place before living here themselves, so I'll have to find new accommodations within the next two months.

There was also yet *another* passive aggressive email in my inbox from the PTO mom at the *stupid* prestigious school my girls go to asking about the holiday party and if I think I'll be able to help out. For whatever reason, that woman has hated me more and more each passing day and even wrote, *we understand more traditional families have more wiggle room in our schedules than you do,* in her email, even though she is *also* a single mom who just happens to be dating some rich asshole who can somehow tolerate her.

And of course, the holidays are looming, the first Christmas since the divorce, and all I want to do is give my girls *everything* and *anything* their little hearts desire to quell the churning, unending mom guilt I feel every minute of every day. Unfortunately, my oldest daughter wants a whole ass *horse* this year, as if we live on a farm instead of in a two-bedroom townhouse in Hudson City. I blame Connor, who loves to tell her about how he grew up on a fucking idyllic *Christmas tree farm* with *horses* and *chickens* and *goats* and so much Christmas magic, his father has a direct line to Santa himself. As if that wasn't enough, my youngest has gotten it in her head that the only gift *she'll* be happy to see under the tree is a *kitten,* as if I'm not struggling to keep the two of them alive enough as it is.

What is it with kids wanting live animals for holidays? What happened to Barbie Dreamhouses and Easy Bake Ovens?

And, of course, the cherry on top of it all, I just got my *fucking* period today.

I would very much enjoy if the universe stopped attacking me, thank you *so* much.

All that to say, I don't make up a fancy lie when I answer Connor's question.

Instead, I commit the egregious act of telling the truth.

"Nothing," I say. "It's the first Thanksgiving since everything went down and I'm just keeping it low-key, you know?"

Last Thanksgiving, I was in protective custody, Damien Martinez working his magic to get me full custody of my daughters, Ruby and Harper.

This year, the girls and I are on our own and happier than ever.

If not a little overwhelmed.

"You're not doing anything?" he asks incredulously, and I sigh.

"I have enough on my plate right now," I say. My fingers touch the handwritten note from my landlord once more.

I've done a bit of searching around, but everything big enough for all three of us is way too expensive or *way* too sketchy. Of course, I could use the alimony and savings I got from Todd, but after using what was needed to settle us, I've refused to touch that money.

It's tainted from that man, from years of letting him push me around, years of abuse. It's all collecting a nice interest for the girls to get when they're of age, to use for college or a home or to spend frivolously—I don't care.

I just don't want it, don't want his poisonous touch on my new life. I don't want my new chapter to be even *slightly* dependent on him. I could, of course, talk to Damien and Abbie about it. He would absolutely either increase my salary at the nonprofit he founded and I work for or offer me a loan or, god, he'd probably buy me a place . . . but they've already been so unbearably generous.

I don't need to feel more indebted to him.

"Come to my dad's ranch for Thanksgiving." Full stop in my head because *what?*

"A ranch?"

"Yeah, he's got a bunch of horses the girls could pet. They'd have a blast."

"I thought you grew up on a Christmas tree farm?" I ask, balancing my phone between my ear and shoulder as I sort through the mail that's piling on my kitchen counter.

Bill, bill, bill, school paper, Ruby's Christmas list with *HORSE!* in bold and caps, an invitation to the 4th grade father-daughter dance that makes me nauseous . . .

"I did, but it's a lot of land. The main house is on the other side of the property near the stables."

"Jesus, Connor, I thought you grew up with a single dad. When you said he had a horse, I didn't know you meant a *ranch*," I say. It's one of the ways he convinced me to let him help me at any given moment—he understood what it was like to raise kids by yourself when life didn't go the way you planned. I always thought one day, I'd meet Connor's father and thank him for raising such a kind, thoughtful son and maybe ask how he accomplished it by himself.

Did he also worry every moment of every day that he was fucking him up beyond repair, or is that something only the *really* lucky ones get?

Connor laughs. "I did. My dad started working there for room and board and childcare when I was born, but he worked his way up and bought the place a while ago. It's a tree farm, but there's stables and boarding on the other side of the property."

*Thanksgiving at a stranger's ranch as the pity invite actually sounds terrible.* "I don't know, Connor. Wouldn't that be weird? No one knows the girls or me."

"It's a Thanksgiving of misfits. Some friends of mine with no family nearby, a handful of employees, my aunt. None of it makes sense, but we make a family of our own, you know?"

*A family of our own.*

It actually sounds nice.

Thanksgiving with Todd was always an ordeal, his entire family coming to our place and me spending the entire week in the kitchen, preparing. Of course, there was *always* something Todd found to complain about no matter how hard I tried. Not to mention, it was always clear to me why he was the way he was, my mother-in-law also loving the sport of finding flaws and making me feel small.

Last year, the girls and I had frozen chicken tenders, French fries, and a boxed cake mix they made mostly independently, leaving the kitchen a total mess when they were done.

It was the best Thanksgiving I'd had in well over a decade.

But I would be lying if I said the guilt didn't creep in, that I didn't feel bad about not giving them the big, crazy family experience I always craved as an only child to introverted parents, the kind my friends always talked about fondly or that were showcased in television and movies as both chaotic and loving and fulfilling.

"Where is it?" I ask, and I know he can sense my hesitation cracking away, my excuses crumbling.

"Cherrystone. About an hour west of Hudson City." I could do an hour . . . "Come on. The girls will love it. Ruby can pet the horses. There's a few barn cats and some goats Harper will *love*." There's a smile in his voice because he knows it's the nail in the coffin to get me to agree—*my girls*.

Ruby, my 9-year-old, would go absolutely feral at the idea of being able to pet a horse. Harper would just be happy to be around new people she can impress with her adorable charm and smile, but add in chasing around a cat and she might just implode.

I sigh.

And before I can talk myself out of it, I ask, "Okay. What time and what can I bring?"

# TWO

## NINE MONTHS PRIOR

### NICK

"How'd your date go?" I ask two days after Minnie, Mickey's foal, was born. I've spent that entire time split between checking in on the mother and babe and planting saplings around the farm, trees that won't be ready for another eight years but, in order to keep the farm going, have to go in the ground now.

I'm *exhausted*.

The good kind where you feel like you accomplished something, but exhausted all the same.

"Good. She's cool." My brows furrow at his words.

"Cool? Doesn't sound like a good date."

Connor laughs, and it sounds so much like my own.

"Yeah, it wasn't a love match, but I like her. I'm meeting up with her again next week."

"So, you're dating the MILF?" I ask.

"I thought I wasn't allowed to do that?"

"You're not." Silence fills the line before we both laugh, and then Connor explains.

"It's not a date. Just friends. I like her, she's cool, but she's not my type." There's a long pause before I can hear the smile in his words.

"She's actually your type." I shake my head even though he can't see it. For as long as I can remember, from the moment he realized his dad didn't have a *someone* like everyone else, he's been trying to find me one.

"I don't gotta type these days, bud."

"Everyone's got a type."

I don't tell him I've been too busy trying to keep up with the growth of the farm, I haven't gone on a date, much less needed a *type*, in nearly two years.

"What do you think my type is?" I ask with curiosity.

"Hot. Older—"

"Jesus Christ, Connor, do I have to have a talk with you every single time you get on the phone with me?" I rub at my temple with one hand, closing my eyes and wondering why the world felt fit to give me a younger version of myself to raise to be a decent human being.

"No, I meant like, not super young, hasn't lived life kinda thing. You're not into the age gap, no history shit."

Fair. That's fair. I couldn't date someone Connor's age or anything.

When he realizes I won't be arguing, he continues, "She's blonde. Has two girls. Divorced, has her shit figured out, though. She's super independent."

"Huh. Seems you know me a bit better than I thought," I say.

"You're my dad. Of course, I do."

# THREE

## 32 SLEEPS UNTIL CHRISTMAS

### SHAE

My phone rings with a number I don't recognize. I *should* ignore it.

It's my personal cell, not a work number or anything like that, and I only give it out to people I know and trust. But today, we are going to Thanksgiving dinner at a relative stranger's house, and my mind starts to jump through hoops, anxiety making me think of all the reasons an unknown number could be calling me.

Maybe it's Abbie calling from her sister's house with some issue.

Maybe it's a work emergency that I need to handle before I can enjoy the day.

Maybe it's Connor at his father's house, telling me Thanksgiving is canceled.

Maybe it's the school calling with bad news, even though I have all of their numbers saved and it's *Thanksgiving morning.*

The answers twist and twist in my mind, barbed-wire edges scraping along the thin wall between my nerves and my peace of mind until I say fuck it and answer the call.

I regret it near instantly.

"Hello?"

"Sharon." The voice is clipped and irritated.

*Todd.*

My ex-husband, who I've successfully avoided for almost a year, is calling me.

I definitely haven't spoken to him outside of the presence of lawyers, despite his occasional attempts to reach out.

Once, he sent a letter, telling me he needed to speak with me about something.

Another time, he sent a note home from school, using the principal he was once golfing buddies with to give it to my oldest daughter.

But sometime around spring, he stopped altogether, like he lost interest in me, in us, and decided to move to greener pastures. I was relieved, and as of the last few months, I had dropped my habit of looking over my shoulder at any given moment, of waiting for the other shoe Todd was holding to drop.

And now he's calling me, proving I never should have done that. That my suffocatingly tight hold on control of every aspect of my life is *right*.

Because he's calling me from a number I don't recognize, on Thanksgiving morning, completely out of the blue, while my girls are watching the parade in the living room, oblivious to my panic.

"Todd," I say, but my voice doesn't sound like mine, not really. It sounds like when you listen to a recording of yourself back and you don't recognize it.

Because suddenly, I sound like the old me. The version I've worked tirelessly for the past year to pack away, to overcome. A single word from this man and I'm back to being her, feeling scared in my corner, afraid to say the wrong word and set him off.

"Happy Thanksgiving," he says casually.

*Happy Thanksgiving*, like he's an uncle who calls on holidays instead of the man I spent twelve years with. Instead of the man who did everything in his power to tear me down, to make me pliable and controllable and whatever he thought I needed to be.

Unfortunately for him, I'm not that person anymore. Even if his voice reminds me of who I used to be, taking a deep breath and looking around this townhouse reminds me of the life I built without him, of the version of me he'll never get the fortune of meeting.

I dig beneath the shock to grasp back onto the strength I've found, to the power I've taken back.

"What do you want?" I ask. He sighs like I'm an unruly child he finds inconvenient.

"Why do you have to be like that, Sharon?"

"Well, maybe it's because I haven't spoken to you in a year. Maybe because we're divorced and you have no tie to my life anymore, as per a *court order*. Maybe because I left you after you hit me hard enough to give me a black eye after years of hitting me emotionally. I think under those circumstances, anyone would be confused as to why you're reaching out." Barely a moment passes before he speaks again, that inconvenienced tone turning into annoyance.

"God, you're so dramatic, Sharon."

I want to respond.

I want to show him the venom the new version of me has, but he doesn't even deserve that. He doesn't deserve to get to know the new me, doesn't get to meet her. And he doesn't deserve the entertainment of riling me, which is what he so clearly loves. Lots of therapy has taught me that, and it also taught me that giving into his taunts means he *wins*.

"Yes, I am. Now, what do you want, Todd? I'm busy." In the pit of my stomach, a tiny glow of pride blooms.

"I want to see the girls," he says. The words are simple, but they shake me. The world stops turning for a moment as they ricochet around in my brain and I try to understand what they mean.

The breath doesn't move in my lungs.

The blood in my veins goes cold.

I go lightheaded.

*I want to see the girls* echoes, and I need to move to sit on the edge of my bed so I don't fall.

Once my brain starts to work again, I shake my head even though he can't see it. "No." I fight to make the word firm, to make it not shake, to make it so he doesn't know his words impact me at all.

"They're my daughters, Shae."

"By blood alone. Legally, they're mine. Legally, you don't even have the right to call me. Legally, you hold no ties to us anymore." The ice in my veins is melting, turning to lava and venom that twists and winds into my words, anger that he would even *dare* to ask bubbling there.

"Except for the fucking money I pay every month, keeping you living nice and cushy. I'm over here, giving you *everything* to keep you from having to work, and I don't even get to talk to the girls. You get to spin some bullshit stories, the girls go to school and act like you're the only parent, and I'm the chump paying for it."

*There it is.*

He's calling because of the money.

The money I don't use—refuse to use, in fact—instead letting it accrue interest for the girls' future.

My mind sifts through his words and the potential explanations as I try to understand the purpose of this call, fighting not to give him the emotional response he wants from me and instead moving with logic.

"Why are you calling, Todd?"

"It's Thanksgiving. I want to talk to the girls. To see the girls. It's a family day." I give him a laugh devoid of humor.

"Todd, we both know you're not calling because it's Thanksgiving or because of the girls. At the very least, give me the courtesy of not treating me like I'm an idiot."

He pauses, probably unsure as to why I'm *deigning* to talk back to him when our entire relationship, I never dared. For twelve years, when Todd Miller said jump, I asked how high and if he'd like chocolate chip or snickerdoodle cookies when I landed.

But I'm not her anymore.

"It's a family holiday—" he starts.

"Bullshit. What's the reason? Was it because you thought I would be softer today? That some kind of nostalgia would take over and I'd be malleable? Listen to your bullshit? Because I'm happy to tell you, the holidays this year hold a much different connotation than in the past. The memories I have of Thanksgiving are not family bonding and togetherness. They're now of my first holiday season without you. When I think of Thanksgiving now, I think of sitting in a hotel room hiding away from you with a black eye, eating fast food but still happier than I ever fucking was. *Freer* than I ever was. Safer"

He doesn't respond, but I don't either, letting that truth ring through the line.

*Safer.*

Finally, he speaks his own truth, seemingly deciding beating around the bush isn't working.

"I want to renegotiate," he says, and the words are heavy weights, each syllable dragging me down.

*I want to renegotiate.*

"What does that mean?" I say, trying to sound offhanded, like those four words, the intention behind them, doesn't terrify me.

"I'm getting remarried." *Jesus fucking Christ.* "And in this new life, I don't want to be paying you so much. If I have visitation with the girls, the number lowers."

Oh my fucking god.

The fact that he isn't bothering to hide his true intentions, isn't *bothering* to tell me he wants to spend more time with the girls, that he misses them, tells me exactly how much he hasn't changed.

And he's getting remarried less than a year after our divorce.

Voices whisper, asking questions whose answers don't even matter. Was he dating while we were married? Does she know about his daughters? What did he tell her about our divorce? Was I painted as the bad guy? Am I the villain in their story?

"Sharon? You there?" he asks, sounding annoyed.

As if he has *any place* to be annoyed.

"No," I say, my voice firm despite the tremble I feel all over.

"No, you're not there?"

"No, I'm not renegotiating because you're getting remarried. You should have thought of that before you abused your wife." My words are clipped, and if I wasn't panicking, I'd feel proud.

"Jesus, this shit again. I—" I stand, walking to the mirror to look at myself as he rambles on about how that was all a big misunderstanding, how I manipulated the courts to get what I wanted. I look at the new me and smile.

My hair is shorter now, messy blonde waves that stop at my shoulders, and I wear less makeup, no longer trying to compete with the wives of his friends, the women he'd compare me to when we were alone. I have more curves now, my hips wider, my breasts fuller. My face looks healthier, despite the ever-present exhaustion in my eyes, but I'm okay with that.

I'll take exhaustion deep in my bones if it means I get to live my life safely, where I don't need to worry about my girls. A life where I'm in control and we're *free*.

Finally, I cut him off, my shoulders back, my face fierce in the mirror as I do.

"Does she know?" I ask, and the line goes silent. "Does your new girl know you hit your wife, that you had a restraining order?" In this moment, I'm regretting saying *no* when Damien asked if I wanted to fight to make the temporary order permanent. "That you lost any scrap of custody of your daughters because I had years of proof of you being emotionally and verbally abusive? Does she know you even *have* daughters?"

"God, you're such a fucking bi—"

I don't hear the rest of the words because Ruby walks in.

"Mommy?" she asks, her little brows pulling together. She probably sees the irritation and anger on my face I can pinpoint easily in the mirror. I force my expression to go soft and smile, tipping my chin toward where she just came from.

"All good, baby, go watch the parade," I say.

"Who is that?" Todd asks, but I ignore him.

"What's wrong, Mommy?" Ruby remembers the most from before the divorce, unfortunately, and because of it, she's both incredibly closed off from other people and hyper-protective of me.

"Nothing, peanut. Go watch the parade."

"Tell her I say hello," Todd says, smugness in his voice. "And that I'll see her soon. You're not being fair to them by keeping them from their father, Sharon."

Ruby stares at me as I ignore my ex in my ear.

"Go," I mouth, then I turn my back to her, waiting to hear her feet retreating on the hallway floor, waiting to hear Harper shout that the next balloon is Poppy from *Trolls*.

"You will not see those girls ever again. You lost that right long ago, and I'm fine on my own, Todd. We are fine without you. I don't care if you get remarried seventeen times, I'm not budging. You do not get to treat us like shit and then start your new, little life like none of it happened. You made your fucking bed, Todd, and you're sleeping in it. If you want to renegotiate, have your lawyer call mine. I'm sure he would just *love* to bring you back to court."

Damien Martinez represented me against Todd and absolutely destroyed him. I'm pretty sure if I had not a lick of evidence against Todd, Damien still would have won, would have turned over every rock in the tristate area to find what he needed to win.

When Todd speaks next, his voice has changed again, reminding me of how he could turn it on and off. The cruelty would swap out for love, the reason I convinced myself for so long that he cared, that he would change.

"I want to do this easy, Sharon. No lawyers, just us. We were a family once—"

"No, we weren't. The girls and I were a family. You were a villain. Goodbye, Todd."

And then I hang up, put my phone on silent, and go to eat cinnamon rolls with my girls.

I'll be damned if I let Todd ruin yet another *minute* of my life.

# FOUR

## 32 SLEEPS UNTIL CHRISTMAS

### NICK

"My friend is coming today. Don't be fucking weird, okay?" Connor says, wandering into the kitchen around 10.

I've been up for hours already, getting shit ready, putting a turkey in the smoker, and making sure I didn't have to send anyone out for last-minute ingredients I forgot, and his ass is just meandering downstairs now, still half asleep but already giving me shit.

"Good morning to you too, son. I slept great, thanks so much. Yes, I *would* love some help making dinner. That would be great."

"Fuck off," he says, pouring himself a cup of coffee and leaning his hips on the counter as he holds it between his hands. "I'm serious. Don't be weird. She's already texted me a bunch this morning asking questions. She's anxious to come here."

"Ah, yes, the MILF you picked up on Tinder." I don't tell him I've been looking forward to this day for quite some time, the day I get to meet the illusive Shae who he talks about way too often for someone who isn't interested. I don't tell him I speculate he actually *is* into her and all his talk about being just friends is bullshit. No young man spends that much time with a woman and her two young kids if he doesn't see her spending a good bit of time in his future.

"If you call her a MILF while she's here, I'm slashing your tires," he grumbles. I smile wider before answering.

"Make sure you only do three. Four and I get a fresh set from the insurance company." Connor groans, but I keep smiling. Raising kids is fun and all, but they forget to tell you how much fun teasing your *adult* children is.

"You're not nearly as funny as you think you are."

"Like father, like son," I say, stirring a pot of cranberries on the stove, still not quite sure how they'll turn into that jelly shit considering they look like rocks in the water.

"Fuck off, Dad," he says, moving toward the fridge.

I've been told since the day he was born and put into my arms that he is my spitting image, but I never saw it. As he gets older, however, I've started to notice it more and more. Maybe it's not seeing him every single day, or maybe it's just his age, but either way, it's indisputable. Connor has the same jaw and dark hair as I do. He's got my eyes, the same light blue that, for better or worse, assisted in me becoming a teen father.

Watching him start his own career, follow a path that wasn't an option for me, living in the city and hanging with friends and dating and not overthinking every penny spent, it's fulfilling in a way I also didn't expect.

I became a father at 18, long before I even really took the time to decide if being a dad was something I would want much, much later in life. But when Connor's mom, a girl I hooked up with on graduation night, called me a few months into the summer and told me she was pregnant, my life changed.

She was having the baby but wasn't ready to be a mom. If I wasn't ready to take him on, he would be going up for adoption.

Even though I had a full ride to Rutgers in the bag, I picked Connor. My parents disowned me almost immediately, but when the owner of the ranch I was working at to earn some spending cash over the summer found out about my situation, he offered me a full-time job with room and board.

I moved into a small cabin on the property and worked my ass off, organizing and managing the barns, making sure everything ran smoothly. In the winter, I'd run the tree farm, keeping tabs on the replanting and the cutting, making deals with tree lots and luxury grocery stores to supply some of their trees each season until it wasn't simply a small family farm running just enough to keep everyone paid and cover the property taxes each year, but a thriving business.

And when I was 35 and Old Man Samuels told me he was ready to retire, we worked out a deal for me to buy it from him.

Thus, Finch Farm came to be.

"So, she's coming? With her girls?" I ask, trying not to seem too interested, even though I am *incredibly* interested. I've heard about this woman for months, how amazing she and her kids are, and even though I think my kid getting wrapped up with an older woman with children and baggage isn't something I should embrace, I'm intrigued.

"Yup. So be cool, yeah?"

"I'm always cool, Con."

"Sure, Dad. Sure you are," he says with a wave of his hand, walking off with his mug of coffee.

"You better be bringing your ass back down here as soon as you get dressed! I'm not doing this shit on my own!" He flips me a peace sign as he walks off, feet shuffling on the wood floors, and I know there is no hope.

I'm absolutely on my own.

"CONNOR!" a little girl with blonde hair streaming behind her yells hours later as she bolts toward my now dressed and showered son, who bends down and lifts her. She has to be eight or nine based on her size, but he lifts her with ease.

"Ruby girl! How are you?"

"Happy Thanksgiving!" she shouts, despite being within inches of his face.

It's cute, watching this. He's still young enough that she could be his little sister in some alternate universe, a child I fathered later in life after finding a woman to settle down with. But it wouldn't be hard to picture her being *his* daughter, someone running into him and calling him *Dad* instead of Connor, and a part of me twists and burns at the thought of my kid having his *own* kids.

Thankfully, I don't have time to dwell too long before another girl runs in, similarly blonde if not a bit lighter and a year or two younger.

"Hi, Connor!" she says with a bright smile, and he puts down the older girl before hoisting up the younger, balancing her on his hip.

"Harper, love of my life, how are you?" She blushes at his words, and I lean back on the kitchen counter, my arms crossing over my chest, a small smile playing on my lips as I watch the show unfold, watch their interactions.

"Did you know there are *chickens* here?" she asks with a shocked look, and Connor smiles.

"Well, yeah, I kind of grew up here." Her eyes go wide in shock and awe, the kind only a little kid can get on her face, before he continues, his head turning toward the older girl. "Later, we can take a walk. I'll show you the horses."

Any slight nerves the older girl had from being in a new place melts away, and her jaw drops open, green eyes going wide. "Horses?" Her voice is small, filled with uncontrolled excitement, and it's really fucking adorable.

"Oh yeah. A bunch. And a pony."

"A PONY?" the little one, Harper, yells. Connor's eyes squint a bit and his head goes back with the noise, like he's joking that she blew his eardrum out, before he smiles and nods.

It's clear he has a connection with these girls, and watching, I have to wonder why he thinks it couldn't work with their mom.

"And a baby horse. Her name is Minnie," he says.

"Like the mouse!"

"Yup." I can't help but laugh at her face, the noise breaking their moment a bit as they all turn to look at me. "Dad, this is Ruby, and this"—he moves to shift the smaller girl so she's on his back, her arms around his neck in a way that definitely cuts off some of his air supply before he readjusts her—"is Harper. Girls, say hi to my dad." I bend a bit to look at the older one and put out my hand. When Connor was her age, he loved this kind of thing, being treated like an adult.

"Hey, Ruby. I'm Nick. Nice to meet you." She looks at my hand and then at my face, examining both like she's evaluating me and this situation, before sticking out her hand and shaking mine. Her face is stern, like she's taking this transaction with the utmost seriousness, and I have to fight a laugh.

"Nice to meet you."

"I'm Harper!" the younger one shouts directly in Connor's ear, making him cringe again. "I'm seven!"

"Wow!" I say, standing tall to look at her on Connor's back. "That's big!"

"I know," she says matter-of-factly.

"Where's your mom?" Connor asks, but there's no time for them to answer because just then, a woman walks through the door as well. She's has a large bag slung over her shoulder, juggling a pie in one hand and a bottle of wine in the other.

She looks unbearably anxious and a bit annoyed, a glare directed at her oldest daughter, I assume. "Ruby, I told you to wait for me," she says, confirming my thoughts. She says something else to her other daughter, and I think she greets Connor warmly, but I can't process any of it.

Because I'm blown away by the woman walking in.

She's wearing a pair of black boots that go just under her knees with a low heel and a deep red dress with a turtleneck and long sleeves that clings to her ample curves. Her hair is a dirty blonde, barely brushing her shoulders, not curled but not straight, like she put some attempt into styling it but then got sidetracked and decided it would have to do.

And she's *fucking beautiful*.

# FIVE

## 32 SLEEPS UNTIL CHRISTMAS

### NICK

Connor gave me a quick introduction to Shae, during which she gave me the kind of tight, uneasy smile you give a stranger you don't want to talk to. Moments later, the girls announced they wanted to see the animals, and Shae agreed it would be smart to let them get some of their jitters and energy out in the cold after an hour in the car.

I spent the next few hours fighting the urge to go into the living room with snacks and appetizers like some kind of Stepford wife trying to win a blue ribbon for entertaining, desperate to catch another glimpse of the woman Connor brought.

After months and months of hearing about her and her daughters, she's nothing like I expected. Not at all. It's clear why they didn't work out—she's not his type in the least, and she looks at him like he's her best friend or her little brother rather than a man she could ever be interested in. Connor interacts with her similarly, which makes the instant attraction I feel toward her slightly more palatable, though no less concerning.

Even more alarming than the attraction, though, is this excruciating desire to . . . take care of her. Comfort her. The desire to make her feel welcome in my home, like she belongs here at this dinner of what Connor likes to call misfits. Some years there are more attendees, some years less, but this year it seems we have just two ranch hands, a friend of Connor's from college, and Shae and her girls.

That urge only gets harder to fight throughout the night, becoming a clawing sensation under my skin when she and the girls come back in, the girls making themselves at home nearly instantly while their mother sits in a chair, completely alert, like she's ready for some kind of pop quiz.

It peaks at dinner when we're sitting around the table, the quiet uneasy despite Connor's efforts to pull conversation out of everyone. Connor's guest seems so uncomfortable, and despite the younger girls' chattering, so do her daughters.

I know the bare minimum of Shae and her daughters' story. A loveless marriage with a narcissist, verbal abuse that unfortunately turned into physical before she left him. This is her first true holiday season as a single mom and despite her efforts to mask it, she looks wiped out and completely worn down.

I remember this age, a time when Connor was both excited and introverted, when everything felt like it took a thousand more steps than it should, simply because I was the only one raising him. The way I'd go to bed tired and wake up with the same exhaustion haunting my bones, the small amount of sleep I could fit around my late-night worrying no help at all in easing it. When I look back on the few photos I managed to get of us together, it's written all over me in the same font as it is on Shae right now.

And I also see my son in her girls, the way they fidget, the way every time they start to speak, they look to their mother for confirmation it's okay, for reassurance,

Connor used to be so quiet around strangers at this age, and I'm sure with their history, it's more difficult to warm up to new people, especially men. An undeniable part of me wants desperately to give them a holiday they'll love and remember, memories of the time they went to the farm with the horses and had a magical dinner and made new friends, even if they're all adults or mammals with four legs.

It's what has me, unfortunately, opening my mouth and speaking.

"So, what grade are you in, Ruby?" I ask the older of the two.

"Fourth," she says, keeping her answer to one word. Like all of her previous answers, she doesn't speak until she meets her mother's eyes, waiting for her to nod her approval. It's obvious this sweet girl is either incredibly shy or slow to trust others. From what Connor has told me, I'm leaning toward option two.

"Fourth grade, that's a good one," I say. "What about you?" The younger girl with a raggedy looking stuffed cat toy in her lap smiles wide. It's so clear, even just knowing them for a few hours, that Ruby and her little sister Harper are complete opposites.

"I'm in second grade, in Mrs. Matrico's class, and we have a class *hamster!*" I smile at her and her exuberance.

"Wow, that's pretty cool. Do you have any pets?" Her face lights up, and she's clearly eager to talk about this topic. Unfortunately, I don't miss the sigh Shae lets out, and I realize I accidentally touched on a sore subject, something she would rather avoid.

Clearly, I'm doing just *great* with this "making her feel welcomed and comfortable" shit.

"I really want to get a kitten, but Mom says she has enough things to keep alive, so I just have my fish Santino."

"Santino, huh?" She nods before returning to picking apart a dinner roll, the only thing she seems to have agreed to eat, and the silence takes over the table again.

I can't help but, once again, want to fix this.

Even though I look to my son for some kind of aid or guidance, he doesn't look at me, using his phone under the table, probably texting some booty call or setting up a visit with friends who are home for the holiday, leaving me out here hanging.

So once again, I attempt to fill in the void, and once again, I think I touched on a subject I should have steered far, far away from.

"Are you girls excited for the elf to come?" I ask the younger of the two. Both look at me, mildly confused. Unfortunately, I am a man, so I don't take in the clear caution flag, instead crashing through into disaster.

"The elf?" Harper asks, confusion written across her face.

This is where I should have stopped.

Or maybe I should have looked to Shae, at the very least. Taken some goddamn context clues and realized what was happening. I would have seen her wide eyes and head shaking, her stiff jaw and the look of panic. I would have stopped, and this all could have been avoided.

But again, I am a man, and as you might know, men are not great at reading signs.

"Oh, you know, the Elf on the Shelf," I say, remembering when I did the silly tradition with Connor when he was younger. The concept didn't come into the mainstream until he was older and didn't believe in Santa anymore, but it was fun to do and always made us laugh. A strange little bonding moment we had.

Up until he went off to college, I'd still set up the little creep every night, making it do dumb PG-13 things to try and get a laugh out of him during a time when he was much *too cool* to find me funny.

"Santa sends him from the North Pole to keep an eye on you guys and make sure you're behaving. Then every night, he goes back to report to Santa and make sure you're on the nice list still," I say, explaining what I think should be relatively obvious to two little girls in the perfect age bracket. Wasn't he on a float in the Thanksgiving Day Parade this year?

"No way!" Harper says, absolutely enamored with the idea, her face the personification of the heart eyes emoji. "Mom, why don't we have an elf?!" She turns to her mother, and I do the same.

It's then that my stomach drops to the floor and I regret every single choice I've made in the past five years.

Maybe more. A lifetime of poor choices that led to this moment.

Because I see it then.

Her face.

The *bro, shut the fuck up please* face I'm almost certain she's been wearing for some time as I chatted with her daughter.

And it's then, I know.

I fucked up big time, and she wants to absolutely murder me.

# SIX

## 32 SLEEPS UNTIL CHRISTMAS

### SHAE

I barely eat for the rest of the dinner, despite it being delicious, instead glaring at the man across the table from me. The man who told my girls about the *stupid fucking elf.* The bane of any parent's existence who is already at a breaking point, trying to plan and organize all of the magical moments and make the memories and curate a perfect childhood.

I made it *nine fucking years* without having to worry about that creepy little fucker, and I was *so fucking close* to being free from the threat of it.

Do you *know* how hard it is to keep little girls from knowing, understanding, and anticipating what has quickly become a tradition across the country? I made it through by the skin of my teeth, their prestigious little school sending a memo each year to let parents know some families don't participate and that it was policy to not talk about it during school hours, just in case.

Now I'm going to have to buy an unnecessarily expensive, stupid, *creepy elf* and put it on a shelf we *don't even have,* and then I'll have to remember to move it each night before I collapse with exhaustion.

As if I needed another *fucking* thing to worry about, another trophy on the shelf of my mom guilt. I can probably fit it right between *leaving their father* and *not letting Harper have a kitten.*

If looks could kill, I'd be looking at twenty to life, for *sure.* And he must know it because he makes a careful effort *not* to look at my face, despite my eyes beaming lasers through him for the entire meal.

Eventually, though, Connor announces he's done eating, and Ruby, who picked at a little of everything, and Harper, who ate nothing but three dinner rolls (as expected), jump at the opportunity he presents to go back outside and check on the animals.

He encourages me to stay inside since I learned before that my boots are *not* made for straw-lined barn floors, an offer I also take because I want to yell at his father.

This means about twenty minutes later, I am able to corner Nicolas Finch alone in the kitchen and give him a piece of my mind.

"Thanks for that," I say with my arms crossed on my chest.

"I didn't realize," he says. To his credit, he genuinely looks apologetic. "I thought it was something everyone did these days, like Santa. Connor was already getting too old when it started, so I don't know how it works."

"Yeah, well, I had managed to avoid it up until now." I continue to glare at him, and to his credit, he is starting to look almost *distraught.*

As he should.

Frustration and irritation are brewing in my veins, and rationally, I can understand it's not his fault and it's not fair to direct this fury at him. Unfortunately, I can't seem to access that rational part of my brain right now. Everything this time of year feels like a personal jab, every shortcoming of mine a reminder of how unfit I feel as their mother, how much I'm letting them down.

There was a time when I wanted nothing but to do all of the cute things, to create the traditions and carry them out so one day, they'd have those memories to wrap themselves in like a soft blanket. But Harper was born so close to Ruby, and when she came into the world, I suffered terrible postpartum depression, making even the most basic tasks beyond keeping myself and my girls alive feel impossible. I'm still shocked we even had a tree or gifts that first year, since we all know Todd was never going to do anything.

As they got older, I realized the concept of doing *all* of the Pinterest-worthy things to *make memories* was a fucking scam and a myth and we were all picking and choosing what activities and traditions we were physically and emotionally capable of carrying out without having a full fucking meltdown.

Even though I understand and accept that limitation and know most other parents are "failing" just as magnificently as I am, it doesn't make the ache of guilt hurt any less.

So, it's not really my anger with *Nick* and the unfortunate situation with the elf that has me drawing imaginary slits across his throat. It's just the time of *year* and he's the unlucky recipient of my unchecked emotions.

This time last year, I left Todd and uprooted the girls' lives entirely and, to them, unexpectedly, and the guilt is seeping into every pore, kicked up with memories from him calling this morning. In my twisted mind, this stupid fucking elf shit is just another example of how I'm fucking up.

"Look, I'm really sorry. I can talk to them, explain how they're good kids and that's why—" he starts, and even though he clearly means to make the situation better, it makes me *more annoyed*, like he thinks I can't handle my own children or their disappointments.

"It's fine," I snap, taking a deep breath and trying to organize my thoughts. I move my budget around, taking a bit from the Christmas fund I set aside and adding it to a new column, an *elf* column, trying to calculate how much the elf will be and adding in any fun adventures it might have to take. It looks like instead of splurging on new pajamas and sheets for myself like I had planned, I'll be buying a creepy-looking elf and whatever else he'll need.

It's not that we're tight on cash—Damien Martinez pays me incredibly well for my work at his nonprofit, and I have the child support and ample payoff from the divorce, but like I said, I refuse to use that.

I want everything I have to be through my own efforts, connections, and hard work.

"Let me make it up to you. I can help," he says, and I think he reaches for me, but I step back, shaking my head and cutting him off with a wave of my hand.

I'm tired all the time, from work and from my kids and from doing it myself and battling my own demons at all times, but this?

This is what I'm tired of most. Everyone is so sure I can't handle things, so *sure* I need their help.

To everyone, I need *something*.

I need money.

I need a new place.

I need a *man*.

But they don't see all I need is myself and my girls.

That's all.

I've given my power to a man by trusting him to take care of us, to put us first, to keep us safe, and I got *nothing* for it. Now, I'm 35, completely starting my life from scratch.

"I don't need your help, thanks. I'll do it myself." I start to turn away from him but stop when he speaks again.

"Taking help doesn't mean you're weak, you know," he says, and it feels like an accusation. I turn on my heel and stare at him, crossing my arms on my chest. I'm sure he thinks this is some *gotcha* moment, a situation where I'll give in and agree and he can go to bed happy, knowing he helped me out, that he did his good deed for the month.

"I know that. I am far from weak. I don't need a *man* telling me I'm not weak or it's okay to accept help, thank you very much." He looks taken aback before he speaks.

"I didn't mean it like—" I shake my head a bit before cutting him off once more.

"They never do, you know? They never mean it, but it still comes off that way. It still sounds like you all pity me, the poor little single mom."

"I don't pity you, Shae. But you need to accept help sometimes."

"Do I?" I ask, slightly confused that he's still pushing it.

"Well, yeah. You're only doing your girls a disservice by—" My entire body goes rigid.

*I'm doing my girls a disservice.*

God, how many times have I heard that over the past year? When people find out I am no contact with their father, I'm doing a disservice to them.

When people find out I refuse to spend the alimony or child support to buy my girls luxury so they fit in at their shitty school, I'm doing a disservice to them.

When people hear I'm not dating because I don't *need a man*, I'm doing a disservice to my daughters.

Even today, Todd told me I was doing a disservice to them by keeping him out of their lives.

Something snaps.

"—I've been you. I've—" He's still talking, justifying as my mind is reeling, but I cut him off.

"Oh, have you?" I stare at him as the dam breaks. Things I've kept in for a year have slowly weakened the retaining wall I built to keep them at bay, and this man is, unfortunately, the unlucky character to get the full blast of it. "Wow, please, do tell me more about pulling your children away from a dangerous situation you put them in by deciding to start a life with a shitty man, about taking them from the only life they've ever known and making them watch you cry in a hotel room while you have a black eye. Please, tell me more about the guilt society puts on mothers to be everything—breadwinner and Susie homemaker and an independent woman and the one who makes the best chocolate chip cookies and knows how to sew a prom dress without even googling it. Tell me *more* about how people look at you when you walk into the pediatrician and tell them there's no father, how the teachers look at you when you roll up to parent-teacher conferences alone." I pause, smiling at his anxious, wide eyes.

"You can't. Because while we may have been in similar seas, you were in a yacht and I'm in the dinghy. You were celebrated for being the father who stepped up while I'm looked at and told the girls really need a father figure to look up to. You don't get it, and that's not on you, but you don't get the opportunity to tell me *you get it* with those pitying eyes. I appreciate you having my family over for Thanksgiving, for letting my girls go look at your animals. It's not your fault about the elf, but I don't need your pity, and I surely don't need your help. Now, if you'll excuse me, I have to use the ladies' room."

And then I walk out to go hide in the bathroom until my breathing regulates, until my hands stop shaking, until it's time to eat pie with a smile for the girls and then get the fuck out of here and away from Nicolas Finch.

# SEVEN

## 32 SLEEPS UNTIL CHRISTMAS

### NICK

I stood in my kitchen for nearly five minutes, staring at a wall and unsure of how to move forward after Shae tore me a new one, rightfully so, before I decided cleaning could wait and I needed fresh air and to clear the house so she wouldn't have to fear bumping into me.

I fucked up.

I fucked up *big*.

It's not even just the elf, which, clearly, I should have shut the fuck up about, but telling her she needs my help, that she needs to accept help, that we were both in the same boat. Because she's right—our lives might be similar, but we are not nearly the same.

It is a different playing field for a single mom versus a single dad. I would go into stores with Connor as a baby and get praised for *stepping up,* as if I were a hero. And then I made a stressful time of year even worse when I opened my mouth and added even more to her ridiculously full plate. I'm already planning how I can send a package to Shae in the next few days, send over one of those stuffed elves and a few gift cards so at the very least she doesn't have to take on the financial burden of my mistake.

When I walked toward the barn where Minnie and Mickey are

along with half a dozen other horses, Ruby was chattering with Connor, her sister parroting phrases and talking incessantly as well, but as soon as I made my presence known, she clammed up.

I know everything there is to know about her little sister Harper by now, even though I've only been in her presence for a few hours. She loves kittens and wants one of her own, but her mom keeps telling her no. She loves rainbow bagels and strawberry cream cheese, but her favorite food is mozzarella sticks, even though she hates the *dip* that comes with them. Her favorite show is something to do with a cat dollhouse, but Connor is much, much too old for me even to have a pulse on today's children's shows. She's in second grade, and her favorite subject is art because, you guessed it, she can draw pictures of cats.

But she doesn't *have* a cat, something that made an epic pout come on her face when I asked a few minutes ago. Thankfully, then she heard a meow, one of the barn cats slinking down to say hello and ask for a treat. Now, she and Connor are off trying to find her again and see if they can give her some pets.

But Ruby stayed behind despite her clear unease and mistrust of me, gently petting Minnie's nose. Her eyes are locked on the young horse who won't be able to be ridden for at least another year but likes people.

And clearly, she adores Ruby.

Ruby, who hasn't stopped looking at or petting the horse, who hasn't stopped whispering sweet nothings to her, scratching behind her ear.

It's been a long time since I've seen someone fall in love with a horse this quickly and for a horse to return the favor. The last time was maybe ten years ago, when Mickey was brought to the ranch and Connor fell for her. Fuck, I'm still convinced the only reason he comes back once a week isn't to see me or get his laundry done here, but to see his horse.

"You like my girl?" I ask, my voice low, the way I would talk to a spooked horse. This little girl doesn't seem much different, especially when her shoulders go tense with my words, like she forgot I'm here or was hoping I would just continue to ignore her. But then Minnie's snout moves to her neck, snuffling there and making her giggle.

Something about it, about that sound, heals something in my chest I didn't know was scarred. Something about that sound, about this closed-off little girl giggling with my horse in my barn when, from what little I understand, she hasn't had much unadulterated joy in her life, feels *good*.

"She's so pretty," Ruby says, not looking at me still.

"She likes you, it seems. You're good with her," I say, keeping my distance. She turns to me a bit more, so she's now facing both Minnie and me, and nods.

"I want to be a cowgirl when I grow up. Or a florist. I like flowers, too."

I fight the laugh that's bubbling inside me because only a 9-year-old could say something like that with a straight face.

"Can't say much about being a cowboy or cowgirl, but I've got a farm with horses. That's pretty good. Maybe a flower farm. That's a thing, you know, a place where all they grow is flowers." She stares at me, and I swear to fuck, it's like she's reading me down to my marrow, taking notes, and writing a thesis about who I am, all of the misdeeds and good I've done in my life.

"That would be good, I guess. As long as there are horses." I don't get closer, still standing a good five feet away and leaning on a beam before I ask a question with an obvious answer.

"You like horses?"

"I love them even more than flowers," she says with awe in her voice, and Minnie snorts into her hand like she's returning the sentiment.

From what Connor told me, Ruby is the oldest and quietest. She's anxious and a worrier and takes the longest to warm up to new people. He told me her mother is concerned that it's caused by the messy divorce and the quick change in her life.

But here?

She looks at ease.

She looks comfortable, despite her nerves about me.

She looks like she's breathing easy for the first time in a long time, and to see that on a 9-year-old is both beautiful and painful.

"You know, when I'm stressed or sad, I like to come out here. Talk to the horses. They always make me feel better. I've been that way for as long as I can remember. I worked at this farm when I was a kid, before Connor was born, and even then . . . this was my happy place." She doesn't say anything but finally breaks her eye contact with Minnie to look at me.

"Anytime you need to, you tell your mom you can come here. Talk to Minnie. She's a good listener."

Finally, Ruby smiles then.

A real smile.

And it's gorgeous.

The kind of gorgeous smile that makes me wonder what a fucking idiot her father is for not to want to see it every single day.

"Really?"

"Yeah. Any time. I'll give your mom my number." With my words, Connor and Harper return, Harper's seemingly ever-present smile as wide as can be.

"There's *kittens!*" she says, and Connor gives me a shake of his head.

"Looks like one of your cats had a litter." I give my son a confused look.

"It's not kitten season, though."

"Tell that to the four up on a hay bale. I'll come out tonight, get them all in a crate so they don't freeze, but for now, the momma's got them safe." I shake my head because that's *just* what I need on this ranch—more animals. But when I look at Harper, who has near-literal hearts in her eyes, I can't be mad.

"They were *so freaking cute!*" She turns to her sister. "You really missed out, Rube."

But Ruby just shakes her head, looking at Minnie, scratching behind the young horse's ear. "No. I'm fine here hanging out with Minnie."

Connor looks between the girls and then back to Ruby, who looks so incredibly at peace, before sighing. "Alright, you two. Let's get inside, get some pie before your mom starts to worry about you."

Guilt churns in my gut as I think about Shae and the way I fucked that up as all of us walk back to the house.

But as seems to happen to me, when I look up at the stars in the sky, the answer comes to me.

"Hey, wait up," I say, slowing my steps.

# EIGHT

## 6 MONTHS AGO

## NICK

"So where does this girl live, anyway?" I ask in my kitchen, Connor tugging on his shoes. He spent the night at the ranch, meeting up with old friends and crashing here, and now he's on his way to take a single mom and her two daughters to the *zoo*.

The single mom he allegedly has *no interest* in.

I call bullshit. What 24-year-old spends a Sunday morning with kids who aren't his *with a hangover* if he's not trying to get into the pants of their mother?

"Over in Hudson City, but I'm meeting them in East Orange," he says. "They added a whole spot where you can feed giraffes, and they're Shae's favorite."

God, the kid is so gone. *So far gone.* He knows her favorite animal and is planning fucking outings to make her happy.

"And the girls?" He finishes lacing up his shoes and stands.

"What?"

"What do they like?" It's a test, another way for me to gauge his interest in this little family. He shrugs, walking toward the coat rack near the door to grab his hat. When he was younger, he had a cowboy hat just like mine, but now he prefers an old worn in baseball hat with his favorite football team on the front.

"The oldest, Ruby, is obsessed with horses. The younger one, Harper, is a unicorn girl. And kittens. She likes cats."

"Hmm," I say, sipping my coffee and staring at him. He rolls his eyes, so similar to my own, and I fight a laugh.

"It's not like that, Dad," he says with a groan.

"It never is at first, bud."

# NINE

## 30 SLEEPS UNTIL CHRISTMAS

### SHAE

"Come on, girls. Shoes, jackets, let's go," I call, glimpses of two sets of pigtails coming into view before their faces do.

"Bagels!" Harper shouts with excitement. Saturdays are her favorite day of the week. She never wakes up early for *anything* except for these mornings when she rolls out of bed quickly, getting both her and her older sister dressed, their teeth and hair brushed before I have to ask. Then, we can head to her favorite bagel shop for rainbow bagels and strawberry cream cheese.

Considering she's the pickiest eater on this planet these days, I will continue this tradition until she decides she can't stand it. Since the divorce, her eating habits have gotten even worse, the list of safe foods diminishing until only a handful of things are left. The pediatrician told me it was relatively normal, one of the few things she's able to control being what and when she eats. The hope is that as she becomes more secure in this new version of our life, she'll begin to eat more, to gain weight once again.

But until then, it's bagels every Saturday.

"Yes, peanut, but you have to finish getting ready first," I say with a raised eyebrow.

"I am!" she whines. I fight a laugh, letting my eyes travel to her feet with meaning.

"I know you're basically a little heater, but you still need socks," I say. "And shoes. Boots, ideally." She grumbles to herself before heading back to the room she shares with her sister.

"I'm ready, Mom," Ruby, my responsible 9-year-old, says. I give her a look because she loves to quietly stir the pot, even if she thinks I don't realize what she's doing. She just smiles her sweet smile. At the very least, it's good to see her bringing some personality back, backing off of her newfound perfectionist who never wants to make my life harder, even when I tell her that it's kind of her *job* as my daughter to drive me a bit crazy.

Before I can say anything, Harper comes running out, one sock on a foot, the other in her hand as she waves it, sliding into the living room and almost falling on her ass.

"Cool it, Harp."

"It's rainbow bagel day. I can't calm down." I smile at her but shake my head, moving to the hook near the door where we keep the jackets, grabbing the girls', and handing them off before putting mine on.

Some days have been difficult over the past year, raising these two on my own when that was never even in my darkest thoughts. There have been a lot of tears—from all of us—and a lot of arguments and so, *so* many fears, but days like this?

It makes up for a lot.

I grab my bag and, once the girls are all zipped up, open the door to leave.

And then I stop.

Ruby and Harper walk straight into my back.

"Mommy?"

"What's wrong?" Ruby says, a hint of panic in her voice. I should tell her everything is okay, that I'm just having a moment, that my girl who fears the unexpected has nothing to worry about.

I should tell her anything, really. Do anything other than stand in the doorway, staring at the old, worn welcome mat we bought when we first moved into the rented townhouse.

But I can't.

I can't do anything but stare in a mix of awe and horror and confusion.

Because on the front step, a little elf in a red outfit, pointy hat and ears, a stupid smile I already hate is sitting on my goddamn welcome mat with two envelopes.

A mother fucking Elf on a Shelf.

Or, in this case, an elf on my fucking front step.

"What is it, Mom?" Ruby asks again, dipping her head under my armpit to see, as if she's going to protect me from whatever horror is plaguing me. But she sees what it is and *screams*.

*"OH MY GOD!"*

That snaps me out of my daze a bit, my eye contact with the elf breaking and moving to look at my daughter.

Unlike me, she doesn't have a look of horror on her face, but one of exuberance.

"Ruby! People are sleeping!"

*"Oh my god!"* she repeats, slightly quieter but not really.

"What *is* it?!" Harper asks, also using her head to nudge me aside to see what has her sister so excited.

"THE ELF!"

I sigh.

There's no hope of keeping them contained and surely no hope of handling this once we get bagels, so we might as well do this in the apartment.

"No!" the girls yell in unison as I bend to grab my new nemesis. I freeze.

"You can't touch her. She'll lose her magic!" I stand and look at my oldest daughter.

"What?"

"If you touch her, she loses all of her North Pole magic." Calm, easygoing Ruby has a look of all-consuming panic on her face, and I continue to stare.

"You know that how?"

"I mean, Catherine was talking about it last week, about her elf coming." My stomach churns with parental failure.

"She was?"

Catherine is a little brat whose parents have more money than God and use it to keep her happy instead of spending *time* with their child regularly and, oh, I don't know, teaching her to be kind.

I don't want to say I have beef with a 9-year-old but . . .

"Yeah, I mean, all of the kids talk about it." She shrugs like it's no big deal.

"They do?" That poisonous guilt churns. God, I should have been doing this over the years. I was so deep in survival mode, I didn't have the energy. But if all the kids were doing it except mine—

"Yeah, but we've always been so good, we didn't need one," Ruby says like it's a fact, and I can't help but let a small smile creep onto my lips.

"Yup!" Harper agrees.

"Well, you haven't been any worse," I say. "To need an elf." I feel the need to clarify that. If, for some reason, they think this is a *punishment* for poor behavior, I might need to drive back to that *stupid freaking farm* and give Nicolas Finch a swift kick in the balls.

I barely know the man, but this has him written *all over it*.

"I *know* that, but Harper and I wished on the North Star for Santa to bring us one," Ruby says matter-of-factly, and I blink at them.

"What? When?"

"With Connor's dad! Nick! When we went outside to look at the horses, he came out and talked to us. He showed us the North Star and told us if we wished really hard, it might happen. And they always seem so fun. Sometimes, they bring presents, and sometimes they make messes and act goofy!"

*I'm going to kill someone.*

I might not be allowed to have beef with a 9-year-old, but this is a grown-ass man.

I can punch a grown man.

I stare at the box the elf is sitting on with deep, unending irritation.

"We have an elf!" Harper says then begins to dance in circles, the kind of dance only a little kid can do, the kind they do when they're so excited, they can't contain themselves, can't handle the prospect of the joy they're experiencing and need to let it out in a different format.

"It seems we do," I say, much less impressed than my daughters.

Goddammit.

We have a fucking elf.

# TEN

## 29 SLEEPS UNTIL CHRISTMAS

### SHAE

The girls are up extra early the next morning, jumping up and down and begging to see the front mat to check if the elf has gone to the North Pole again.

I'm also filled with an uneasy excitement I beat back because this whole thing is *annoying*, not endearing. But as we walk to the door, the girls all dressed for the day despite it usually taking a century on a Sunday, I realize I should have woken up before them to check. If the elf isn't there, I'm going to have to scramble to make up for it.

The only person I can rely on for my girls is myself. Even though there are people in my life who love and adore all three of us and have proven they care for us, I'm the only one I know who undeniably, always, and forever will put Ruby and Harper first. I can't expect some random man who feels guilty about getting my kids excited for something to do the same.

Yesterday, we stepped back into the house after I grabbed the stupid elf with a pair of kitchen tongs, put it on the counter, and read the notes he left. It turned out there was one for the girls and one for me.

The first was in a thick red envelope with a *fucking wax seal,* all official and shit. I have to wonder what kind of man has thick cardstock envelopes and the ability to wax seal things.

The note was typed up rather than written, and a name tag with *Hello, my name is . . .* fell out when Ruby ripped it open and read the text.

> Hi, Ruby and Harper!
>
> I'm so excited to visit you this Christmas! I've heard you both are always on your best behavior, but Santa heard your wish on the North Star and wanted to make sure you got a little extra holiday magic this year. I'll visit you every night after you've gone to bed, so you have to make sure you go to sleep quickly—my magic only works once you go to sleep! Each night, I'll go back to the North Pole and report to Santa about how amazing you've been and maybe even bring you back a few surprises.
>
> Love, your elf.
>
> PS: I need a name! I left you a name tag to write my new name on. Make sure you leave it on me before you go to bed.

It was sickeningly sweet.

Too fucking sweet.

And before I even opened the second letter with *my* name on top, I knew who it was from.

Nick.

> Hey, Shae,
>
> I'm so sorry about bringing up the elf at Thanksgiving. I know you have a lot going on, so

```
I  promise  this  won't  be  another  thing  on  your
list.  Just  leave  the  elf  on  your  front  step  each
night   and   I'll   come   move   her   around,   drop
presents,  that  kind  of  thing.
    Connor  told  me  where  to  find  your  place,  by  the
way.  I'm  not  a  total  stalker.
    -Nick  Finch
```

I wanted to let that anger continue to rage, continue to brew. I wanted to feel *indignant* he even *bothered* to come to my place after buying a fucking elf.

But I couldn't.

It was kind.

It was thoughtful.

And most of all, it did what he intended, taking a bit of the burden off my shoulders.

I hate him for that.

And right now, as I watch Ruby turn the handle of the front door with excitement, I am ready to hate him for letting my little girl down.

But then she squeals.

She squeals and jumps up and down and flings the door open, letting it hit the wall with a loud thunk, as I've told her not to do a million times.

I want to be annoyed, but I can't because just *look* at her. Her face is awash in joy and pure fucking Christmas cheer and *god*.

I can't be mad.

And I surely can't be mad when Harper joins in.

Because there that dumb elf sits, this time on a stack of boxes. That small red elf with the creepy fucking smile and dead eyes is staring at me like she knows something I don't know. Taunting me and all of my failures as a person. As a mother.

I hate her, I think.

She's sitting next to two boxes, and when I get closer, I see they're Advent calendars for the girls to start on December 1st.

Unicorns for Harper and horses for Ruby, the expensive kind with little toys instead of candy. I have *no idea* how he got them so quickly or how he knew which girl liked what, but regardless, I'm . . .

I'm grateful.

# ELEVEN

## 28 SLEEPS UNTIL CHRISTMAS

### SHAE

The third night, I wait for him.

This morning, the girls ran to the door to find the elf they've named *Holly* and there were *gifts*.

*Gifts*, all wrapped up in paper (kittens for Harper this time, horses again for Ruby) and topped with bows, the elf sitting on top with that god-awful smile. Really, who designed this thing, anyway? It's like it was made with nightmares in mind.

Oh, and there weren't just gifts for Ruby and Harper.

There was a third for me. The girls both received a cute package with pajamas in their size and a book based on their interests, and in the small box for me there is a *gift card* for a spot where I like to have lunch near my work.

Clearly, I need to have a chat with *Connor*, who not only is giving his father information about where I work and where I like to eat when we grab lunch together once in a while, but also *where I live* and what my girls like.

I also add *Connor* to my list of people and things I hate.

Just call me *Scrooge*, I guess.

So on night three, I'm sitting on my couch with a much-needed glass of wine and waiting. I sit in front of the TV playing some trash show, working on crocheting a pink stocking, hyper-fixating on my phone screen showcasing a live feed of the security camera and jumping each time someone walks by. My neighbors probably think I'm insane, considering I keep cracking my door and looking out, staring down the street each way to see if Nick is here.

But eventually, a truck drives past, moving toward the parking area, and before I even see him, I somehow know it's him.

It's Nicolas Finch.

And when he walks up the front steps, I'm already at the door, opening it and standing there, crossing my arms on my chest and staring at him.

"Hey," he says, and when the edges of his lips tip up, I decide another reason he's annoying is because he has a good smile. He can't be the bane of my existence *and* have a good smile. It's just *rude*.

Instead of giving him a greeting, I step back and wave my arm to gesture to my home. "You can come in. You don't have to . . . do your thing outside every day. The girls go to sleep at eight on the dot, so you can come after then. Or you can just go on about your life and I'll move the elf each night. You don't have to drive all the way here every day." He stares at me before walking into my house.

"I do," he says before glancing around my tiny townhouse. Instantly, self-consciousness fills my veins when I remember just how gorgeous and breathtaking his home is.

"I just said you don't. I'm letting you off the hook." He looks at me and shakes his head.

"Are you always this stubborn? Connor didn't mention that." I'm actually shocked by that, since his son loves to inform me I am, in fact, incredibly stubborn when I *always* refuse his help.

*Everyone* says it, actually. I wear it as kind of a badge of honor at this point.

"Yes. Now, you can happily move on with your life and your December without trekking here every night. Save the gas and the headache." Finally, he stops the perusal of my place, turning to me and crossing his arms on his chest, a reusable tote with his farm's logo across the front in one hand.

"You said yourself you're a single mom who is overwhelmed. I'm not going to make that worse, Shae. I'll be here every night until Christmas." My stomach churns.

I can't tell if it's because of the guilt I *refuse* to feel at the thought of this man driving an hour each way every night because I complained about him making my life more difficult or if it's because that means I'll be seeing him *every single night* and despite my best efforts, with him standing in front of me with his broad shoulders and that worn cowboy hat that doesn't fit in in my living room, I have . . . mixed opinions.

"It's an hour's drive," I say.

"Yup."

"Each way," I clarify, just in case he hasn't yet figured that out.

"Yup," he repeats.

"And you run a Christmas tree farm," I remind him.

"Yup."

There goes that tiny bit of attraction I had.

This man is *utterly annoying*. No wonder Connor says he's still single. Can you imagine *choosing* to spend excessive amounts of time with *this*?

"Do you know other words than *yup*?"

"Yup." I groan and look at the ceiling, ignoring how he's now *smiling* and *definitely* ignoring how it's a really good freaking smile.

*This is funny to him.* He finds my irritation *funny*.

"Are you always this obnoxious?"

"Yup," he says, his definitely not handsome smile getting so wide, it's a shock it fits on his face. He undoubtedly uses it to get his way and does it often. In fact, I'd bet he's used that smile to get his way since he was a kid.

*Well, too bad it won't work on me,* I think. *Ruby and Harper have much cuter smiles and their bullshit doesn't work on me.*

"You're a pain in the ass, you know that?"

Somehow, his stupidly handsome smile widens *still*.

"Yup."

I groan, throwing my hands up before moving to my couch and going back to my project. He chuckles as he goes into the kitchen, placing the elf and shuffling a bit, but I ignore him.

In fact, I don't speak to him for the rest of his short time in my home, barely even bothering to lift a hand when he says good night and that he'll be back tomorrow.

I decide then the only way to survive the next month is simply to pretend Nicolas Finch doesn't exist.

# TWELVE

## 26 SLEEPS UNTIL CHRISTMAS

### NICK

On Wednesday, she opens the door before I even knock then moves straight to the kitchen, working on drying a pile of dishes before putting them away. I watch from afar as she then moves to making lunch for her daughters and herself, writing a note for each girl before placing it into a lunchbox and into the fridge.

When I think she might be done, she heads for the living room and grabs a laundry basket, starting to sort and fold clothes as if I'm not even there.

This is how it was yesterday as well. The door was opened before I could even knock and she gave me a small, polite smile before moving into the kitchen to go back to what she was doing and barely speaking a word the entire time I was there.

Yesterday, I set the elf up to look like she was fishing in the sink and caught some candy fish for the girls. When I asked if it would be okay, not sure about space or if the girls were allowed to have candy, something I forgot to ask Connor ahead of time, Shae nodded without making eye contact before telling me she didn't care either way.

Tonight is the same, Shae opening the door before I even knock, like she's watching for me, and me going into the living room to set up the elf while she goes about her night.

I wish I could say it didn't bug me, but it does all the same. And it's stupid since I'm only here because I fucked up, telling her girls about an activity she doesn't have the mental wherewithal to execute.

From what Connor told me, this is her first Christmas post final divorce and, while she's financially stable thanks to the man she works for, she's clearly burning the wick at both ends to give her girls everything she thinks she's slacking on.

The dark circles under her eyes each night and the way she jumps from task to task as if there just aren't enough hours in the day for her to do it all confirm that.

And honestly, I don't know if it's seeing her exhaustion from doing it all herself or if it's from months of Connor telling me about her and her girls, but I'm pretty sure that night, as I watch her finish her laundry then collapse on the couch to work on what I think might be a pink Christmas stocking, I decide that no matter how hard she fights it, I'm going to help Shae give her girls any and everything they need.

She officially has another person fighting in her corner for her.

# THIRTEEN

## 25 SLEEPS UNTIL CHRISTMAS

### SHAE

The third day of letting him into my place, I break my silence. I don't even mean to. It just kind of . . . happens after I finish writing a silly joke on Ruby's lunch note and putting everything in the fridge for the morning.

I've spent three nights now going about my normal routine of trying to set everything up for the next day before I go to sleep, including cleaning and laundry and lunches, despite having a visitor in my home while I do, but yesterday, I was off so I was able to catch up on the basics.

"The girls are so excited," I say as I walk toward the couch to work on Harper's stocking. "They've been on their best behavior, too, so I guess . . . thanks for that." Nick smiles and for some reason, it eggs me on. "Harper hates waking up. It's always a mess. But every morning, she's up and out of bed without me having to hound her. They're . . . They're going to remember this. The magic of it. So, thank you."

A lump forms in my throat at the thought, and not for the first time, I have to fight back the guilt I feel from not being the one executing this. When the girls were born, I thought I would do all the things, nurture that magic while I could since, as everyone just *loves* to remind overwhelmed moms, *they're not young for long!*

But what they don't tell you is while your kids are young, young enough to enjoy magical moments without questioning them, the world is also turning. The outside world is still moving, and bosses and deadlines and shitty husbands don't really care about the narrow window of magic-making.

I had to pick and choose my battles, which magical moments I'd orchestrate, and the elf never made it onto that list.

But because of this man, this virtual stranger, they're getting it anyway.

"We're a team. Santa's team of magic makers," he says with ease, like it's the obvious answer, and I just *don't get it*. I don't get why he's spending so much on this, time and money and energy. Why he's devoting time, during what I can only assume is an incredibly busy time in his year, to two girls and a single mom to whom he has no attachment to.

"Why are you doing this?" I finally ask the question that's been plaguing me since the elf showed up on my front step. He hesitates before answering.

"I, uh . . . I'm trying to make these marshmallows look like a fort. For the elf, you know?"

I roll my eyes because why are men . . . men? I can't tell if he *really* doesn't know what I'm asking or if he's playing dumb, but either way, I clarify.

"No, I mean, why are you doing this? Driving an hour each way to come and set an elf up for my kids. You don't even know me. I'm sure you have much better things to do."

He stops what he's doing, manipulating the arms of a stuffed elf to make it look like she's drinking hot chocolate and making a snow fort out of marshmallows (too fucking cute, especially since it looks like he brought the girls their own mugs with their initials on them), and looks at me.

And when he does, he *looks at me*. It's the kind of look that burns to my soul, like he's using some kind of X-ray vision to read down deep, to scan me and see what answer I'm *really* looking for.

*I don't like it.*

Not one bit.

And I like it even less when his face softens, when he stands straighter, leaning his back against the cabinets and crossing his arms on his chest. When he looks like he enjoys or, at the very least, appreciates the answer he found in my subconscious.

"I've been there," he says, shrugging before continuing. "Young kids, raising them on your own. It's not easy. It's really fucking hard. And you're doing it with *two* kids."

I'm not buying it.

"There are a million single moms struggling to do all of the things in the tristate area alone. In fact, all things considered, I'm pretty privileged. I've got it mostly under control and I've got a good system backing me up. Why aren't you over there, making marshmallow forts for an elf?"

He stares at me for a minute, a small smile playing on his lips and a shake of his head before he answers, like I'm not getting some obvious piece of context that explains everything.

"Because they're not *you.*"

"What does that even mean?" I ignore how my belly flips and how his eyes go a bit warm with his words, with his look.

"It means your girls are cute and sweet and they've somehow got Connor wrapped around their fingers. And you're also cute and sweet, and it's not a burden to drive here and spend a bit of time with you. Especially now that you let me inside and I get to see you with your hair down, relaxed in your sweats." His smile goes wide. "Even if you ignore me and shoot daggers with your eyes at me while I'm here."

I swallow, not sure what to do with *that*. I would very much like to ignore this man calling me cute and sweet, *thank you very much.*

"So, that's why I'm doing this." Then, he turns his back to me and finishes up moving the stupid elf, conversation closed. I watch him with avid fascination as he continues for a minute or two before he nods at the little scene he created on the kitchen table, like he did his job well, and turns, grabbing his jacket.

"I'm doing it for you, Shae. And the girls. But if I'm being completely honest? I'm doing it to see you."

I don't respond.

I can't.

"See you tomorrow, sugarplum," he says then tips his stupid fucking cowboy hat he grabbed off my coat rack like this is some old Western movie and not fucking *Hudson City, New Jersey,* and walks out my door, letting it click shut behind him.

I don't know what makes me do it.

I should let him leave, should let him do whatever it is he's doing until the end of December then move on with my life.

But instead, I open a can of worms and my front door and shout at his retreating back, trying to ignore his ass that looks abnormally good in those faded jeans.

"The hat looks stupid! You're in New Jersey, not the Wild West!" I shout down the sidewalk, loud enough for my neighbors to hear, I'm sure.

He doesn't stop.

Instead, he lifts a hand, his laugh filling the dark street as his boots (stupid fucking *cowboy boots*) click against concrete as he does.

"Tomorrow, Shae."

I stand there for a full three minutes, long after the I can't see him anymore, before I return to myself and go back inside to get ready for bed.

# FOURTEEN

## 24 SLEEPS UNTIL CHRISTMAS

### SHAE

My phone buzzes on my desk with an incoming text and my entire body goes tight because even though it's barely ten, it's been a *morning*.

As we were getting ready for the day, Harper decided her normal lunch I *already made* of a PB&J was on her list of foods she absolutely hated, and it took everything in me not to lose my mind, instead making the teary-eyed girl an *only* peanut butter sandwich right before the bus came to grab her.

Then I got to the office to find not one, but *two* emails that made my entire body go rigid.

One was from my ex-husband, requesting I "stop being such a bitch" and ignoring his calls so we could "have a conversation like fucking adults," about the "bullshit support I shouldn't even have to fucking pay for."

As I put that one into my *deal with this on a day when I have more energy* folder, I became resigned to the fact that once the insanity of the holidays passes, I'll have to bother Damien once more with all of this communication. The restraining order from last year was temporary and we didn't feel it was necessary to seek a permanent order, but now it's looking like, once again, I'll have to burden my friends with my issues.

The second email was from Molly McGee, the PTO mom at the girls' school who can't stand me for one reason or another, sending another passive-aggressive reminder that the father-daughter dance that the school will be selling tickets for in January is for *fathers and step-fathers only*. Considering I'm the only single mom on the email chain, it's incredibly clear she's singling me out. I've only ever been kind to her and her god-awful brat of a kid, so I have no clue why she hates me so much.

So when a number not saved in my phone pops on my screen, I assume it's going to be more of my shitty luck. But I'm proven wrong when I read the message.

> Hey, it's Nick. Connor gave me your number. I'm going to be in the area a bit early. Mind if I bring dinner?

I want to say no.

I want to say *hell fucking no*. I don't want to have to worry about entertaining a not-quite stranger after a long day of work, and I don't feel like having to do the entire bedtime routine with him around, waiting for the girls to go to bed to move the elf or whatever.

But he's going so far out of his way every single day during the holiday season when his business is quite literally *the holidays*, and I might be a bitch, but I'm not *that* big of a bitch.

> That's fine. Don't worry about dinner though. I can handle it.

> I owe you.

> Let me get this one. Next dinner can be on you.

*Next dinner*, as if this isn't going to be a one-time thing.

> It's really no big. The girls are picky. It's easier if I handle it.

> Are you always this difficult when someone tries to help you?

I can almost *feel* my eyes rolling into my skull as the irritation this man intrinsically brings to me consumes me once more.

> Excuse me? I'm trying to make it easier on YOU.

> Then make it easier on me by telling me what the girls will eat.

I stare at my screen for long minutes.

Long, long minutes. So long, he sends me another text.

> Please, Shae.

It's simple.

Just two words, written in a way somehow portraying if I tell him what he wants to know, I'll be helping *him* out instead of him helping *me*.

Nothing about this man makes sense to me.

Still, I sigh and reply because, again, I'm a *bitch* but I'm not a *cunt*.

> Ruby is easy. She'll eat just about anything. Harper is . . . incredibly picky right now.

> What does she eat, sugarplum? I'll grab it.

My stomach turns at the sweet endearment he used last night. I wanted to hate it because *really? Sugarplum?* But also . . . I couldn't. It's so . . . Nick.

I should tell him to stop.

I should tell him I can handle the elf shit.

I should tell him we're moving to Aruba and taking the stupid elf with us.

Instead, I tell him the name of the only pizza place Harper eats from, telling him to grab her garlic knots and mozzarella sticks, and he confirms he'll be at my place at six.

I sit at my desk for long, excruciating minutes after, staring at my computer screen but seeing nothing at all.

What the fuck am I doing?

"So, Harper's a picky eater?" Nick asks later that night. It's been an interesting one, to say the least.

He ate dinner with the girls and me, having conversations with them, making them giggle, asking them about what they like, what they don't. Chiming in about some of their favorite shows even though there's no universe where he's seen them.

When the night got late, he helped get them ready for bed, watching over them while they brushed their teeth, making it a fun game for Ruby, who usually despises the task, making them giggle as he looked for monsters in their mouths that needed brushing, and then reading them not one, not two, but three books while I cleaned up around the kitchen.

I'll deny it if asked and take that lie to my grave, but it felt so good to have someone, to have *anyone* come and help handle the workload.

It's something that always felt like a myth media showed to make people feel shitty about their relationships. When you're surrounded by women all living the same reality as yours—the husband going out to *make the money* while you stay home with the kids and parent and cook and clean, then he sits on the couch after a long day at the office while your day continues—you think that's just the way it is. It's easy to tell yourself any other reality is a fantasy.

But tonight showed me *potential*. Some new version of life I should reach for.

And now, I sigh, setting aside the stocking I'm working on, having finished all of my nighttime chores before the girls were even asleep so I have more "me" time. "Yeah. She used to have more foods she'd eat, her safe foods, but they're diminishing."

"Has she always been like this? Or is it a phase? Connor went through a good month where he would only eat blue box mac and cheese. I still can't look at the stuff twenty years later." I smile at the thought, wondering if that will be me in a few years, talking about rainbow bagels and mozzarella sticks.

"She's always been a princess, a bit picky and particular about, well, everything. She knows what she wants and won't bend to anyone telling her otherwise. But the intensity of it . . ." I pick at my nails, suddenly uncomfortable. "That's new."

He doesn't respond, his back to me as he positions the elf on the mantel between framed photos, a marker in her hand. He drew silly faces on the girls' photos with a washable marker and framed the elf with the task. They're both going to *love* this one—I can already hear the giggles as they run around the house to see which pictures have been defamed.

His back to me gives me the freedom to speak more, something about not having his all-seeing eyes on my face when I open up a comfort.

"The doctor says it's a control thing. She's been through so much in the past year, with their dad and moving and a new school . . . It's been a lot. Eating is the one thing she has control over and she's holding on to that."

I expect to hear what a lot of parents who haven't dealt with this say: I just need to ignore it or that *kids won't starve!* I expect him to tell me what worked for his kid, what foods he could get him to eat, and how he snuck in vegetables. How he simply refused to make separate meals and eventually, his kid just *got over it.*

I've tried it all, of course, but it got to a point when I needed to prioritize both my and Harper's mental health. If making an extra stop means she gets to feel in control and heal a part of herself *and* she's going to get calories into her little body, what does it matter?

But as seems to be his way, Nick surprises me.

"That makes sense. There's not much a kid has control over. When and what she eats is easy for her." My brow furrows at his words as I continue to stare at his back. He's been playing with the goddamn elf for a full three minutes, and I'm starting to wonder if he's doing it on purpose, buying time as if he somehow knows by doing it, I'm more comfortable speaking.

Like he's giving me the same sense of control over the situation as feeding Harper her safe foods gives her.

And with that, I confess to this stranger.

I'm not sure if it's easier to confess to him *because* he's a stranger or because he seems to understand and he's doing so much to help my girls, or if maybe I just need *someone* to know what's going on in my mind, but regardless, I do.

"I get it—the need to have control over things when everything else is so unsure. I'm the same. It's my coping mechanism." I don't admit it's why I feel so much guilt about Harper's *lack* of control and stability in her life and how it feels like just *another* thing I gave her that hurts her.

"Yeah, I can see that," he says, looking over his shoulder with a smile, and I give him a look. It's one thing for me to say it, another for him. Like when someone calls your sibling annoying—only *you* can say it. "You think I could just let that one waltz by and not say anything?" He laughs, and it makes some of the irritation melt away.

"You know, if you want me to talk to you instead of just ignoring you again, you should really try being nicer to me." He finally stops working on the elf, and I notice he only does it once the moment is broken, once my oversharing is complete.

"Noted. I won't pick on you anymore. At least, not much." The fucking boyish smile that makes him look closer to Connor's age than mine lights the room up, and I fight the urge to do something stupid.

Like walking over and hugging him.

Or kissing him.

That would be really, *really* fucking stupid.

Thankfully, he speaks instead. "Alright. I should get out of your hair, get back to the ranch."

I definitely *don't* have to fight the urge to tell him he's not in my hair, he's not annoying me, and he doesn't have to leave right away.

Nope.

*No way.*

But I *can't* fight telling him how much appreciate his help before he leaves. "You coming with dinner . . . I know it isn't huge, but it means a lot," I say as I walk him to the door—his brow furrows as he turns and looks at me.

"What?"

"Bringing dinner. I know I said thank you, but it really means a lot to me. It takes a lot off my plate, you know?" I shrug, feeling silly saying it. "And you helping put the girls to bed."

"It's just dinner, Shae. Not paying your rent or anything."

"I know. But . . . I make all of the decisions. Breakfast and lunch and dinner and if they get dessert any given night and if I'm going to fight them on how well they brush their teeth before bed and if they get a book. I decide what they can and can't wear to school and if they can go to a friend's house for a playdate, and then I decide on *more* dinners. It's . . . It seems little, but it means a lot. It *helps* a lot. I get decision fatigue but it's just me and the girls and I can't put that on them. So it all falls on me." It's a constant conundrum in my life, wanting to be in control and then feeling like it is a burden I can't handle.

I shake my head, realizing what I'm saying can definitely come off wrong, come off needy or begging when I just meant it as a simple thank you. "I'm not saying I want you to bring us food all the time; I don't, really. I swear. Actually, please *don't* do that. I would offer to pay for tonight's dinner, but I know you'd give me that look."

"Not even sure what *that look* is, but you're right. I wouldn't be okay with you trying to pay for dinner."

I grumble, and he smiles before I speak again. "I'm just saying . . . thank you. That's all. Deciding what's for dinner sounds like a small thing, but sometimes . . . I get tired of being in charge all the time," I say. I don't know why I say it. "I'm tired of making every decision, of being the only one that *can* make choices, of not being able to delegate. So . . . thank you."

He stares at me as he tugs on his thick dark-brown jacket, more utilitarian than fashion, and he tops his head with that stupid cowboy hat before he does the unthinkable.

Nicolas Finch reaches out, cupping my cheek in his hand, callouses scratching at my skin in a way I can feel all over my body, and brushes his rough thumb over my cheekbone.

"Anytime, sugarplum."

And then he leaves.

And just like the night before, I don't move for long, long minutes as I try and digest what the hell just happened.

# FIFTEEN

## 23 SLEEPS UNTIL CHRISTMAS

### NICK

> What do you drink?

I send the text on a whim, mostly because I can't stop thinking of the mysterious woman more closed off than the Federal Reserve and the way she's slowly softening toward me.

Just a week ago, she looked at me with absolute *venom* in her eyes. But last night, I stayed there for a full thirty minutes after the girls went to bed, talking to her about anything she was willing to talk to me about. This was after she let me bring her dinner and help take some of the burden of the bedtime routine off her plate for a night.

Going there is quickly becoming the highlight of my day. I spend a good chunk of each morning searching for silly things the girls' elf can do instead of working during my busiest time of year and the rest planning how to get her to talk to me about . . . well, anything.

To let me in.

Shae is nothing like I thought she'd be and everything Connor told me she is. When she came on Thanksgiving, I fully expected to see something he couldn't or wouldn't admit, some pull they had, but instead, I saw he was right: everything between her and my son is completely platonic, and she's an amazing woman to her core.

Convenient for me, since what I'm feeling for her is anything but. After months of listening to my son tell me all these amazing things about this woman only to meet her and find she actually *is* gorgeous and strong and independent and fucking *stubborn* . . . I want her as my own.

My phone buzzes with what I assume is her response.

> What?

> Wine? Beer? Apple juice?

> Why?

See? *Stubborn.*

> I'm bringing some.

> Why?

God, she's also *such* a pain in my ass.

> Because I want to.

> Are you trying to get me drunk?

> I offered apple juice, so no. What do you drink, Shae?

It takes her a while to answer, and for a moment, I start to second-guess myself, thinking I fully fucked up without intending to, before she replies.

> Wine. White. But I'm not getting drunk with you.

I smile to myself.

She might think she's still being standoffish, but I see this small win for what it is. It's just another example of Shae letting me in, little by little.

And I can't fucking wait until she lets me in all the way.

"Are they asleep?" I ask when she lets me into her place later that night. It's barely after eight, ten minutes past the bedtime she told me about, but when I look around and see they must be tucked in already, I feel an acute sense of disappointment.

As much as I'm enjoying spending time with Shae, I also really like her girls. They're goofy and sweet, even if they're a bit standoffish, and the stories they told me when I brought dinner, all exaggerated and extravagant, were a fucking delight.

Bonus, they both give *huge* belly laughs at all of my terrible jokes, and considering Connor finds me precisely zero percent funny these days, I can use the ego boost.

"Yeah," she says, sitting back down on the couch and picking up the pile of yarn she seems to be always working on. Every night I've come here, she's working on it after she does her laundry list of chores, and every night she looks mildly annoyed that she is, in fact, working on it.

I watch as I grab the elf, moving him— her, as Harper reminded me last night over mozzarella sticks and pizza—until she's happily set up with a few other little toys I bought, having a "pizza party" with gummy pizzas they can eat at some point tomorrow.

When I'm done, the last thing I want to do is leave Shae, so I move to the kitchen, finding her wine glasses and pouring her a glass before grabbing a beer for myself, sliding the others into her fridge.

I like the look of it, my beer nestled in her fridge between kids' snacks and the three prepacked lunchboxes, each a different color for the different women in this house. Then I move back to the living room to watch her turn yarn into . . . something.

"Can I ask what you're making?" I ask, moving to her and handing her the glass of wine I poured.

She groans and accepts the glass, and I fight the laugh from her clear exhaustion, both in the literal sense and with whatever it is she's making.

"Stockings for the girls."

"Like Christmas stockings?"

"No, for under a dress," she says with an eye roll, the words filled with sarcasm. I smile. "Yeah, Christmas stockings. Sorry, that was bitchy. I'm just hating everything about making these." She takes another long sip of her wine before placing it on the coffee table in front of her and laying her head back on the couch, the yarn and stocking a mess in her lap.

"Why are you making them then? Why not just buy the cheap ones from the store and add some glitter glue. I bet they'd love that," I ask. A look crosses her face, a mix of frustration and pain and sorrow, and somehow I know where it's going without her even having to say a thing.

"My ex's mother made the girls each one when they were born. She passed away not long after Harper was born, but they loved those stockings." I stare at her, waiting for more. She continues to stare at the ceiling like answers or a script are up there, guiding her through this conversation she clearly doesn't want to have but also, for some reason, wants to have all the same.

I wonder if she works the way I do, if confessing her issues and mistakes and fears makes them less powerful and, if somehow, I'm the person she's trusting with this info.

I'd be honored if she were.

The universe gives me an answer with her next words, spoken to the ceiling in a quiet voice.

"When I left Todd, I left almost everything. I got the kids' clothes and toys and anything they needed but left most of my shit. I had a police escort later, and I got about twenty minutes in the house to grab what I needed. But even that, Todd was allowed to veto things, so I only grabbed what he couldn't argue. It wasn't worth it to me. Some things, like those stockings his mother made, I knew he'd fight me on just to be an ass. So they stayed."

Jesus, this guy is even more of a jerk than I thought, and I thought he was the worst kind of man already. Anyone who could look at gorgeous Shae and not only not want to give her the world but to cause her pain is an ass.

"Once you won your case and got the divorce, I'm sure a judge would have let you go back and get whatever you want." She sighs and shrugs but sits up once more to take a sip of wine, like she's trying to avoid the conversation or keep busy.

"Damien, my lawyer and friend, would have taken it back to court in a heartbeat, but he'd already done so much for me. It wasn't like I was missing their baby pictures or anything—I had those. It didn't seem worth it to get everyone riled up on my behalf. Plus, it meant less time dealing with him. More time spent moving on, you know?" I stare at her, taking her in, and for a moment, she returns the look before she quickly shifts her focus to her lap, playing with the yarn in her fingers. "So instead, I'm making new ones. A fresh start."

"You do that a lot, don't you?" I ask.

"Do what."

"Sacrifice shit you want in order to not feel like a burden, to not make waves." Her head snaps up and she gives me a new look, one that's half defensive, half teasing, a confusing mix I should expect from his woman at this point.

"I make plenty of waves, trust me," she says with a self-depre-cating laugh.

"But do you really?" I ask, staring at her. I don't know what makes me do it, but I do it all the same. I reach out and grab her hand, smooth and soft, the ultimate contrast to my rough, calloused hands and so freaking small in mine. My thumb gently brushes against the back of it.

"Trust me, I do."

"You wouldn't let me help with the elf shit. I had to fight you on dinner."

"Not wanting help does not equate to not wanting to make waves, Nick," she says, her voice low.

"Doesn't it?"

"No, it doesn't." She's starting to get annoyed, and fuck, it's cute. She might not like making waves, but I sure love making a wave in her waters, watching her carefully crafted boat rock a little.

"What's your explanation for not wanting help? Because you don't want to bother people, right?" When she smiles a look of triumph, I know I got it wrong. She looks like I've proven a point I didn't realize she was intending to make, and somehow it feels like a loss after a few wins.

"No. It's because I like control. I like to be in control of what I do and how it happens, and the best way to do that is to do it all myself. I gave up my power for over ten years, letting my husband have it in order to appease him, to try and save a marriage that was only going to get worse. Giving others control put my daughters in danger, and I'll never forgive myself for that. *That's* why I don't want help."

"You take the help; you lose control," I say, understanding. She smiles and takes another sip of her wine before tipping her glass to me.

"Exactly." Then she moves back to her project, and I watch this confusing woman, trying to work out how to break through those walls of hers but also make sure she keeps that control she clearly desperately needs.

"I should head out," I say maybe thirty minutes later, after checking my watch. I have to be up with the sun tomorrow, all of the tasks I usually do at night this time of year suddenly becoming morning errands. She sighs before standing with a nod.

"And I should get to bed myself," she says, standing and grabbing her wine glass as I grab my half-empty beer bottle. "The girls will be up with the sun to see what kind of trouble Holly got into." I move instinctively to apologize, but there's a teasing smile on her face telling me she didn't mean it in irritation.

I think the elf might be growing on her.

I spent the entire thirty minutes on the couch watching her, admiring the lines of her face, the way she'd get angry each time her hair fell out of the small ponytail, the way she'd occasionally lift the half-made stocking to look at it and would smile in pride and satisfaction.

And each second over those thirty minutes confirmed how fucking much I want this woman.

We both walk to the kitchen, and I pour the remains of my drink down the drain. That's when she bumps into me, her hand brushing mine and sending electricity racing down my arm.

I think it might be the confirmation I need in my decision to make her mine, to make this little family my responsibility. Or maybe I decided that when she walked into my house on Thanksgiving, looking annoyed, her girls racing in like it was normal. Maybe I looked at them then and knew, decided to make them mine.

They don't need a man, a father to protect them—Shae is clearly doing that and so much more—but I still felt the tug to be that for all of them. Something innate, like a piece of the universe slipping into place, like the plans of some higher power I don't necessarily believe in are going exactly as planned.

But that brush of her skin on mine, the sparks it sends, the look of shock on her face—it makes me decide I won't just be the guy who helped out for the holidays, another friend with a helping hand in her life.

I want to be *hers*.

"Sorry," she whispers.

I don't say anything.

Instead, I drop the beer bottle into the sink, grabbing her glass from her hand as well and placing it in, then I grab her wrist and turn toward her. Her hips are on the counter as I step closer, our chests just barely touching. My head dips down so I can look at her as she looks up at me, her mouth slightly open as she does. Moving her hand, I twine her fingers with my own before sandwiching them between our bodies as my free hand moves to the counter.

I want to use it to touch her, to tangle my fingers in her soft-looking hair, to tug her closer to me, but I'm terrified of scaring her off.

I've never felt like this with a woman. This need to protect and nurture and move slowly. I've never had the knowledge that the wrong move could destroy the tentative peace between us, could ruin even the smallest chance I have with her.

If I'm being completely honest, since I was a kid, women have gravitated to me to the point I never really had to try much. Fuck, that's how Connor came to be, a stupid teenage decision with a girl who wasn't ready to be a mother. Even as an adult, I've never had to chase a woman, never had to convince her to give me a shot.

But I've also never been able to envision any form of *more* with a woman. And even though I barely just met her, I'm picturing *more* with her so fucking vividly, I can almost touch it.

"Can I kiss you?" I ask, my words barely a whisper. My eyes are locked on hers, a bright spring green both of her daughters have. Hers are on my lips, and it takes everything in me not to smile, not to let my lips tip up at the lost look in her eyes.

But mostly, I have to fight not to say *fuck it* and kiss her until she can't breathe.

That would ruin everything because like her daughter, Shae needs this control. Needs to know it's all in her hands. She's the master of our destiny.

"What?" The word is a single breath of air touching my lips, an erotic caress making me want her even more.

"Can I kiss you, Shae? Say no and I'm on the other side of this room in a heartbeat." She swallows and stares behind my shoulder like she's picturing where I'll go if she says no.

I don't dare move.

I barely breathe.

"Kiss me?" she asks. "You want to kiss me?" I let myself smile then.

I can't *not*—she's so fucking cute and so unaware of her impact on me.

"Very much so. I want to do a lot of things with you, but we'll leave it at a kiss for tonight." Her eyes go impossibly wider, and in my hand, her pulse goes wild.

"Oh."

I don't reply.

Instead, I wait. I wait for her response, wait for her to give me the go-ahead or to knee me in the balls or to tell me to leave right this instant.

I would, too. No questions asked.

But I don't need to ice my groin or head for my car because she does something unexpected.

She doesn't say yes.

She doesn't say no.

Instead, she moves to her tiptoes and kisses *me*.

# SIXTEEN

## 23 SLEEPS UNTIL CHRISTMAS

### SHAE

I think I've lost my mind.

That's the only explanation for why my arm is moving up and wrapping around Nick's neck, why I've moved to my tiptoes, why I'm pressing my lips to his like I haven't been kissed in years.

To be fair, I can't remember the last time I *was* kissed, but that's neither here nor there because I'm kissing Nick and the world is spinning around me.

His lips are warm as they meld to mine, soft and pliant, and as he takes a short breath of surprise, he steals the breath from my lungs.

I like that. I like how I surprised him, how he didn't see this option coming out of the ones he probably mapped out in his mind. And even more, I like the way he feels against me.

The kiss radiates through my body, and warmth, sweet and comforting, flows through me, leaving heated tingles in its wake as his hand tightens on mine, holding me like I'm a lifeline. My free hand moves up, playing with the hair at the back of his neck. The hand he had on the counter moves to my jaw, holding it gently as he deepens the kiss, as my lips part in invitation, as he *takes* that invitation.

And fuck, does he take it.

His tongue moves into my mouth, tasting me, the flavor of beer and something so *Nick* I can't even put my finger on it filling my mouth and adding to the desperate nature of the kiss that started so sweet, so innocent.

I mewl as I tighten on his neck, trying to get closer, trying to let him consume me. He groans in response, like he feels it, too—the flood of emotion and need and lust coursing through me, coiling tight in my belly.

He nips my lip, and I moan into his mouth as he moves even closer, pinning me between his body and the counter, the kiss taking another turn into something more volatile as his cock presses against my belly.

The man is hard.

*Holy fucking shit.*

This man—all cowboy and rough edges wrapped in cotton candy sweetness and silly Christmas cheer—is hard just from *kissing me.*

*I can't help it.*

I move to take it further, using my hand on his neck to tug him closer and moving my body so his cock grinds against my belly.

Somehow, this kiss has me forgetting about reality and *should dos* and *bad ideas* and housing issues and . . . well . . . everything except how I want to get closer to him and how I want to touch him and how I just *want him.*

But as it has a tendency to do, pesky reality breaks in with the sound of a door opening, the painted frame sticking a bit in the quiet apartment, and my body freezes.

Nick does too and instantly, he drops his hand from my jaw, stepping back as the sound of little feet on creaky floors travels to us.

"Mommy?" the voice asks, and I don't have to look to know its Ruby. When I turn, she's standing there in her purple pajamas, a bit too short on the ankles, her hands on her eyes as she rubs, the lights in the living room too bright.

"Hey, honey, a bad dream?" I ask. The nightmares were almost a nightly occurrence a year ago when I first separated from Todd, but they trickled off until we spent nearly the entire summer without them.

But then the brats at school started giving her shit, and I can only assume the anxiety is what started them back up. I add a sticky note with *call Ruby's therapist* to my mental wall and pray it sticks before moving closer to my girl.

"Alright, go back in your room and I'll tuck you in, okay?" I ask. She stands firm before shaking her head and looking behind me to Nick, a reminder of just how much I've lost my mind.

"No, I want Nick to," she demands. My stomach drops. I shake my head, a mirror of hers.

"Honey, he can't—" Nick cuts me off before I can finish my sentence, his hand going to the bend of my arm, calloused fingers wrapping there in a gentle, easy touch.

"If you're okay with it, I am," he says, his voice low so only I can hear, his thumb brushing on my skin in a soft caress.

I look at him and all I see is sincerity.

"Please, Mom?" she asks, her voice nervous.

I want to give her this.

I want to give her this, but I also so deeply *do not want* to give her this because it feels like another failure of mine. Another shortcoming, the inability to give her a stable male relationship or father figure, and, knowing Ruby, there's a good fucking chance of her getting attached.

It's just who she is.

I desperately want to protect her, to keep her safe after all the harm I've already exposed her to, but I can't.

I don't have it in me to say no.

So I nod.

"Okay. Quick, though, okay? He'll tuck you in and you go to bed."

"Can he read me a story?"

"Not tonight, baby. Your sister's still asleep, right?" She nods, her eyes going watery with the refusal.

Fuck.

*Goddammit.*

Harper is handling all of the changes by reaching for control, but Ruby is coping by going out of her way to make everyone's life easy, rarely arguing, and barely making a fuss.

And yet, she's choosing *this moment* to ask for something for herself finally.

"I'll be quiet," Nick says, squeezing my hand. "And only one book, yeah? A short one." Ruby nods, the tears still shining in her eyes, but the risk of them falling has passed. "Get in your bed, I'll be right here." She runs off back down the hall before Nick turns to me.

"If you don't want me to, you can say I had to go. I understand."

God, he's good.

Too fucking good.

And it's in that moment, and again when I watch him tuck in Ruby and read her a story from the shadows of the hallway, I make my decision.

A painful one, considering that kiss, considering how having him in such a small way has felt.

Because I decide then I can't have Nicolas Finch.

I can't have him because I'm giving him to my girls.

We can't be anything more than adults working together to make magic for two little girls. Being "more" always comes with heartache, and Ruby and Harper have already had enough of that in their lives. So long as I ignore the pang in my chest each time I think of him, we should be good.

Nick returns just a minute or two after I leave the hall, walking in on me drying my wine glass, my mind made up.

"She's out, I think. Barely made it through the book."

"She does that," I say. "Nightmares wake her up, but she falls back asleep easily once she knows she's safe." He reaches for me, his hand moving to grab mine and pull me in, I suppose, but I step back, shaking my head.

"That was a bad idea," I whisper, the words tasting sour in my mouth.

He looks at me, confusion written on his face. "Putting Ruby to bed?" I shake my head then clarify.

"We can't kiss."

He smiles that boyish smile, that ache in my chest intensifying. "But we did."

"Okay, fine. We can't kiss *again*," I clarify, crossing my arms on my chest.

"And why is that?" He doesn't look mad. No, instead, he looks almost . . . entertained.

"Because . . ." I sigh. "Because Ruby likes you. And so does Harper." The amusement slips off his face, his brows furrowing in confusion.

"You can't kiss me because . . . your kids *like* me?" I sigh, trying to put my thoughts into words he'll understand, words he can't argue with.

It's becoming increasingly obvious Nick Finch *loves* to argue with me.

"I can't kiss you because, for me, kissing leads to emotions. I can't kiss you because my girls like you and emotions lead to breakups, and if they like you, if they get attached to you, they'll lose you." His face softens, but I continue, armor on and deflecting anything that might make me waver. "So instead, you can come every day and do the elf thing and show my girls that not all men suck."

"But I can't do it kissing you." His arms cross on his chest, his face moving to contemplative.

"No."

"And why's that?" I step back from him even though he hasn't closed the gap at all. He's just *too close*, and nearness means he's going to cloud my judgment.

I think any distance from Nick is too close, though, if we're being honest.

"Because I'm choosing to give you to my girls instead of taking you for myself." He stares for long seconds that feel like an hour, decoding me and reading between the lines of what I'm saying before he nods.

"Got it," he says.

"Got it?"

"Yeah, you're setting your boundaries and putting your girls first."

I refuse to think about how my gut drops when he doesn't argue, when he doesn't fight. Instead, he walks backward toward where his jacket is hung on the hook next to my front door.

"Just means the next time we kiss, it's all on you, sugarplum."

I ignore the first part of that sentence.

I don't have the bandwidth for it.

"What's with that? The sugarplum thing."

"It's you," he says simply.

"What? Sugarplum is *me?*"

"Oh, absolutely," he says then shrugs on his jacket. "I most definitely have visions of you dancing in my head all night, every night."

And then he grabs that *stupid fucking hat* and leaves.

# SEVENTEEN

## 22 SLEEPS UNTIL CHRISTMAS

### NICK

"I like her," I say into the phone, and fuck if my stomach isn't churning just a bit with nerves. As if I'm not 42 and the man who raised him, but some buddy who's interested in dating his ex.

"Who? Shae?"

"Yeah." I balance my phone on my shoulder and tug one of my boots on. It's early still, and I don't need to put them on just yet, but I need to keep my hands busy.

"Well, no shit," he says, and I stop what I'm doing, letting the boot fall to the floor with a loud thunk.

"What?"

"I said *no shit, you like her.*" I lean back on the couch, my brow furrowing as I run a hand through my thick hair, trying to understand what he's saying. I've been nervous about this call for a week, trying to find the right words to tell him I'm going to try and make Shae and her girls *mine.*

I keep trying to figure it out, when it happened, when I decided I'd fight for Shae. Was it when her girls ran into my house and tackled my son like they were always some part of this family? Was it the daggers she shot at me when I mentioned the elf to her daughters?

Was it when she let me into her place instead of leaving me in the cold every night? Was it when she let me stay for dinner and I fit in like I was meant to be there?

Or maybe it happened slowly, over months and months of Connor telling me about this woman he met on a dating app and her daughters he was taking out on day dates. All of the calls where he'd say, *Shae is so strong, she doesn't even realize it*, or *Harper is a goof and you'd love her, Dad*, or *Ruby's a little shy, but once she warms up to you, she's Velcro.*

"What do you mean?"

"I mean, *no shit, you like her*. You've been driving an hour each way every fuckin' night just to see her ass." I hadn't actually told my son about that, thinking there was a high chance of him being annoyed I was going to his friend's place or that I had accidentally added more stress to her plate.

"How do you—"

"I'm friends with her, Dad. That's how you met her, remember?" He says it like I'm a moron.

"Yeah, well. I'm going to help out with the elf and . . ." My lie trails off as Connor laughs.

"I'm not 9. I can see right through your bullshit. I'm also not a 35-year-old woman buried under stress and the fear of letting go of control. I know exactly why you're going there every night."

I don't respond because, honestly, I don't know *how*.

"I invited her for you, Dad."

That's when the ringing in my ears starts.

"What?"

"Thanksgiving? I invited her because I thought you two would be good for each other. You're the same and different in all the ways that matter, and I'm not an idiot. I know you wanted more kids after me but didn't have time to date between me and the farm. Those girls need a dad, and you're a really good one."

A long stretch of silence fills the line as I try and process his words, as I try and figure out how to respond.

"So yeah. I know you like her," he says, but his voice is different, tinged with something new. "Don't hurt her, okay? And be patient. She thinks she's over all the shit with her ex and she is, but she blames herself for a lot of it. Blames herself for how the girls were impacted."

"That's not—"

"I know, trust me. And I've had this conversation with her a million times, but she's a brick wall. I'm only telling you because I don't want you to hear her say some version of *no,* or *this won't work,* or *this is too much for you* and take it at face value. She tries that shit with me nearly weekly, telling me not to bother helping her or spending the day with them. It's just how she is. She's selfless to a fault."

That fits what I know of her, with the little I've tugged from her. She might be past her irritation with me and might not be telling me every day I don't have to be doing this, but it's in her eyes, in the way she talks to me.

She's waiting for me to be over this, waiting for me to get bored.

It's my job to show her I won't.

A part of me saw Shae for the first time and it was like I knew, one way or another, she was sent to the world to be mine. I was brought here to take care of her, to make sure she always comes first.

And I'm going to do that.

"So, let's say I want to pursue her," I say, once more running a hand through my hair. "What should I do?"

There's a smile in his voice when he speaks, and a mix of joy and trepidation creeps into my veins with his words.

"I've been waiting for this day, old man. You got a pen to take notes?"

# EIGHTEEN

## 20 SLEEPS UNTIL CHRISTMAS

### NICK

The first two nights after the kiss and my decision to make Shae and her girls mine, she doesn't speak to me.

In a way, I expected it, somehow already knowing her well enough to know she would absolutely freak the fuck out the first time I kissed her and crawl into her little hole of overthinking and panic and reading too far into things.

That's fine. She can hide, overthink, and panic because this is all new and strange, and I'll be here waiting for her to be ready for us. Because I know down to my bones, they were meant to be mine.

It might be strange, thinking of a man knowing a woman and two young girls for just a few weeks and deciding to make them a permanent fixture in his life, but it's not to me. I've always been this way, all or nothing. I heard Ashley was pregnant and I knew in that instant Connor was mine.

I heard Mr. Samuels was selling the farm and I knew, somehow, some way, it was going to be mine.

And I think I watched Shae walk into my house in that red dress on Thanksgiving and I knew then.

She was going to be mine.

So the first night after the kiss, when she lets me in and clearly avoids me, barely saying hello, repeating the action again the next night, I let it go. But considering I only have a month to prove what I already know in my bones to her, when she doesn't even greet me the following day, I decide to push her a bit.

"You can't keep ignoring me, Shae," I say after setting up the elf and moving to sit on the arm of the couch.

"I can," she replies, not even looking up from the stocking she's still working on. This one is almost done, it seems, and I wonder if she has another to do or if Ruby's is already done. This pink one is definitely Harper's.

"You can't. I'm a hard man to ignore." Her hands stop moving, and she gives me a look that should kill but instead just makes me laugh. I don't miss how her face softens with the sound of my laughter, like I have the same effect on her as her laugh does on me.

*How can she not see this? Feel this? A fucking Christmas miracle is what we are, two people finding each other randomly and fitting so perfectly.*

"Don't you have better things to do than drive an hour into Hudson City and move an elf every night?" she asks with a groan, and I smile, moving to the actual couch but still a good three feet from her.

"Nope. Got all the time in the world to convince you to spend some time with me."

"Ugh, god, does that actually work on women?"

"Don't know. I've only ever tried it on you and clearly, the results are . . . mixed." She fights a smile.

I don't.

She rolls her eyes. "You look tired. Maybe you should go home and sleep. Go to bed early tomorrow," she says, and I laugh again.

"God, you really know how to make a man feel good, don't you?" A blush takes over her face before she starts speaking quickly.

"I didn't mean it . . . Shit, you definitely still look *good*, don't get me wrong. I—fuck, I didn't mean it like that. Not *good*, good just like, good, you know? Like healthy? But tired. God, this is—" If she wasn't genuinely getting worked up and nervous, I'd let it go because she's cute like this, nervous and panicking.

"I was joking, Shae. Don't panic. I'll be sure my sarcasm comes across a bit more clearly next time," I say to appease her.

"You're an ass," she says, throwing a couch pillow at me. When I smile, she rolls her eyes, and I see it then—what the future will look like once we cross this hurdle, once we cross the line she needs to get over in order to give us a chance.

"It's my busy season," I say as an explanation. "The drive here is actually really fuckin' nice, a decompression of sorts. I spend October through December stressing about making sure we hit numbers to keep the ranch and the farm open all year. People ask me questions all damn day—on the drive here, my phone's on silent. I don't answer shit until the next morning. It forces me to . . ." I don't really know how to explain how she's given me a bit of peace, that I usually run myself ragged all November and December and spend all of January recovering, usually sick as a dog by Christmas. "Relax. Enjoy the season."

"Are things tight?" she asks, clear concern in her eyes, and it makes me like her even more, the way she worries.

"No, not like that. But there are markers we need to hit every week in order for me to feel comfortable with shit."

"Do you do anything any other time of year?" she asks, putting her needle aside and turning her body to look at me better. I shake my head.

"It's always just been the Christmas tree farm. Mr. Samuels, the old owner, used to keep it simple. I've added the Christmas shop and brought in more horses so we can do carriage rides. The horses used to just be pets. Same with the animals—they used to be exclusively personal animals. So, we added the little petting zoo. Helps me hit those numbers easier."

"But come January, everything's done?" she asks, confused. I nod. "Have you thought of . . . adding anything?"

"We're a Christmas tree farm, Shae. Not much of a business outside of that." She shakes her head like I'm a stupid man, and it makes me smile.

"You have to think bigger picture. In fall, people would kill to be able to go into the farm and take their holiday photos. A couple of weekends, make it an event—get photographers to come, charge a base price, and have stuff for the kids to do after. Hayrides, apple cider, bounce houses, food trucks . . . It would go over really well," she says then perks up, clearly getting excited. "Or in the summer, horse-back riding lessons. I'm not sure how that works. I'm sure the insurance would be expensive, and you'd have to hire instructors, but kids want that. Shit, *Ruby* wants that. I was looking into it for her and it's not cheap by long shot, and people pay it. It would be a good way to keep the ranch profitable all year and take the pressure off the holiday season."

I smile at her, and then suddenly, something in her face changes. "I'm sorry. That was a lot, and I totally overstepped." I shake my head.

"No, no, it's good. I've been trying to think of new things to add to lessen the holiday pressure. I'm tired of working all season and not *experiencing* the season. What else do you have?" I ask, and she gives me a small smile, tucking hair behind her ear, that short, shoulder-length hair that never stays in the ponytails and clips she puts it in.

"I'm not . . . I mean, I'm not an expert or anything—"

"You've got ideas, share them." I stare at her for moment, watching a wash of emotions cross her face—nerves, excitement, embarrassment, then determination and she moves even closer, like she can't wait to share her ideas, like she's been sitting on them for a while.

Then she spills, talking about pumpkin patches and summer camps and retreats. Some are more or less impossible, others are things I've thought of before, but even more . . . they're smart. Good business decisions that would help the ranch be more financially stable.

"You're good at this, thinking up business ideas," I say, and she absolutely *beams* this time at the praise.

"I love it. I do it a bit for my work, but I've always loved brainstorming business ideas." I remember Connor telling me she worked for a lawyer, but not really what she does.

"What do you do now?"

"Administrative stuff for a nonprofit. Nothing too exciting. I love it, though, don't get me wrong."

"But it's just not your passion," I state, and she doesn't argue, so I know that's the truth. "Why aren't you following your passion?" The scale in her head tips left and right as she moves her head toward each shoulder, balancing and weighing her response.

"Security, obviously. And Damien, my boss, kind of saved me, so there's that. Plus, I wouldn't know where to start. I'm a single mom who, until last year, thought I'd be a stay-at-home mom forever. I thought I had another, ten, twelve years before I had to figure out *what comes next.*" She shrugs, her face tipping down to look at her hands playing with the frayed edge of her worn shirt.

"You seem to be doing well regardless." She scoffs out a laugh.

"Yeah, I'm not too sure about that, but I appreciate it."

"You clearly don't give yourself enough credit."

"I'm a disaster. Harper won't eat anything but bagels and mozzarella sticks. Ruby has nightmares about her father. They both always look at me like I'm about to completely fall apart, and my own personal life is nonexistent." I shake my head because she clearly doesn't get it.

"None of that means you're failing. It means that the world is going on around you, for better or worse, and regardless of the punches thrown, you're still standing. That's impressive. That's something to celebrate." She shakes her head like she doesn't agree but doesn't expand, just sitting there, letting her finger play with a loose string at the collar of her shirt.

I let her for long minutes, enjoying her sitting here with me, happy to let it be like this, until a question enters my brain, niggling and eating at my consciousness until I have no choice but to blurt it out.

"Do you date?" I ask, and she clearly doesn't expect the question because her head moves back in shock and confusion.

"What?"

"Do you date?" I repeat. Suddenly, I need to know. I need to know if she's dating, if she's been open to a partner in her life recently, or if this is truly a lost cause. I'll push my way into her life, help her with her girls, and wish she could be mine, but if she's genuinely just not ready to date, I'm going to have to accept that. To *endure* that, watching her from afar instead of making her mine like I really want.

"Uh, I mean. I met your son on a dating app," she says, and I groan, my head hitting the back of the couch as I glance at the ceiling.

"Not gonna lie, if I'm continuing on this path, gonna need you to stop reminding me of that," I say, giving Shae a smile that tells her I'm not fully serious.

"What, do you feel weird about kissing your son's sloppy seconds?" I smile wider because she thinks she's winning, and she has no clue at all. No clue that when she smiles at me like that, I just want to say fuck morals, fuck her making the next move, and press her into the couch and have my way with her.

"Not in the least." Her eyes go a bit wide with shock. "If I get to kiss you without your walls up, when I finally con you into giving me a shot, any man who kissed you before is absolutely nonexistent." Her mouth drops open as she stares at me. "So. Do you date? Are you dating right now?" I ask, the question churning in my gut in a way I don't necessarily enjoy very much but just is.

"Do I date?" she mimics, clearly still stuck on my previous words. I brush her hair back, letting my fingers linger on the skin of her neck before smiling.

"Yeah. Online dating, dating apps, blind dates . . ." She blurts out words I didn't expect.

"Online dating was created by the devil himself, and I will die on that hill." My eyes go wide at her outburst, and she blushes. "Shit, sorry. I have very strong feelings about modern dating."

"I can see that."

"It's just . . . I hate it. You have to make a *resume* for someone even *looking* your way, and I'm convinced there has to be some kind of dopamine response that connects app dating and swiping. Like, you hear about people using these apps behind their partner's back and you're kind of like . . . well, yeah, it makes sense. App and online dating have created a universe where you can always convince your-self you could do better, that instead of going to your partner and working out an issue, you can just start fresh. Make a new bio, shift it a bit to fit what or who you're looking for better this time, and move on."

She sighs and throws her hands up.

"And everyone is highlighting the best parts of themselves, and you have to pretend the bad parts aren't there, and the ones who show their bad parts are secretly *really fucking bad* because, just like everyone else, they're only showing what they *think* is their best. The only difference is, they have *so many bad parts* that even in this incredibly curated state, the bad slips through. Which, in a fucked-up way, makes the medium bad ones look slightly better. It just seems . . . pointless." She takes a deep breath before continuing.

"So, yes. I try and date. But it's hard, and I hate it, especially considering I have the girls to think about. I met my ex in college at a frat party in a basement. I married the first guy who liked me and always said how lucky I was I never had to *do* this online dating bull-shit. I must have jinxed myself. I never had to do this *new* version of dating before. And it's . . . It's rough out there," she says then finally stops. "Oh god, that was embarrassing. I fully just gave a dating Ted Talk." She tries to move away, but I grab her wrist, forcing her to stay and shaking my head.

"Do you really think I don't get exactly what you're saying? I've been trying to date for twenty fuckin' years with Connor. I get it, Shae. It's not easy. Somedays, it seems like it would be easier to just . .

. not," I say, confessing my own truth. "To just live life single, let that dream go."

She stares at me, then she smiles shyly, like she's nervous I'll think she's silly or something. "But also . . . I don't want the girls to see me not trying to move on, to not find love. I don't want that life for them."

It's like I'm a fucking middle schooler, my stomach filling with flittering butterflies when the girl I like smiles in my direction.

"So you want that? To find love?"

"I mean . . . isn't that what life is about? Finding a partner to spend your days with?"

"I think so," I say, reaching up and letting my thumb swipe across the apple of her cheek, hoping she understands what I'm saying.

*I think I could want to spend my days with you.*

*I'm glad I waited so long for you to find your way to me.*

*Please give this a chance.*

Because whether it takes a week or a month or a year or a decade, I'm going to make Shae mine.

But I'm hoping a Christmas miracle will make that wait go quickly.

# NINETEEN

## 19 SLEEPS UNTIL CHRISTMAS

### NICK

On Wednesday, Shae unlocks the door, letting me in, and I get to work, placing the little elf on the kitchen counter and sprawling cotton balls around.

An elf snowball fight.

By the time I'm done, I'm pretty impressed with myself—the girls are going to absolutely love this. To be fair, it wasn't my own idea. In fact, I ran out of those just a few days into this project. Thankfully, the internet is filled with elf scenes much more creative than I could ever hope to be and for that, I am *grateful*.

The entire time, Shae is sitting on the couch, music playing low while she continues to work on crocheting a stocking, this one purple. I watch her for a few minutes once I'm done with my task, her tongue sticking out once in a while in a way that's really fuckin' cute, like she's concentrating on what she's doing and not really sure if she's doing it right. She's so lost in her thoughts that when I finally speak a few minutes later, she jumps, dropping her needles and yarn.

"How was your day?"

"What?" she asks, her face confused.

"I said, *how was your day?*"

"Oh."

"Oh?" I ask with a smile.

"I just . . . I don't know. I didn't expect that."

"I realized today I haven't asked you that yet and I see you every day. So, I'm making that right."

"Huh," she says, then her fingers move to a spot on the couch where a few threads are loose, touching it gently.

"So?"

"So?" She's dazed, lost in her thoughts.

"Jesus, Shae. How was your day?" She smiles a small smile before shaking her head.

"Sorry, it's been a . . . day."

"That's why I'm asking."

"Because you know I've had a day?"

"No, because I want to know about your days." She stares at me, confused, reading me, like she's trying to understand what she's supposed to say, how she's supposed to respond. "I don't know what you look like when you have a good or bad day. Only way for me to learn is by asking."

"It was . . . fine," she lies. This must be a leftover reaction from her ex or maybe even further, some kind of habit ingrained in her. I shake my head, reaching out and grabbing her hand, the only unprovoked contact I'll allow myself.

"I want you to tell me the truth, Shae. The mess and the stress and the good and bad shit."

"You don't want that, trust me," she says with a self-deprecating smile.

"I do. I very much do," I say. "I want the good, the bad, the in-between. The boring, inconsequential things, the little things that made you laugh. All of it." The challenge in her eyes burns, like she's hearing my words but not believing them and is ready to prove me wrong.

Because Shae still doesn't believe I want her, want this.

"I woke up at four this morning because the neighbor has this little yapping dog on the wall connected to mine and it was barking at something, and then I couldn't fall back asleep so I stared at my ceiling, thinking of all the things I could be doing, should be doing, but I was paralyzed because I couldn't decide where to start. My list is *that* long. It's always that long. Then I got up and made lunches for the girls because I forgot to the night before. Harper will never eat school lunch, not these days, and Ruby brings her lunch because she wants to avoid standing next to the mean girls in the lunch line. Then I had to fight the girls to get them up and fed and out the door in time, and I saw the little brat who bullies Ruby outside the school and I had to bite my tongue even when she said *nice shoes* to Ruby in front of me in the bitchiest way and her mother didn't even say anything. Nothing! Which isn't a surprise because the mother used to be nice but then she got engaged to some rich guy and thinks her shit doesn't stink." She pauses and takes a deep breath before continuing.

"Then I sat in traffic until I died because I wanted to go into the office even though Damien tells me I can work from home, but, really, how will he know I'm actually *doing my work,* and I need to prove to him I'm not just fucking around, that his trust in me isn't for nothing. And I got yelled at by donors *all fucking day.* You'd never believe it, but the rudest people on this planet are the ones who donate to nonprofits for clout. You'd think they would be nice since they support worthy causes, but no. They're *mean.*"

Her cheeks are going red, and I think she expects me to intercept, to stop her, but when I don't, wanting her to get it all out, she continues.

"Then I got an email that Ruby was in with the guidance counselor, crying over the mean girls at her school *again,* and they never do *anything* about it because, you guessed it, her mom's new man donates to the school so they let that little brat do whatever she wants. I really want to pull my girls from that stupid school, but public schools in Hudson City *suck* and they don't have affordable aftercare, and Todd pays for the private school still. But that meant Ruby was in a shit mood when I picked her up and I was her emotional garbage can, which is *fine* because she needs it to regulate and she keeps everything in all day so when she's safe with me, she loses it. But now I have all of this emotional *garbage* and nowhere to toss it because I'm the parent and I need to be mature and put together. And when I put the girls to sleep, Harper wanted to cuddle and stay up with me, but I was so drained, so *tired*, so burnt out, I just wanted to be *alone*. And isn't that fucked? I spend all day away from them, dealing with everyone's problems, and I miss them to my *bones all day long*, but because of the world we live in, I'm too exhausted to *be* with them at the end of the day. And then you came, and I just know tomorrow morning that dumb dog is going to bark and wake me up early and repeat this entire dreadful process. But also, I know when we find a new place, it'll be even *worse* because do you *know* how expensive it is to live in Hudson City? I'll never find anything this nice without dipping into Todd's money, and I refuse to dip into that money and . . . I'm just so fucking *tired.*"

I stare at her until I know she's actually done with her monologue, her chest rising and falling, and fuck, there are tears shining in her eyes. It's been a long time since she's done that, vented and unpacked it all to someone without worrying about being a burden to them, a long time since she's given *that much* to someone, and it's clear she's not sure what to do with herself.

To be fair, I don't really know what to do, so I just do what feels right and hope that's the answer.

I lean over on the couch, wrapping an arm around her waist and tugging her until she's in my lap, and when her head moves right to my chest, laying there, an ear to my heartbeat, I know I made the right choice.

My arms wrap around her, holding her, protecting her with a firm grip like I'm holding all of the pieces she holds so tight in for her so she can finally let go and relax.

And slowly, so slowly I almost don't realize it at first, she does just that. The muscles in her body release their tension. First her jaw, then her neck, her shoulders, and her back until she's loose in my arms, her breathing slowed once again.

I ignore the wet spot on my shirt from the few tears she let slip because somehow, I also know she wants that. Wants me to pretend they didn't happen, that this crack in her fearfully put together facade didn't occur.

That her tight grip on control didn't falter.

To Shae, I'm realizing, any break in her carefully collected facade is a weakness. It's a fault line she doesn't want anyone to know she has. Her coping mechanism is the tight grip she has on everything in her life. If I'm going to make this work, I need to be the one place she can comfortably and safely loosen. The person she can confidently give her stress to and know I'll take care of her.

Once her body is lax, I move the hair covering her face to the side and behind her ear and speak. "When was the last time someone took care of you?"

"Sexually?" she asks then blushes, and it takes everything in me not to react to that, to her. I shake my head and smile.

"In any way," I ask, brushing the damp track her tears left aside. She shakes her head, her face going fierce, a bit of that stiffness returning to her shoulders.

"I don't need anyone to take care of me." I fight the urge to sigh.

"When was the last time, Shae? And by that, I mean *you*, not your girls. When was the last time you *let* someone take care of you?" She huffs and shakes her head, but I don't let her brush off the question, instead staring at her, waiting for an answer.

"Why does it matter?"

"Because I like you," I say, my response coming quickly and precisely, and it's clear my words shock her.

"You like me?" I shake my head with a smile.

"I thought I had made that clear." Again, she doesn't respond, instead choosing a different tactic, clearly still not believing me.

"But I dated your son," she says, and I roll my eyes.

"You went on one date with him before deciding to be just

friends. You instantly decided it would never work between you because he's a *boy*. I'm very much a man, Shae. And you need a *man* in your life."

Her eyes go wide, fire pooling, and finally, the hand she holds up between us has dropped and she's there.

And for the first time, she's mine.

She's mine and she's not worried about anything but being *mine* and it's fucking glorious. And then once more, Shae's lips are on mine, smooth and soft, her lemony lavender scent filling my nose, and her hands are moving back behind my neck just like last time. Those fingers scratch at the nape of my neck as our lips slide against each other's, the world going quiet until it's just her and me, together. For once, her walls are down and she's open to me, and it's so fucking obvious.

She could be mine.

She *should* be mine.

In fact, I'm not fully sold on the idea that she *isn't* mine behind those skyscraper-high walls she uses to hide. That feeling builds as her soft lips move against mine, as heat fills my body, starting in my chest and spreading as my hand tangles in her hair, holding her close to me.

And then she moans.

She moans, and it breaks the spell she put herself under, letting reality creep back in, and she breaks the kiss.

But on the bright side, she doesn't pull back.

"Shit," she says, her breathing heavy as I press my forehead to hers. "We can't keep doing this."

"Why not?"

"Because I can't have you," she whispers, pain laced in the words.

"Why the fuck not?" I ask. I can't help but let my fingers move the long hair over her shoulder.

Something crosses her face like she's trying to decide if she's going to say something or not. Something inside her wins, though, when she blurts out her next words.

"Because I want the girls to have you." I stare at her, trying to decode what she just said, not understanding.

"You mentioned that. I still don't get it, Shae." She sighs and groans to the ceiling, sliding out of my lap and putting more distance between us on the couch. She doesn't stop staring at the ceiling when she finally speaks.

"The girls like you."

"And I like the girls."

"The girls don't like people, not unless they've known them for a while."

"Okay . . ."

"And they don't have any kind of positive male influence, not really. Ruby had a nightmare and wanted *you* to tuck her in because she trusts you. She feels safe with you. That's so rare, especially considering everything they've been through. So I . . . I decided I'm giving you to them."

"I don't understand, Shae. Why can't I be with you and there for the girls?"

"Because we won't *be*, Nick. We'll hook up, and something will happen, and we won't be. And by then, the girls will be attached to you and I'll rip that from them, too. So, after everything that happened last year, they get you."

"I'm not some kind of toy you all have to share, you know." She sighs, shaking her head.

"I know. It . . . It came out wrong, I guess. I just don't want to get in the way of the girls having someone like you in their lives. If we . . . do . . . stuff . . ." I smile at the use of the word *stuff,* like she's 15 instead of 35. "Then it complicates things."

"See, what I don't think you're getting, Shae, is that I am a man, but I'm a man who doesn't play games. I'm a man who gets what he wants, when he wants it, but I don't go around picking *who* I want for shits and giggles. I don't just find the first piece of ass and hop on it. The last time I kissed a woman was well over a year ago," I confess.

Her mouth drops open slightly, and she gapes at me in a way that really makes me want to kiss her again.

It's not a line, either—I haven't kissed a woman since Halloween of last year and haven't fucked one in much longer. After Connor was born from a drunken teenage night, back when I didn't take things like sex and commitment as seriously, I changed the way I saw things. Kisses became something I shared only with women I could see myself with.

"So, if I'm here, driving an hour each night, using an excuse of moving a toy every night so you'll open the door for me and let me try to win you over, it's because I fucking like you." There's a long pause before she speaks.

"You knew me for half a minute before you started coming here."

"And Connor has been talking about how fucking amazing you are since April."

"That's another reason we can't do this," she says with scoff.

"What?"

"I dated your *son* first!"

"Again, you can use that as an excuse as much as you want, but we both know the truth. He was a pathway for you to make your way to me, for you to find your way to me. And for that, I'll forever be thankful." She stares at me with wide eyes, confused and shocked.

"You barely know me."

"I know what I need to. I've always trusted my gut from the day I was born. It never pushed me in the wrong direction. You walked into my house on Thanksgiving, and my gut knew you were mine. I'm not going to push you into anything you're not comfortable with, but I'll wait here patiently until you're ready. Until you're ready for an us. Until then, I'll be here, your . . . emotional trash can. Give it all to me. I promise I can take it."

She stares at me with shock all over he face, shaking her head.

"You don't mean that," she whispers, and I think she doesn't even realize she said it out loud.

"You've been let down a lot over the years. I get that. I don't expect you to trust what I say. But let me stick around a bit and you'll see my actions support the words." And then I move, standing before bending in front of her and pressing my lips to her hair. "I'll see you tomorrow, sugarplum," I say, voice low, and then I move to the front door, grab my hat and my coat, and leave.

# TWENTY

## 18 SLEEPS UNTIL CHRISTMAS

### SHAE

He sits with me after he moves the elf the next night.

He just . . . sits with me. Moves to the couch and sits on the other end, leaning back, his ankle on his knee like this is normal. Like I didn't just turn him down last night after we made out, like we're not living in some weird limbo where he's driving an hour each way every night to move an elf and spend time with me and I'm not adamantly trying to ignore this undeniable pull to him.

"How was your day?" he asks casually.

Ruby's stocking is in my lap but I'm not working on it, too distracted by his tanned forearms in the ever-present flannel shirt he has rolled up to his elbows.

"Fine. How was yours?"

It's the strangest mix of uncomfortable and unbearably comfortable, like we were made to do this—to put the girls to bed and sit together on the couch for hours just making small talk until it's time for us to go to bed together. It's like we're just waiting for time to catch up, waiting for our minds to remember that's what we're always supposed to do.

"Good. Next week is usually the busiest, and then it slows."

"Are you excited for it to slow down?" I ask, genuinely interested. I'm long past the hill in my mind where I'm convincing myself he's a nuisance, that I don't want to know anything about him or I'm not interested in his day.

Unfortunately, I'm still hyperaware of the fact that we cannot be.

"Yes and no. This is my busiest time of year, which is great income-wise, and I love the holidays, the people coming all excited and happy, the look on the kids' faces . . . It's great. But I also have no time to enjoy the holidays myself. I have all of my shopping to do still. It was more concerning when Connor was younger and I had to balance it all. You know what it's like, I'm sure," he says, tipping his chin my way.

"Yeah, I get that," I say with a laugh. "Obviously."

And then I don't know what comes over me. Maybe it's because the kiss from yesterday won't stop playing in my mind or maybe it's because I am a glutton for punishment or maybe I'm just an idiot.

Probably a little bit of all of the above.

"You've got something," I say, reaching over to his thick flannel that has a bit of fluff from whatever little elf presentation he set up on it. I've started avoiding the elf before the girls see it, for some reason wanting to see it for the first time with them, to get that excitement just like they do.

I move closer to him on the couch, an excuse if I ever saw one, pick it off, and drop it onto the floor, but his hand grabs my wrist.

"You're a conundrum, you know that?" he asks, his rough thumb on the sensitive underside of my wrist.

"What?" I ask like I don't know what he's talking about. His smile goes wide and my belly flips.

"God, come on, sugar. If you want to sit with me, just do it." My hand moves back and I shake it, feigning confusion but still biting my lip.

"What? I don't—oof!"

Oof because his arm is on my waist, lifting and tugging me until I'm in his lap, my hands moving to his neck to hold me still.

"Much better," he says before moving his head back to watch whatever is on the television, his hand traveling up and down my back like a slow, casual caress. We seem to get into this position often, and as much as I refuse to tell him, I really freaking like it.

I shouldn't, not if I wish to keep my sanity and my heart intact, but I do all the same.

Time passes like molasses, my heart beating like I'm 17 and this is my first date, but I'm sitting in the lap of a man who is continually driving me insane and who I absolutely cannot have in any context beyond being friends.

That's what we are, I remind myself.

We're friends.

Friends who kissed a few times but are both very understanding that we can't do that. Right?

And friends always sit on each other's laps. This is . . . This is no big deal. None at all.

My inner voice gives me a pitying, be so real, kind of look and I try a new tactic, a new way to convince myself this is anything but him flirting, anything but some kind of relationship starting when I can't have that.

He's only here because he told the girls about the elf and he feels bad.

*Then why is he sitting on your couch every night, long after the girls are asleep, after he's done his little Christmas magic task?*

*Why is he bringing you food?*

*Why is he enduring you and your suitcases of trauma? He could have anyone.*

*Everyone, really.*

*And yet he's driving an hour each way to move an elf, to sit on your couch and wait for you to soften enough to let him in.*

I can't help it.

That version of myself who sees all the signs and really likes them, the version who can ignore the potential destruction wins.

My finger moves to the hair at the back of his neck, twirling the soft strands beneath my fingers.

"So . . . ," I start, confused and unsure of what to do, what to say. "How was your day?"

"Good," he says, staring at me. Staring at my lips, to be exact. The gaze sends lava into my veins, flooding my system with thoughts and ideas I can't afford at this moment. "Uneventful. Was counting down the minutes until I could get in my truck and head here."

"Yeah?" I ask, trying to leave the eagerness, the excitement, the joy those words bring out of my voice.

"Yeah," he whispers, moving hair behind my ear.

It's intimate. More intimate than any small touch should be when both people are fully clothed, and I wait with bated breath for his lips to touch mine, for that electricity to flow through me like it did the other night, to awaken parts of me I buried deep, deep beneath the surface, safe from harm. Parts he's slowly rediscovering.

And . . .

It doesn't happen.

Instead, he just keeps staring at me, his thumb swiping along the apple of my cheek, his face completely unfazed, like he's not waiting for another life-changing kiss.

I try. I really do. I try to be patient and sweet and girlish, try not to get annoyed, but patience was never my virtue.

"Are you going to kiss me tonight?" I ask finally, my voice breathy. I'm in his lap, after all. His thumb is brushing against my knee.

He's so unbearably unaffected by this that it notches up my anxiety.

"What?" His head turns to look at me.

"Are you . . ." I pause and swallow. "Are you going to kiss me? I'm sitting in your lap and . . ."

"And what?"

"And you kissed me yesterday. And before that. So, you know. I was just wondering . . ."

"Do you want me to?" he asks.

I pause before answering, my heart beating like crazy. "I don't know," I whisper.

"No, you do. Tell me the truth."

A moment passes and I battle all of the potential answers, but the truth wins.

"I want you to kiss me," I say, and when he doesn't immediately do as I say, I continue. "I want you to kiss me, but I'm desperately afraid of getting too used to it, of liking it too much."

"What's wrong with liking me kissing you?" he says with a smile.

"We can't be that," I say. He smiles and shakes his head.

"I'm not kissing you tonight, Shae."

"Why not?" Even to my own ears, I sound like a begrudged child not getting her way.

I feel that way too, if I'm being honest. His rough hand moves to cup my cheek, forcing me to look at him as he gives me his answer.

"Because for me, this is real. This is something I want to work at and I'm not gonna push it, not gonna let you twist it in your mind to be something it's not. I'm not a fling, not some pity fuck—"

"Fuck?" He smiles.

"Oh yeah. Fuck." A blush burns on my cheeks and heat simmers elsewhere. "But until you tell me you're ready, until you're ready to take the jump, we're doing this. Hanging out, getting to know each other. Sitting on this couch and just talking."

"But . . . just talking?" I ask, clarifying.

"Just talking," he says with smile. "Now tell me about your day, Shae."

And something about that is so mundane and sweet and wholesome, something I don't know if I've ever had before, a man asking me about my day with no other ulterior motive to get in my pants or get his way or anything other than to get to know me, I smile.

And I tell him about my day.

# TWENTY-ONE

## 17 SLEEPS UNTIL CHRISTMAS

### SHAE

I call him on my lunch break, the salad I packed from home sitting in front of me, nearly untouched. The nerves have been twisting all morning since I opened that note, since the girls squealed in excitement.

"Hey," he says, his voice low and rough.

It travels straight through me in a way it really, really should not.

His voice shouldn't be hot, not in the least. The simple act of a man talking to me over the phone should not give me butterflies. What am I, 14?

"Hey," I reply and stop there because his voice not only traveled to my belly but did some kind of *Men in Black* mind wipe, so I can't even begin to pull myself together and remember what I called him about.

"How's it going? You on your lunch?" he asks like this is normal, me calling him during my lunch on a Friday with no intent beyond saying hi and listening to his voice.

*That could be nice,* the voice in my head says.

It reminds me how this can't be nice, which reminds me of why I felt the need to call him on my lunch break.

Because today's elf mayhem was a note inviting us to Nick's ranch for the weekend. Holly the elf was sitting on three boxes holding cowboy boots—pink for Harper, purple for Ruby, and a gorgeous dark-brown pair for me, all three of which fit perfectly.

"Fine. Yeah, it's my lunch." I take in a quiet breath, hoping he can't hear my nerves over the line before speaking again. "So . . . the boots."

"The boots," he says without expanding, like he's waiting for me to fill in before he decides which way to take this conversion.

"Are you sure?" I ask finally. "About the girls and me coming there for the weekend?"

"I wouldn't have asked if I wasn't sure, Shae." It flips my belly again, and I want to hate it.

"Technically, you didn't ask. A small plush elf did." He laughs, and somehow I know the sound alone could turn any shitty day on its head.

"You know what I mean, Shae."

"And you know what I mean, Nick." Another laugh, another warm bolt through my body.

"I do. And for transparency, I also know I should have asked you first, but I'm quickly learning taking away any chance for argument is the key to getting you to do what I want." His words feel barbed, old wounds coming out to play, and that sweet warmth turns sour.

"What, so you thought cornering me would get me where you want me?" I fight the irritation, knowing the true meaning of what he's saying, but still . . .

"No," he says with a sigh. "Fuck, I'm screwing this up, aren't I? I just knew if I asked you, you'd go all Shae on me. Telling me all the reasons you'd be a burden, all the reasons I shouldn't invite you over, not the reasons you can't come. You haven't gotten past the part that you and the girls are not a burden or a nuisance to me yet, so I need to kind of play the game. But you're right. I should have asked you before I invited you and the girls." It comes out in word vomit, like he knows if he doesn't say it now, there won't be a chance for further explanation.

As much as I want to be mad, I get it.

I get why he would have gone this route. It's why I didn't instantly tell the girls no, why I didn't call him first thing this morning to yell at him.

"It's not that, Nick," I say with a sigh. "Okay, maybe it is. I don't know. It's more that I don't want my shit to add more to your plate. I've known you for a couple of weeks and you've spent that time making your life as complicated as possible on our behalf." I shrug even though he can't see it, using my fork to push the food in my Tupperware around. "I feel really freaking guilty for all you've done for a relative stranger."

He laughs then, loud and full, like he just finally understood some joke I wasn't privy to.

"I've been hearing about you for the better part of a year, Shae. You're far from a stranger to me."

"What?"

"I told you. Since that first time you met him, Connor's been nonstop talking about you and the girls. How sweet they are, how kind you are. How much you sacrifice for them, how you refuse help from everyone. How strong you are. Fuck, if I didn't see how you two act like fuckin' siblings together with my own eyes, I'd be a bit concerned." He finishes, and I pause, trying to move his words into the picture I have of him, of us.

"Why would you be concerned?" I ask.

"Before I met you, I was sure you and Connor were eventually going to have some kind of big whirlwind romance, the way he'd been talking about you. That you just needed to get over the hump of your divorce and then you'd let him in. But now that I've met you, I want you for myself."

I can't breathe.

My words come out stuttered.

"You . . . You want me for yourself?"

"Thought I made that pretty clear the other night."

"When you refused to kiss me?" I spit out without meaning to and instantly regret it. "I mean—"

"Yeah, when I refused to kiss you because I want you to be absolutely sure of me before we go any further. But I was talking about a few nights before that, when I had you moaning into my mouth on your couch."

My tongue comes out and licks my lips as I remember that moment, remember that night. Remember how much I liked it and how I wanted more and how I've been struggling since, trying to figure out how to get what I want without the inevitable disaster.

Instead of responding, I change the subject. I'm not mentally prepared to argue with Nick, that much is clear.

"How'd you know my size?" I ask, my voice rough and low, even to my own ears.

His laugh is booming through the line with my question.

"If I told you I just take note of everything about you, would you think that was really sweet or psychotic?"

"Psychotic," I say with zero hesitation. "Especially since you got the girls' sizes right."

"Smart girl," he says. "No, I asked Connor, who asked a friend of yours—Abbie?"

Fucking Abbie. I'm surprised she hasn't called or texted me yet, begging for all the dirty details.

"Hmm," is all I say.

"So, are you coming?" he asks, and he must have moved to where there's more noise, as there are people talking now in the background and I think I hear a horse.

He's at work, Shae. It's his busiest time of year, and you're wasting all of his time.

"Yeah. The girls are very excited."

"Good," he says. "So am I." A beat passes before I clarify, so we're on the same page. Setting expectations from the start and all.

"I'm not sleeping with you," I say, and a blush comes over my entire body with embarrassment as another laugh comes out.

"You've got your own room at the ranch, sugar. All ready for you." Now, why am I disappointed by that? I'm supposed to be relieved. "Not that I'll say no if you want to cuddle in my bed at any point."

Disappointment rolls out and annoyance rolls in, even if it's a bit feigned, and I fight a smile.

"Go," I say. "Go work and curate Christmas cheer or whatever it is you do." He gives me one last rumbling laugh I feel down to my toes.

"See you tonight, sugarplum," he says.

"I much prefer sugar," I say without thinking.

"Sugar it is," he says, and then the line goes quiet, leaving me to contemplate everything over my boring salad.

# TWENTY-TWO

## 17 SLEEPS UNTIL CHRISTMAS

### SHAE

We pull up to the ranch, and just like the last time we were here, the girls gasp every three seconds. Unlike last time, they're adding names and facts to various gasps, like they belong here. I pull up to the driveway where Nick told me to park. Harper tells me one barn is where there are goats, and Ruby shouts about seeing the horse she hasn't stopped talking since Thanksgiving.

All this to say, the girls are beyond excited to be here.

I, on the other hand, feel nothing but anxiety twisting and pulling in my stomach with each stone that crunches under my tires on the gravel driveway. The entire area is surrounded by trees, some at least a hundred years old, some clearly much newer.

Last time we were here, my anxiety was different, more of the *I don't know these people* variety. This time, it's more, *I think I know this man pretty well and I might be catching feelings, which is a terrible idea, and spending time here is only going to make things worse.* But this brand of anxiety allows me to take in the land and the area we're driving through much better than I was able to last time.

It's clear the plots to the right are where the Christmas trees are grown, and a building far in the distance must be the actual farm where you go to purchase your tree. Thanks to my covert googling, I know that is where you go for horse-drawn carriage rides with hot cocoa, a small shop with ornaments and decorations, and a building with occasional Santa and Mrs. Claus visits.

My mind reels with new ideas to share with Nick, different ways to spin this land to help grow his business.

When we finally pull up to the ranch, Nick is standing outside, despite the cold, wearing that stupid fucking cowboy hat that suddenly doesn't look as out of place as it does at my townhouse, a smile on his lips as he watches us pull up.

"Nick!" the girls shout in near unison, and he smiles like he can hear from where he stands. It's then I realize just how fucked any hope of not getting tangled with this man is.

The night is a surprise, to say the least.

We walk into Nick's gorgeous house, and unlike on Thanksgiving, the entire place is decked in holiday cheer, from Santa statues to garlands on every surface to four—yes, *four*—full and completely decorated trees throughout his home.

But most surprising are the rooms. Nick had mentioned on the phone we would get separate rooms, but I didn't expect to find one guest room with two twin beds, one with pink bedding and the other with purple, decorated gently with a few things I know for a fact were bought just for the girls: an equestrian helmet on each bed, a unicorn nightlight in the corner, and a pretty pink and purple polka dot rug in the center of the room.

The man decorated a room in his house just for them, and as much as I really, really want to deny and ignore it, it's sweet as all get out.

And the room next to theirs is mine, with burgundy bedding and a pretty bouquet of flowers on the bedside table that I really, really want to pretend isn't there but is all the same.

Now, I'm sitting on what might be the world's comfiest couch in Nick's living room, watching his back flex beneath a worn, emerald-green Finch Farm tee as he stokes a fire in the fireplace.

We had dinner after we got here, pasta and meatballs for everyone but Harper, who had plain Christmas tree-shaped noodles with butter and cheese and a side of mozzarella sticks.

It was the first time in months I'd seen her eat pasta, but when Nick showed her the bag of dried shapes, she squealed and then continued to laugh and giggle and smile as she helped him prepare the rest of dinner.

She had two servings, and I almost cried.

Over fucking *buttered noodles.*

Then he made the girls big cups of cocoa in mugs he had clearly bought for them, pink for Harper, purple for Ruby, before putting on *The Santa Clause* and continuing to top their mugs off with extra marshmallows.

Finally, when it was time for bed, he helped them brush their teeth and hair before reading them three new books he bought—*so you have something to read when you're here,* he had told them, implying this wouldn't be a one-time thing—before telling them goodnight and closing the door behind me after I kissed them each before bed.

"Thanks," I say with his back to me, a comfort in not having to look at his face when I do. "For tonight. The girls were so excited when I picked them up and told them we were coming here, but I don't think even they understood how special you'd make tonight for them." He looks over his shoulder but doesn't turn all the way, keeping the illusion of space between us.

"No problem, sugar," he says. "They're good girls, deserve the world." I sigh at his words.

"Yeah. We haven't . . . We haven't had the opportunity to do anything since last year. No vacations or anything. We went to the beach once last summer because Damien, my boss, has a condo down in Long Beach Island, but that was it. This is a real treat for them."

He turns back to the fire, doing God knows what with it, and says, "No problem."

"And Harper . . . she hasn't eaten pasta in months. That was a real step forward."

"I'm sure part of it was because she's somewhere new and someone new was making her food," he says.

"Or because you took the time to let her cook with you. I . . ." I pause, feeling the guilt swirl. "I should do that more, but by the time dinner rolls around, I'm so exhausted that I have to fight not just ordering takeout, much less have them help me cook."

"You gotta stop that," he says, poking a log. Sparks erupt, the wood hissing and cracking as he does. "Being so hard on yourself." I don't reply because if he doesn't like *that*, he definitely won't like my response. "Being a parent is hard enough without the constant pressure to do all of the things, especially when you're doing it by yourself."

"Yeah, but they're only young once. I want to pack in as many memories as possible while I can."

"I've always hated when people say that. *They're only young once,* as if parents who are stressed the fuck out aren't already painfully aware of that. As if it doesn't stir the never-ending pot of guilt. It's always old people, whose kids probably fucking hate them now, too." I laugh because he's not wrong.

"That and *let them be kids!* when you know damn well if your kids were *actually* acting like kids, you'd get the *you should really parent them better* look." Nick smiles over his shoulder again, and just looking at it changes something in my chemical makeup, I'm sure.

"I'll never understand it," he says, poking the fire again. "But regardless, you're doing an amazing job, Shae. Those girls love you and they know they're safe and taken care of with you. And that's all that matters." His words coat me like a soothing balm, protecting the abrasion the world and my guilt have created, giving me space to heal.

But it's then I also realize he's doing literally nothing in front of that fireplace but using it as a barrier for me to continue talking to him, continue opening up to him.

I laugh and say, "You know you don't have to play with the fireplace to get me to talk to you, right? I'm in your house, Nick. I'm not going to ignore you anymore." He turns and smiles sheepishly at me, like I've caught him in the act. "I think we're kind of past that, don't you?"

He stands then, closes the safety grate to the fireplace, and while I wonder if that was always there or if it's a new addition, he moves to the couch, sitting beside me.

Then he surprises me by pulling me onto his lap without hesitation, my legs draping over his, my arms going to his neck instinctively.

It's so comfortable, so perfect like this, like it was always supposed to be. Always supposed to be us at his place, a fire roaring, my girls sleeping in a room upstairs.

Like this isn't all new and scary and exciting, but run of the mill and ordinary.

Like I'm already past the point of *we can't do this* and moving toward *this is us*.

"You caught me," he says.

"I kind of trained you at this point to handle me with kid gloves, so it's mostly my fault."

"Mmm," he says, his voice a rumble against my body. "I don't think you've begun to understand how I'm happy to do whatever I have to to get you to talk to me, to trust me."

I don't know how to respond, so I go back to my original topic.

"Thanks for tonight. And for this weekend. I'm sure you have a ton of work you could be doing instead of hosting us."

"Could be? Maybe. Want to be? Absolutely not."

That stops me in my tracks, such a simple sentence that somehow means so much to me.

"Hmm," I say, because it's all I have. He smiles, his hand moving up and brushing my hair that fell out of my tiny ponytail back behind my ear. And as he does it, he stares into my eyes, the moment much more intimate than it was just seconds before, and I'm hyperaware of everything.

His chest rises against my body with each breath, and I can't help but focus on the way his tee feels on my wrists where the skin is thin and sensitive.

The way his calloused hand feels against my cheek.

The way his fading tan from the summer makes the lines near his eyes slightly more prominent.

The way my heart races. The way his gaze keeps moving from my eyes to my lips and back again.

And the way his chest rumbles when he speaks.

"I want to kiss you, Shae," he whispers.

*I want that too.* It's all I've been able to think about since the other night, completely consuming my every thought.

"It's not a good idea," I say. I don't know *why* I say it. I don't know *why* I don't just lean in and let his lips touch mine. Or, at the very least, why I don't tell him we *can't* kiss because it doesn't make sense.

Instead, I sit in the middle, not saying yes but surely not saying no.

Because that's the spectrum I'm sitting in—my body and my heart saying *yes, yes, yes,* and my head saying *oh no.*

"Yes, it is. It's a great fucking idea, really." I can't fight the way my lips tip up. His free hand moves my hair behind my ear, rough fingers leaving a trail of heat in their wake.

I can't help but wonder what that trail of fire would feel like on other parts of my body, what his fingers would do on other stretches of skin.

My chin tips up, begging him without saying it, and his body reflects the need mine feels, and I just know at any microsecond he's going to—

"I'm not kissing you until you tell me," he says, his voice low and ragged, his breath grazing my lips as he does, and it takes a long minute of staying locked just like this before his words register in my brain.

"What?" I ask, but I don't move.

Instead, my eyes pop open, no longer drifting shut and filled with lust and want and need. I don't miss how even at this close distance, I can see his lips tip in a smile like he finds this *entertaining*.

*Entertaining!*

"I said I'm not going to kiss you until you tell me to."

It hits me like a ton of bricks, what he's saying.

I told him we couldn't do it again after we made out and Ruby interrupted us, and he told me I would be in control from then on. And apparently, he meant it. Either I have to kiss him or I have to ask him to kiss me.

"Why won't you just give in to this? To us?" he asks, once more pushing that piece of hair behind my ear. I usually curse the bangs my stylist cut in at my last appointment as per Abbie's suggestion, but right now, I'm almost thankful for them and the constant excuse for him to touch me.

"Because I'm scared," I admit, my words low, and there's a bit of shock on Nick's face, like he also can't believe I just told him this truth.

"You're scared?" he asks. It seems so obvious to me, I can't even fathom how he hasn't understood yet. Because *of course*, I'm scared. This man could be a comfort, a welcome hand, a confidant and friend, or he could be the biggest mistake I've ever made. If we do this and it goes wrong, it won't just hurt me.

"I'm terrified," I whisper. He waits a moment before asking the question burning in his eyes.

"What are you so scared of, Shae? Really?"

"Everything," I whisper.

I mean so much when I say that—I'm scared of him, and I'm scared of the way he makes me feel. I'm scared of how safe he feels to me and the way my girls love him so much, so soon. I'm scared of how hard he's trying and how easily he seems to fit into our lives. I'm scared because I don't trust my own opinions on things, and I'm scared because a part of me really, really wants him.

He must see all of the thoughts ping-ponging in my mind, already so able to read me.

He opens his mouth to ask something but doesn't get the chance because a sob breaks through the hallway and into the living room and he stands, moving toward the sound before it even registers in my brain that it's Ruby.

# TWENTY-THREE

## 17 SLEEPS UNTIL CHRISTMAS

### SHAE

I move quickly once I do, but by the time I get to the hallway, she's standing there crying and Nick is already on his knees in front of her, face-to-face, large hands on her cheeks and speaking low.

"Are you okay?" he asks, and she nods with a sniffle, and even though I want to interrupt, to move to her and pick her up, hold her until she stops crying and tuck her in myself, I stand a few feet back and watch. "Nightmare?"

"Yeah," she says in a tiny whisper.

"I'm sorry, peanut. You wanna talk about it?" I ask carefully because I never know which way she'll go. Sometimes, she wants to talk about it. Others . . . Her eyes go wide, and her head shakes fervently, the idea clearly terrifying to her. "Alright, alright. We don't have to. Do you want me to tuck you in?"

"No," she says.

I know *exactly* what that means, so I move to my daughter, leaning down and lifting her, her arms wrapping around my neck. It's bittersweet holding my oldest like this, the way I did when she was tiny, and knowing there's not much time left where I'll be able to easily lift her like this, knowing eventually and probably without me realizing it, there will be a moment when I pick her up for the last time.

It's a place in me that aches, an ache I know intrinsically will never, ever heal.

"Wanna sleep with me?" I ask. This has been the way for a year now, ever since we left Todd. I think there's a good shot Harper doesn't remember much of *before*, doesn't remember much about the black eye that was my tipping point or the numerous outbursts over the years before that, not yet, at least, but Ruby . . . Ruby does.

And she has nightmares about them. It hasn't been as often lately, but when she's somewhere new or stressed, they tend to creep back in.

Her head goes to my shoulder and she nods. "Alright, let's go," I say, moving toward the room and giving a *sorry* look to Nick.

Sorry for ditching you.

Sorry we can't finish this conversation.

Sorry my life is and always will be *complicated*.

"No, no!" Ruby shouts, and I stop. "I want Nick, too!"

"Rube, that's not—" I start.

"No! I want Nick!" Her voice is ratcheting both in sound and panic.

"Ruby, I—"

"I need him! He'll keep me safe!" A part of me breaks in a way that will never be repaired.

A break that, even when I glue it back, will show a hairline fracture, a weak spot for the rest of my days because *I did this*. I did this to my child, my daughter. I put her in this position by choosing a terrible life partner for myself, a terrible father for my children.

"Okay, okay, no problem," the deep voice behind me rumbles. My head turns to look at Nick, and Ruby's does as well.

I expect a look of panic.

I expect a look of *what the fuck have I gotten myself into?*

I expect a lot of things I don't see in the least.

He's standing there, and instead of a look of panic and confusion and regret, there's one of surety.

Stubbornness.

Resolve.

"What?" I ask low, even though I'm holding Ruby so there's no chance of her not hearing our conversation.

"I said okay, no problem. My room, though, the bed is the biggest."

"Nick, no—"

"Not arguing with you, Shae. I'll give you anything in the world, but right now, I'm giving her this." He tips his chin toward my daughter, who is still shaking in my hold with nerves and anxiety, her arms latched around my neck and her legs tight at my waist, but her eyes are locked on Nick like he's a calming point in the room.

And I will always give my daughter whatever she needs most in the world. Right now, it looks like that's Nick.

We walk into the big room, and I see he was right. The bed in the center of the bare bedroom is gigantic—a king, or maybe even a California king. I could lie in this bed with *both* girls and we'd still never touch Nick.

The bedding is a dark navy, a comforter pulled over mounds of pillows, and the frame is rustic-looking dark wood. The room is also shockingly tidy for a man.

"You two, under the covers. I've got a blanket. I'll lie on top," Nick says, grabbing said blanket out of a trunk at the foot of his giant bed.

"Nick, this isn't—" His voice goes low as he pulls the blankets back, lifting my daughter from my arms and placing her in the bed. She doesn't even question it, just rolls over, waiting for me to climb in, too. Then, Nick steps back, giving room for me to climb in behind her.

"Nick, I—" I say in a low whisper, hopefully quiet enough Ruby won't hear our arguing. He cuts me off, his look stern and serious and *shaken*. I've seen Ruby have this kind of reaction to a nightmare before, but he hasn't, and that's clear in the look in his eyes and his words.

"I saw her. I heard her. Whatever her nightmare was spooked her good. I'm not arguing with a 9-year-old who looked that scared, sugar." My gut does a strange mix of twisting and floating, both anxious over his words and thoroughly thrilled by them.

"Nick . . . ," I start, unsure of where to go, but he knows.

It seems he always does.

"But I'm also not comfortable with all three of us sleeping like that since, if we're being completely transparent and honest, you don't know me *that* well, no matter how sure I am that I'm gonna be in your life for some fuckin' time. I'm not offended or anything, just being honest."

Warmth blooms in my chest with his understanding.

"Mommy, get in," Ruby says, her voice sleepy.

Even though I haven't brushed my teeth or put on my moisturizer or any of the things I normally do right before bed, I nod and climb in behind her, tucking an arm around her belly and snuggling in. Her hair tickles my nose, and the smell is comforting, my Ruby.

"Now, Nick," she says, and despite her bossy words, I can tell she's already starting to fall asleep. Nick smiles in the dim light, leaving the small lamp on as a night light without me even asking before lying on top of the blankets, leaving a good foot and a half between himself and Ruby, tugging his blanket up over his body.

"Closer," she says, patting the bed next to her.

"Ruby, I think—"

"It's fine," he says, moving slightly closer and rolling on his side so he's looking at me over her head. Then he whispers so low, my sleepy girl can't hear, "I'll move once she's out."

All three of us lie there in silence, my thoughts going crazy as I try to figure out why whoever is in charge up there loves to put me in these situations.

*What the fuck did I do in a past life?*

My mind registers my daughter's breathing slowing, going more even as she falls asleep quickly, and I look back at Nick finally.

He's staring at me and somehow, I know he hasn't stopped since he rolled closer. My hand moves to Ruby's head, brushing her long blonde hair back gently so it's not in her face.

"I'm sorry," I whisper, guilt eating at me. This poor man just wanted to have Thanksgiving with his son and he's now stuck with a grown woman and her two kids. He doesn't say anything, instead just continues to stare at me. "I might be able to move her in a bit. She's not the heaviest sleeper, but maybe she won't need both—"

"Does this happen often?" he asks, cutting me off.

I contemplate how to answer.

I'm not sure, to be honest.

"Not as much anymore, but it happens. When things happened with her father . . ." I sigh. I hate talking about this, not because it hurts or bothers me, but because I always feel so *stupid*.

I dated Todd for two years before marrying him in a whirlwind of a wedding, and a year later, Ruby was here. We had Harper barely a year later, and in all of that time, I now realize it was never . . . good. Not the way it should be, at least, not the way I hope my daughters one day have in a relationship. It was always tumultuous, so much stress that he blamed on his job, leading to angry outbursts and too high expectations. I was to stay home with the girls, which I was happy and grateful to do, make sure there was always a hot dinner on the table, keep the house in perfect order, and be ready and willing whenever he wanted me in our bed, regardless of how touched out I was from the kids or how unloved he made me feel. I told myself it was because he was climbing the corporate ladder, desperate to provide for us, but it wasn't that. I know that now.

He was just *mean*.

And cruel.

The things he would say to me, picking me apart until I didn't know who I was at all, giving me expectations I'd never meet, and tearing me down anytime I tried to reach said expectations weren't actions of a shredded, overwhelmed man who loved his wife. They were actions of a manipulative narcissist who loved to watch me struggle and loved to dangle the carrot of *well, what would you do without me?* over my head.

"Connor told me it wasn't a great situation. Did he hurt the girls?" Nick asks the question so openly, so basically, for a moment, it's like he screamed it instead of whispering it in the dark of this room.

But it only *feels* loud because people don't do that.

People in my life, people who know me, and people who just met me *don't do that.* They walk on eggshells, tiptoeing around what happened like they're afraid one wrong word will send my carefully constructed facade tumbling down. They might ask small, useless questions from the periphery of the real issue, but they never just *ask it.*

And it's fucking *refreshing.* A relief, almost.

"No," I whisper in reply, leaving the truth of it hanging in the air between us because he didn't. Todd never laid a hand on the girls, barely even acknowledging their existence unless it was to continue his hold on me.

"But . . ." There's a pause, and then it becomes clear to me Connor didn't share all of it, not in the least. "But he did hurt you?"

I wonder for a moment how to answer his unspoken question. I've been very careful to navigate my thoughts since that day, to carefully tiptoe over different subjects so my mind doesn't go back unless it was absolutely necessary for court. Once that case was closed, so was the door I keep all of it behind.

But for some reason, with my daughter tucked into me, already fast asleep, this man in the same bed only because he wanted to make her feel as safe as humanly possible, I carefully open that door up and peek in.

I remember the ten years of our marriage, the years of dating before it. I see the red flags I ignored for so long and all of the little things I brushed aside, telling myself he was under a lot of stress, or he didn't know better, or it was my fault.

I remember the end of our relationship, when I started to find myself, when I realized I didn't want our girls to see this and think it was normal, wanted better for them, and he became even more cruel. When he would tell me I'd be on the streets, that no one wanted a washed-up 30-something with no real work experience and a half-finished college degree. When he would pick apart the baby weight I was never able to lose. When he'd point out other women he wished I were more like.

And as I walk further into the room in my mind where I packed this all away, the memories don't burn and ache as intensely as they once did, but they hurt all the same. A reminder of why I hid them so well. I don't have the energy to ask myself why I am choosing now with this man to walk in. Why I feel safe to do it, feel empowered to now.

"Yes and no," I say.

"If the answer is yes, there is no *no*," he says. There's an unexpected sharpness in his words, something I've never heard, his soft teddy-bear nature outlawing any and all harshness typically.

"What?"

"If someone hurts you once, you can never again say they didn't." I see it now—he's angry on my behalf. Annoyed and irritated. I give him a soft smile, liking that he's jumping to my defense but needing to clarify.

"Well, I didn't mean it like that—" He cuts me off again.

"You didn't have to say it out loud. I saw it on your face. You're contemplating all of the times it *could* have been your fault. It was never your fault, Shae. It doesn't matter if you were the biggest pain in the ass, if you were a bitch at every turn. If you give a man your trust, trust him to love you, to care for you, he doesn't hurt you. Not in any way, shape, or form. And if he does, no matter what, it's not your fault. He was an adult, not a child unable to control his actions."

I lie there in stunned silence at his words, words I would tell a friend but never myself. And I realize, of course, he's right.

Todd *did* hurt me, and he chose to hurt me, and whether it was physical or emotional and whether he was stressed or overworked *doesn't matter.* I have been stressed and overworked and annoyed, and I've never lashed out and called someone stupid or ugly. I've never gripped their arms so hard it left bruises, never backhanded them and left a black eye in my wake.

*But he did.*

So I tell Nick the truth, the truth he helped me better grasp. "Yeah. He hurt me. It was just words for a while. When he finally hit me is when I left."

This part always feels embarrassing, another reason I like to keep that door slammed shut and locked at all times. There's inherent shame in realizing my husband, the father of my children, *had to strike me across my face* in order for me to realize that wasn't a loving situation and he wouldn't change.

And most importantly, if I didn't get out, the girls would be next.

That's the part that scares me most. Because if I'm being honest, and, truly, what else do I have to my name other than honesty anymore, if I didn't have the girls, I'm not sure I would have left. It's the opposite of what I feel is expected in a world of *stay together for the kids,* but for me, it was *leave for the kids.*

"I left because of the girls," I admit, my voice so low now, it's almost inaudible, but his eyes tell me he can hear me. "I knew one day, it wouldn't stop at me. At the very, very least, they would see it happen. I didn't want that for them in any way. Not to think it was okay, and definitely not for him to lay his hands on them."

I expect the normal conversation next. I've told this story three times and have always gotten the same response. The *expected* response.

*You did the right thing.* I hate it because if I did the right thing, I never would have fallen for Todd in the first place. Sometimes, I get, *you were so brave,* which I hate even more because I have never felt brave. *Your girls deserve better* is what cuts the deepest because, in my mind, if I had chosen better in the beginning, they would have *had* better.

But instead, he asks, "How long were you married?"

It sounds strange in this context, a basic, simple question in comparison to the heavy topic, but I'm grateful for the lack of *cheer-up* or *good-job* banter.

"Almost ten years. We got married when I was 23—had Ruby a year later. It was six months before our ten-year anniversary when he hit me and I finally got the courage to leave," I say. And then, because I want to give this to him, because I think it might help him understand, I expand. "It was just over a year ago now. Last Thanksgiving, I had a black eye and was in protective custody, waiting to get a restraining order and custody of the girls."

He widens his eyes in the dark.

"The way you act, I thought it had been a lot longer ago."

I laugh without humor. "Because I'm *so* well adjusted?" I ask, the words full of sarcasm, but his thick eyebrows come together, confused.

"Well, yeah."

"You're delusional or I'm a better actor than I thought," I say with a smile.

"You should stop that," he says, his voice low and conversational.

"Stop what?"

"Playing shit off. Acting like you're not doing a fantastic job. Your girls are amazing, Shae. You've built such a great life for them in just a year—"

"We had help," I argue.

"Yeah, you're right. You've worked hard to build a community you can trust who loves and supports you. That wasn't easy either. Any of them, the people who help you, who you reply on—are they from your old life?"

I scoff out a laugh.

"Absolutely not. Once I was out, all of my old friends abandoned me. The playdates dried up, no more calls to have coffee. Most of my 'friends' were wives of Todd's coworkers or friends. So . . ."

"So they chose him," he says. I shrug. "You're better off."

"I know," I say, because I do, and the surety in my voice makes him smile.

Then he reaches out, moving to the hand I have tucked under my chin, and grabs it, holding it over Ruby and letting his rough thumb brush over my skin.

It's calming, a metronome that could easily put me to sleep, a soothing motion somehow exactly what I need right now as the unearthed thoughts swirl around me, slowly sinking back into the recesses of my mind, no longer locked behind that door.

I'm contemplating if that's better, if having them out and more available to deal with is healthier or if I should try and shove them back behind that locked door when Nick speaks again.

"You all can have me, you know," he whispers in the dark. It surprises me because his thumb had stopped moving, his breathing easing until I thought he had fallen asleep, Ruby still between us.

"What?"

"You can all have me. I'm not some kind of a limited quantity."

At first, I don't understand until it clicks.

*I'm letting the girls have you.*

Now he's saying we can all have him.

But we can't, can we? That's not how this works, not how the *world* works. I shake my head and try to explain.

"It's not about quantity, Nick. It's about crushing them if we become something more and it ends."

Silence fills the room once more, and I concentrate on Ruby's soft breaths, letting them regulate my own. A blanket of sadness, of hope-lessness, has come over me with the reminder I can't have him, can't have this, with the reminder that the girls need him more than I do.

Minutes pass and finally, I start to succumb to the exhaustion leaking into my bones, but right before I fall asleep, curled into my daughter, I hear his voice.

"Then we'll just have to make sure it doesn't end, won't we?"

# TWENTY-FOUR

## 16 SLEEPS UNTIL CHRISTMAS

### SHAE

I underestimated how freaking cold it would be here. Somehow, despite it being barely an hour west, the temperature outside is a full eight degrees lower than it is at home. The girls are fine, considering I inevitably and *thankfully* overpacked for them, but me?

I can barely feel the tips of my ears.

I should have brought a hat, at the very least, but even though I'm fighting whatever pull Nicolas Finch has on me, I desperately didn't want *hat hair* while staying here.

Alright, so I'm a bit of an idiot and didn't bring a hat because I wanted to impress a boy.

I'm adjusting the thin hats I brought that fit perfectly under the helmets Nick bought the girls, making sure their ears are covered, when he comes alongside me, reins in his hand, a gorgeous brown and white horse walking beside him. A second all-black horse is behind it, Nick not holding onto his reins but his eyes locked on Nick in a way that even someone as clueless about animals as I am can see he is *Nick's* horse.

There are two smaller horses already ready for the girls, and we've spent the last hour in the cold, Nick teaching them all about the animals, how to care for and treat them, and the basics of what to do while riding. He's also informed me they are two of the kindest, sweetest, tamest animals on this ranch. He may have just said it to appease my very obvious nerves, but if so, mission accomplished.

"Alright, girls, you good? Warm?"

"Yes, Mom," Ruby says in an irritated voice that she's slowly leaning into more and more, a clear indication the preteen years are upon us.

"I'm your mother, Ruby. It's my job to *mother you*." She rolls her eyes and I want to argue, to tell her to stop the sass or her eyes will get stuck like that if she keeps it up, but then a hand is on my waist. Even though I'm wearing three layers, it feels warm, like his bare hand is lying directly on my skin, and sends a shiver down my spine.

*Fuck.*

"Where's your hat?" he asks, his voice a low rumble as he tugs on my braid.

"Hats equal hat hair.

"Hats equal a warm woman when it's freezing out." I glare at him.

"The horse doesn't have to wear a hat." Now he glares at *me*.

"It's a fuckin' horse, Shae." I shrug. "You really don't have a hat?"

"It's not a big deal. I—"

My words are cut off when he takes his own hat off, placing it on my head. It's a bit too big, dipping down in the front before he shifts it so it dips in the back instead, but it's *warm* both because of the thick leather and the heat from his head.

"Wear this," he says, pushing a stray piece of my hair that fell from my little braid behind my ear.

"I can't. It's yours."

"And I've given it to you," he says matter-of-factly.

"What are you going to use? It's freezing out here," I say, my hand on my hips.

"I'll be fine, Shae." He's smiling now, like he thinks my irritation is cute, like he thinks this is all a game and he's winning.

"Seriously, Nick. Take it back." My hands move to the wide brim, but his hands move to my wrists, cool fingers on my newly exposed warm skin, and I shiver.

"You take that off, I'm going to be really fucking disappointed, Shae." Suddenly, he's not joking and smiling, but serious, like he'd *genuinely* be disappointed if I try and take his silly hat off.

"Why?" I ask in confusion.

"A cowboy puts his hat on a woman, he's marking his territory. I need everyone who works for me, everyone whose eyes won't leave your ass in those jeans to know just how off-fucking-limits you are."

I gape like a goldfish, my fingers going loose, loose enough that when he tugs one of my hands, it comes free easily as he pulls it toward his mouth, pressing his lips to the inside of my wrist.

"Wear it," he whispers there, and I don't answer because I can't. Even when he drops my hand and I come back to my senses, I can't because he's moving, walking over to help the girls onto their horses while I stare at him and try and figure out what is happening.

# TWENTY-FIVE

## 16 SLEEPS UNTIL CHRISTMAS

### SHAE

The girls fall asleep easily in "their room," and I'm hopeful Ruby won't have another nightmare, if only because she's absolutely *exhausted.* Both girls picked up riding their horses with an ease I didn't expect, especially Ruby.

She took to it so well and looked so natural and at peace in a way I haven't seen in at least two years, I instantly started to play with my budget in my head, wondering just how much horseback riding lessons and camps cost and if I could pull it off with my salary. By the end of her lesson, I was convincing myself pulling from the settlement from Todd for this one would be absolutely worth it. He gave her the trauma, so he could pay for the healing.

I guess I should have known it—Ruby has always known what she wants. I'm sure a part of her always knew she'd be amazing at it, that it would heal something in her, and that's why she's loved horses from such a young age.

And by the time we came back inside, all four of us were chilled to the bone and exhausted from a full day of moving our bodies; even Harper ate her entire dinner of pizza, another shock.

Turns out, horses and ranches are just as therapeutic as they're made out to be.

Even if part of me thinks there's a good chance that it's Nick and his presence changing up my girls' attitudes.

"Today went well," I whisper, staring at the fire he built, the fire he helped the girls roast marshmallows on while I sat in the comfy love seat, reading a cozy book.

"It did." He reaches over to where I'm sitting, a full couch cushion away, hooking his arm around my waist before tugging me into his side. "We gotta work on that," he murmurs into my hair.

"On what?"

"On you not feeling comfortable enough to sit right next to me."

"I just . . . want to give you your space," I say, biting my lip as I look up at him, his thumb on my waist strumming, spreading heat even through my pajama shirt. The girls insisted we all get into pajamas before their s'mores, and who was I to say no? Plus, that meant I got to watch Nick in low-slung flannel pajama pants and a thin, worn tee shirt that clings to muscles and sinew gorgeously.

"The last thing I want between you and me is space, sugar. Take up as much of it as you want."

"Hmmm," I say, but I don't move. Instead, I surprise even myself by turning to face him and putting a hand on his chest.

"There she is," he says, and his words rumble against my hand in a way I *really* like. It's in that moment it hits me straight in the face.

I *like* Nick.

I really like him.

I like him in a way that I might be okay with the risk of the girls getting wrapped up in him, of him becoming a fixture in our lives. Because no matter if he leaves us today or in a month or in five years, we're all going to feel it.

And maybe *that's* the lesson I should be teaching my daughters. That life is too damn short to play it safe all of the time. That even when it scares you, love is worth it. The promise of being in love and *being* loved is worth the risk.

"I think . . ." I whisper the words, my mind swirling with realization, and I also wonder for a moment if this is what he meant when he told me he wouldn't kiss me again until I was ready. Maybe he was waiting for me to feel this all-consuming acceptance of an *us*, waiting for me to be willing to brave the uncertainty. "I think I want you to kiss me." A wide, boyish smile lights up his whole face, and I can't help but let it reflect on mine.

It's contagious.

"You think, huh?"

"Yeah." The word is breathy with anticipation, my entire body moving slightly closer to him.

"I'm not kissing you until you're sure, sugar. When you're ready for me to kiss you, it'll be more than an *I think* situation."

I roll my eyes.

I groan.

I contemplate running off and leaving him behind.

But I do none of the above.

Instead, I lean in and kiss him.

For a split second, his body is still, like he's unsure of what to do, and I realize I just *surprised* him. I surprised Nicolas Finch, and something about that feels really fucking good. Good enough to give me a burst of confidence, my hands moving to his neck and tugging a bit to deepen the kiss, my tongue slipping out to graze the line of his lips.

His moment of surprise doesn't last very long, though, the shock wearing off quickly as he opens his mouth and sucks on my tongue, pulling a moan from my chest. It seems as soon as this man's lips are on mine, all sexual tension and need spiral, intensifying almost instantly and building with each day of no relief.

And now that I've let myself come to terms with the fact that I *like* this man, there's surely no point in denying it any longer: I *want* Nick. I want him in a physical way, and no matter how terrified I am of it, I'm starting to understand I want him in other ways.

There's no time for overthinking, though, because as my hands grip his shoulders and his neck, as my breaths become gasping and my heart beats faster and heat pools in my belly, Nick moves my body so I'm straddling him, his hands moving from my waist to my ass and gripping there tight. My hips shift instinctually, grinding down as my lips move on his, and I gasp.

Nick's *hard*.

Not a little either—I can feel every inch of him, stiff and long and pressing right against my clit. There are just a few very thin layers between us, between utter bliss.

And right now, there's a brick wall erected between logic and desire in my mind so I move, grinding my clit against him as we kiss, and I moan into his mouth. The move has his fingers tightening on me and a deep groan coming from his chest, the sound traveling through me to add onto the pressure in my belly. His hands grip my hips, shifting them again to recreate the movement and sending a lightning bolt of desire through me.

"Oh," I whisper against his lips, and his hands continue the circuit, guiding me back and forth along his hardness as pleasure blooms and builds in my belly in a way I haven't felt in years. Maybe ever, if I'm being honest.

"That's it, sugar," he whispers, his lips on my neck just under my ear, his words rough and breathy and driving me higher. "Take what you need." I'm in another world, one where I'm consumed by lust and need and utterly lost in Nick. "You're in control of this. Use me."

Those words do something more, making my swollen clit throb as I dig my fingers into his shoulders and groan, my hips moving faster along the shaft of his cock over our clothes, and I tip them so he hits where I need it most.

"Oh, shit, fuck." I groan, my head dropping to his shoulder as I continue to move, to writhe frantically. The fire is spreading, heating my lower back and expanding through my belly, through my veins, taking over everything and anything, and *oh god . . .*

"That's it, baby. That's it. God, you should see how fucking beautiful you look like this, taking control. Taking what you need."

I moan again into the shoulder of his shirt, and his hand moves up into my hair, tugging hard so my head tips back. His grip causes tiny pinpricks of pain and pleasure on my scalp and grounds me.

And when his eyes meet mine, hooded and dark and so turned on and enamored and *enthralled* by what he's seeing, it happens. The scale tips, the fire consumes me, and I come on Nicolas Finch's lap, moaning his name as I do, my hips grinding on his hard cock.

"Fuck, you're beautiful," he murmurs, and it's not for my ears, not for my benefit, but more like a prayer he didn't mean to say aloud. It causes another ripple of orgasm to tear through me, my hips jerking on him before I collapse and bury my face into his neck with a groan.

That hand in my hair tugs once more, gentler this time, until I'm looking at Nick, and his lips move to mine in a frantic press, like he needs to bookend this connection with one last kiss, a wax seal to make sure it doesn't leak, that I can't forget what we just did.

It's like he's afraid if he doesn't, I might move back to avoiding him, back to telling him no, that this won't work, that *we* won't work. He's afraid I'll let the fear consume me and take over, and that fear is valid, all things considered. There's not a small chance that once the high is gone, once I'm not in the safe, comforting bubble of his presence, I'll start to let my anxieties creep back in, but for now . . .

It's him. It's Nick. And it's me. And I think I'm finally ready to give *us* a real chance.

And it's only about one third because of the ridiculous orgasm.

Fine. Maybe half.

Nick's lips travel from mine as my breathing eases, and he kisses the edges of my lips, my cheek, moving down to my neck, my body shifting as he does, and it's then I feel him beneath me, still hard and very much not experiencing the same blissful relief I am.

Guilt and anxiety fill me as he starts to kiss under my jaw, sweet presses of his lips to my skin, but all I can think is, *I'm not ready.* That might make me a bitch, considering I just got off, even if it was in a high school, fully clothed kind of way. He's here hard and needy, and I'm unwilling to return the favor just yet.

But I'm not ready.

I'm no longer the woman who does shit because I feel guilt or because I want a man to love me. I no longer am a woman who gives up my power to secure that love and affection. And I think—I really fucking *hope*—Nick isn't the man who only gives that affection when he'll get what *he* wants.

"Hey," I whisper between kisses as his lips move down my throat.

"Mmm," he says against my neck, and I giggle as his stubble scrapes against my skin.

"Hey, hold on," I repeat, and he moves his head up, looking in my eyes with concern. His hand, callused and warm, pushes my hair back over my shoulder. It's then nerves take over, nerves that what I'm about to say will land wrong, that he'll be disappointed, that it will ruin this beautiful moment we're sharing.

"I'm . . . ," I start but can't finish.

"Whatever you want to say, Shae, this is a safe space. With me, you're safe. Always."

Somehow, I know that's the truth. It hasn't been long enough for it, but somehow, I feel *safe* with Nick, like I can trust him with anything—everything—and he'll take it in stride. He'll take care of me.

"I'm really sorry. So, *so* sorry, but I . . . I'm not ready. Not yet. For anything . . . more than this." He looks at me and smiles like he thinks I'm cute and not a total buzzkill.

"That's okay.,"

"It's not that I don't . . . want to. Do things with you. I do," I say, scrambling to explain what I don't necessarily understand myself. "It's just . . . I'm not ready."

"Shae, it's all good."

"I mean, I know you're saying that because you're a gentleman and sweet and way, way too good for me, but—"

"Alright, we're stopping this now," he says then stands, his hands on my hips so I move with him. I squeal, my hands going around his neck and legs wrapping his waist as I do, and he begins to move with surety toward his room.

"What?" I ask, tightening my hold around his neck even though I know he's strong enough to carry me wherever.

"We're stopping this now." He pushes the door to his room open before stepping in and kicking it shut behind him.

"Stopping what?" He doesn't answer, instead tosses me to his bed. I bounce once before he climbs on, holding his weight on his hands on either side of my body, looming over me.

"For one, we're stopping this *too good* bullshit before it even starts. I don't want to hear it." I open my mouth. "If anything, Shae, you are too good for me. Fuck, just look at you. Gorgeous and kind and so fucking strong. If anything, I don't deserve you, don't deserve the trust you're slowly giving me."

"You don't have to say that kind of stuff, Nick. My ego isn't that fragile."

"I'm not saying anything to stroke your ego, Shae." He moves, his hand tucking hair behind my ear and a smile on his face, before doing a pushup and pressing his lips to my forehead. "I'm just telling you the truth, and you're letting your twisted mind get in the way. So it ends now."

"Nick—"

"You are not too good for me, Shae. Relationships like that, where one person thinks the other is better or one person thinks the other is lesser? Toxic. Doomed to fail. And I know you're not there yet, but I am, and I don't want this to fucking fail."

I don't know how to respond to that.

My body is still buzzing gently with the high of my orgasm, anxieties hiding in the dark corners, unseen but not unfelt.

He means so well and has such high hopes, and I know he doesn't say these things lightly as a single parent himself, but I can't help but think he doesn't know what he's agreeing to if he decides to take on me and the girls.

"I've got a lot of issues, Nick."

"Then we'll have a lot of talks. We'll go slow. We're playing by your rulebook." Warmth flows through me, but I, of course, can't let anything be.

"I don't know when I'll be *ready*." I mean this in so many ways— ready to give him my all, ready to trust in a relationship. Ready to let someone fully in or just ready to do more than dry hump on his couch.

Though, to be totally honest, I think it won't take much for me to be ready for *that*.

My body already wants more, just waiting for my mind to get on board. But still, I'm not there.

"That's fine," he says.

"It could be never." It's a challenge, in a way, and I wait for the hesitation, the uncertainty . . . anything.

"That's fine," he says easily. I feel the need to clarify because him hovering over me like this with that *smile* makes me think there is no world where I would *never* be ready.

In fact, if I had sat on it for a few moments before blurting out I wasn't ready, I could probably have convinced myself to let it be, to just go with it and see where the night takes us. I'm glad I didn't, but . . .

"Okay, it probably won't be forever. But it could be a while." He looks at me, shakes his head, and smiles.

"I'm a patient man, sugarplum. I'll wait for however long it takes for you to be ready. A day, a week, a month, a year? Fine. So long as I get to spend it with you, I'm good."

I stare at him.

I stare at him and look, really look, trying to understand what he's saying.

If he means it.

He does.

"What is *happening* here, Nick?" I ask. "You've been in my life for no time at all and you're consuming me." I whisper the confession like I'm afraid to scare him off because I *am*.

He rolls us once more.

"Sometimes, things are just right. Sometimes, things were always *meant* to be. You didn't find Connor because you were meant to date him or because you needed him as a friend, Shae. You found your way into his life so you could find your way into mine. And I've been hearing about you, falling for you by proxy, for months. So, it's gonna take you a bit longer, but I told you, Shae. I'm a patient man. And for you, I'll wait a decade." I lie there, confused and elated and warm and a bit scared, but then he presses his lips to mine once more and it all washes away, leaving just the warmth and the elation before he rolls us both so we're on our sides, facing each other.

I smile, and he lies like that for long minutes in silence before I speak again.

"But I, uh . . . I'd still like to make out with you. If you're up for it." A beat passes before his head tips back, his neck long and lean as he laughs before using his hands to roll over me again and showing me just how up for it he is.

# TWENTY-SIX

## 15 SLEEPS UNTIL CHRISTMAS

### SHAE

We spend the day at the farm, mostly cuddled up on Nick's big couch, watching movies in new pairs of cozy slippers Holly brought as snow falls gently, the girls still in awe that the elf followed them to the farm, while Nick runs around, putting out fires.

A part of me feels unbearably guilty this man is wasting so much time on me and my little family during his busiest time, but also . . . I don't.

It could be some kind of Stockholm syndrome, could be the holiday season, could be the excessive amount of time together or his constant reassurances, but for one reason or another, this . . . relationship, friendship, whatever you want to call it feels like it was always in place. Like this isn't new, the girls and me coming to spend a weekend with him. It feels natural.

"I don't want to go," Harper says, her hands on her hips, her face near anger.

"Me neither," Ruby says. "Minnie is going to miss me!"

I don't mention that the small horse she has grown worryingly attached to in less than two days most definitely will not miss her and will not even notice she is gone, but instead, I let her live in her delusion.

It's good for girls to have a healthy sense of delusion.

"I'll make sure I tell her every day you say hi," Nick says, grabbing the big bag of our stuff off the kitchen table and hoisting it over his shoulder to bring it out to the car. I look at him and open my mouth to tell him no, I've got it, but he instantly glares at me. "If you try and tell me you'll carry this, I'm gonna lose it, sugar." I roll my eyes.

But I don't fight him on it.

Progress, I suppose.

"Alright, girls," I say, looking to my daughters in their coats already. "Let's go. You've got school tomorrow, and Ruby, I'm pretty sure you still have homework."

I expect an argument.

An "I don't want to go to school tomorrow" or a "no, I don't have homework" or any of their normal complaints and arguments.

But instead, Harper's eyes go wide and start to water.

"I don't want to go," she says, her voice low and whining in a way I haven't heard in years.

"Harper—"

"I want to stay here forever."

God. This girl.

She never asks for anything, not like this, and having her choose this moment to do so hurts.

"I know, honey," I say because I do. There's some kind of magic at Finch Farm I can't quite put my finger on, but it's in the air. A feeling of calm and comfort.

Maybe it's just Nick. I think I'm at a point where I can admit that now, if only to myself.

Nick feels like home.

Not in the way that he feels familiar, but in the way that he just . . . fits.

In the way where I feel like when I'm by his side, I can both do anything and be anything and do it all safely. In the way I know he'll protect me no matter what comes, and I'm safe to . . . to try.

Isn't that kind of what he's asking me to do, after all? To give us a chance? To push my fears and anxieties aside and give him a try?

This morning, I woke to kisses on my neck, having fallen asleep in Nick's bed last night. Part of me prepared myself to have to tell him no, not yet, to hurt his ego or have him get annoyed or frustrated with me, but that didn't happen. Instead, once he realized I was awake, he trailed his lips up my neck, his short beard scratching my skin as he did before he let his lips hover over mine.

"Morning," he whispered, his breath brushing my lips. I thought I would worry about morning breath or morning hair or puffy eyes and pillow lines, but I couldn't bear to. He had the same sleepy eyes, the same first thing in the morning puffiness to his face that comes with age no matter how many treatments, the same creases in his cheek from his pillow, and it just . . . didn't matter.

"Morning," I said, my voice just as croaky, but even I could hear the smile on my face leaking into the single word. He moved again, until he was hovering over me, an arm on either side of my face, his arms holding him up.

"How'd you sleep?"

"What?" My mind was bumbling, a mix of sleep and chaos from having this gorgeous man hovering over me.

"How'd you sleep? In my bed? Cause I slept better than I have in a fuckin' year," he whispered, and the words traveled through me, leaving trails of heat and warmth as they went.

"Good," I whisper. "Great."

"Good," he whispered. And then he just stayed there, above me, his body not even touching mine. As I continued to stare at him, as I continued to wake up, I started to wonder what we were doing and why his lips weren't on mine.

"Can I kiss you?" he asked me finally, and I think I melted then and there.

Because we had made out the entire night, I had slept in his bed, and still, he was hovering over me first thing in the morning, asking to kiss me.

I, of course, smiled and told him yes.

And after he kissed me, he looked at me, pressed his lips to my forehead, and said, "You wake the girls up. I'll start breakfast."

"You don't have to—" I had started, but he shook his head and gave me another quick kiss to shut me up.

"We're a team now, Shae. Go get the girls. I'll make breakfast." And then he rolled off me and did exactly that.

Which leads us to now, midday and arguing with my daughters who, just like me, already feel way too at home on this ranch and don't want to leave.

"Can we stay, Mom?" Harper asks, eyes wide and pleading. I give her a small shake of my head.

"I'm sorry, honey. No, we have to go home. You guys have school tomorrow." She stares at me, eyes watering and lower lip trembling.

"But you guys can come back this weekend," Nick says. All three of our heads move to look at him with various expressions. Ruby is so full of hope, it makes my heart hurt, while Harper is skeptical. I'm sure I'm a mix of irritation and, just like Ruby, hope.

"Really?" Harper asks.

"If it's okay with your mom and you don't have anything else going on, you can come over anytime you don't have school the next day."

I could kiss him for the clarification, for knowing if he said anytime and left it at that, Harper would go on a tangent about staying today.

But then her look changes again, going from curious to the kind of calculating look only a 7-year-old can have when she has a plan, and before I can argue or shut her up or stuff her in the car, she speaks.

"You should have dinner with us tonight," she says. "At our house."

I sigh. "Harper, Nick has—"

"I can do that," he says. I look at him like he's insane.

"Nick, that's not necessary, really. You've done more than enough already."

"And let these two down?" he says, moving between them both and putting an arm around each, pulling them in to his chest. "Never."

"YAY!" Harper yells, pumping her fist like she won some championship instead of guilting a grown man to drive an hour to our house to have dinner with her.

"Pizza!" Ruby says, disregarding that we had pizza last night.

"And garlic knots and mozzarella sticks for Harper," Nick adds.

And even though I want to argue, want to remind him it's so very unnecessary, when I see all three of their smiling faces, my heart grows and warms.

So I roll my eyes like they all drive me insane (true) and they're nuisances (false) but don't argue anymore.

And really, what right do I have to complain when, after we get back to my place, he runs out to get the food while I unpack the girls and start laundry, then does the dishes while I help the girls shower and get ready for bed? I can't complain when he tucks them in at their request while I get their lunches together for the next day.

And then, of course, I can't complain when we make out on the couch like teenagers for almost an hour before I finally kick him out of my house, but not before he promises to come back in time for dinner the next day.

And even though logic tells me not to get comfortable with this, not to lean into it too much, I can't help but think how freaking nice it would be if I had this every day.

# TWENTY-SEVEN

## 14 SLEEPS UNTIL CHRISTMAS

### SHAE

"Mom, when can we get a tree?" Harper asks the next night, barely three minutes after Nick walks into our house. He once again bought dinner and though I feel guilty, I'm learning to let it go.

"Maybe we can get one from the farm," Ruby says, looking at her sister, and in that moment, I know this was orchestrated. Some kind of sister-plan spoken of in the middle of the night while they were supposed to be sleeping. Instead, they were plotting how to get themselves a tree from Nick.

"You guys—" I start with a sigh.

"I'll see what I can do," he says, and I turn my ire to him.

"That's so very not necessary."

"Why, you got a tree hiding in your car I don't know about?" he asks.

"No, but I was going to go to the store and get—"

"If you say you were going to get an artificial tree, I'm gonna lose my shit, Shae." I stare at him for a beat, then I look to the girls who are holding back giggles.

"It's cleaner. No needles," I explain because I absolutely was planning to buy a fake tree.

"Adds to the fun. I'm sure the girls will help," Nick says.

"This isn't a dog you're trying to convince me to get by telling me you'll walk him every day, Nicolas."

"Oh, can we get a dog?!" Harper asks excitedly, and I look to the ceiling, counting to ten to try and find a semblance of patience.

I don't get there.

"I've been looking to get a dog for the ranch, you know," he says.

"Nicolas, can you please come with me into the kitchen?" I ask through gritted teeth.

"Absolutely, sugar. Girls, you go wash your hands for dinner, yeah?" They look at each other with smiles before nodding and running toward the bathroom, a feat I've never been able to accomplish without at least a moderate amount of pleading and bargaining.

"How do you do that?" I ask, standing in the same place and staring at where they once were. He moves to me, grabbing my hand and leading me into my small kitchen.

"Do what?"

"Get them to listen to you in a heartbeat? The don't listen to me no matter what." God, am I that shitty of a mom, I can't get them to do a thing I say?

"Stop, it's because you're a *good* mom, Shae. Because you're always telling them what to do, and, as you've pointed out, they occasionally will need to fight you for power. I'm new and fun. Give 'em a few months. The shine will wear off."

*Give 'em a few months.*

The words pool, slow and sticky in my belly, like sap from one of Nick's trees, and I can't ignore them even if I want to. That sentence, like so many before it, tells me he thinks he's going to be here, telling the girls to get ready for dinner into the new year.

"In the meantime, give me a kiss while they're still preoccupied," he says then spins me so my front is to his, an arm is wrapped around my waist, and he's stepping back until my ass hits the countertop.

"Nick," I whisper, but my chin tips up, my body giving him every sign that even if I'm arguing with him, I want him to kiss me.

He doesn't, though.

"Not kissing you until you do it first, baby. You're in control."

He loves to show me that, I'm learning. To both give it and take it away, somehow knowing exactly how I need to take the reins in any given situation.

Nick loves to give me control of our relationship, of how this . . . thing between us is going, and takes it away in the things I'm starting to get burnt out on—dinners and decisions and life in general.

So I smile.

I smile and I move to my tiptoes, him still needing to bend a bit when I'm in no shoes and standing in front of him, and I press my lips to his. He makes a low *mmmm* sound as I kiss him, and one hand moves to the back of my neck, taking back that control he gave me, taking over the kiss.

I'm so very okay with that.

# TWENTY-EIGHT

## 13 SLEEPS UNTIL CHRISTMAS

### SHAE

"What the fuck is that?" I ask when I open the door. Nick is standing on my welcome mat, holding a big ass Christmas tree in one hand, a red plastic stand in the other.

"It's a tree," he says matter-of-factly, like I'm the crazy one.

"Yeah, I see that. What are you doing with it?" It's fucking giant, way too big for my small townhouse, but now he's stepping over the threshold with it, looking around like he's contemplating where would be the best spot.

"Gonna put it up in your place." I should tell him no. I should tell him *hell* no. I should give him the commonsense answer of *that will never fit* and then violently fight the urge to say *that's what she said*, but instead, I ask a different question.

"Why?"

"Because you don't have one." That, too, he says so incredibly matter-of-factly, like it's the only option and he's bored with how long it's taking me to process his actions while he stands in my home, holding a *huge fucking Christmas tree*.

"Nick, this is crazy. You don't have to do this. I was going to—"

Finally, he looks exasperated with me and my antics, cutting me off to speak.

"I own a fucking Christmas tree farm, Shae. I promise it's not a hardship. Barely even had to leave my house to get it." I glare at him.

"And the stand?" I ask with a raised eyebrow, and he smiles.

"We sell them in the shop. There are a few tree skirts in my truck, too. Wasn't sure which you'd like. Figured you can pick one and I'll bring the rest back, but I didn't have enough hands."

Guilt curls in my belly at his words, with how much he's going out of his way and the fact he's spending money on me and the girls.

"I'll pay you back. You don't—" He was starting to move into my place, seemingly looking over my head to find a place to lay down the tree even though I'm still standing in the doorway, but he comes to a full stop, turning to look at me with a fierce face of irritation.

"You start up that shit again, I do not care if we're playing this safe and slow, I'm throwing this fuckin' tree on the ground, tugging your sweet sweatpants down, and spanking your ass until you drop it."

My mouth is open and my eyes are wide as I stare at him, shocked at his outburst, but I also can't fight the burn on my cheeks, a blush that isn't embarrassment or anxiety but something so completely different.

Arousal.

Jesus Christ, what's wrong with me?

But even now, all I can think is Nick sitting in the worn love seat, my sweats around my ankles, his hand coming down on my ass, rough callouses on my burning skin and—

"Well fuck," he says, breaking me from my trance. "Not the reaction I expected, but I can work with that."

My blush stays but the shock melts, and I glare at him with daggers in my eyes.

"Go set up the stupid tree, Finch."

And then he laughs, the sound filling my headspace in a way I refuse to think about how I could get used to. "So, what, are the girls supposed to think this is from the elf? I'm not sure how realistic this elf bringing a mountain of a tree into our home with zero help is, Christmas magic or not." He looks at me and shakes his head.

"No, I'm gonna tell them it's from me." I furrow my brows in confusion.

"I thought the whole point was to create some kind of magical season for them."

"Fuck that, I want them to know I brought this. I gotta get some street cred for all of this work." I scoff out a laugh. "Plus, we have a deal," he continues.

"Me and you? All deals you think you have with me have been crafted in your own little head, Mr. Finch." He smiles and shakes his head, clearly *entertained* by me. I haven't moved, glued to the door by the shock of the tree in front of me.

"No, you pain, me and the girls. Now, can you move so I'm not just standing in your hallway with a fuckin' Christmas tree?"

"With *my* girls?" I ask, ignoring his request.

"No, the girls down the street. Yes, your girls. Now, please move. You're letting all your heat out."

That breaks the semi-fog I'm in and I step aside as he walks farther into my house, and I close the door behind him.

"What kind of deal did you make with my girls?"

"Nothing nefarious, calm down," he says and places the tree carefully onto the floor, leaning it on a wall. "So, I'm thinking right there," he says, pointing to the window in the living room. There's a love seat there, but it can be moved. I'd just been putting it off because it weighs a million pounds and I hadn't bought the tree yet.

"I can help you move the love seat," I say, forgetting I was going to argue, to tell him it wouldn't work, that I don't want a live tree and the mess it brings. He looks at me like I'm insane then walks over to the sofa, bending to grab the arms and lifting.

The man is un-fucking-real, that much is for sure—that love seat is heavy as fuck and took two delivery people to bring it inside. And then I watch in awe as he moves it right to where I would have suggested without me saying a thing.

It's unnecessarily hot, and I need to change the subject *immediately*.

"So you made a deal with the girls . . . ?"

"Yup." He grabs the red tree stand and moves to the spot he just cleared out, ignoring my question for the most part.

"What was it?"

"Last weekend, they begged me for a tree from the farm, before they even brought it up yesterday. I told them I had a feeling you didn't need more shit to clean up and that real trees made a mess, but they said they'd clean the needles up every day." I stand in shock, a seemingly constant state when he's around, and whatever part of me that wasn't already liquid melts. "Of course, I know they're gonna miss most of 'em, so like I told you, when I come here at night, I'll sweep up whatever they miss. But there's no universe where I'm letting a woman of mine have a fuckin' plastic tree in her house when I've got acres of 'em begging for homes."

God, this man.

*This man.*

"*Wait.* You convinced *Harper* to clean up?" I ask, the warmth melting into shock because Ruby, *maybe.* Harper? Hell no.

"Well, I mean, there wasn't much convincing to be done. It was her idea." *When did they have this in-depth conversation about Christmas trees?*

"How did you know that? That I wouldn't want to deal with the needles?" I ask, and he stands from where he was loosening the screws of the stand and walks over to me.

He pulls me in close, a thick arm wrapped around my waist, tugging until our chests are pressed together. My body tingles anywhere he touches me.

"One of these days, you'll realize I'm not doing this shit because I feel guilty. I'm doing it because I really fuckin' like you, sugarplum. I like you, and I take note, and I'm here to make *your* life easier." He leans down, pressing warm lips to my forehead. "Until then, I'll be here every night, doing whatever I can to help you out and categorizing every little sliver you show me of yourself."

# TWENTY-NINE

## 13 SLEEPS UNTIL CHRISTMAS

### SHAE

The tree is huge in my small living room, but I can't say it doesn't look amazing. It's full, the branches not giving any room to see the trunk in the center, and Nick even strung up white lights around it. He only needed to show me one of the tree skirts, knowing the red one with little horses running around the edges would be absolutely perfect, and even though I'm going to add what ornaments we have with the girls later, he hung one round ornament reading *Finch Farm* on it, dead center.

It's been an interesting hour or so, us working together on this little sliver of Christmas magic, me guiding him to make sure the tree was straight and choosing the white lights over colors (because, *of course*, he brought those too) and adding water to the tree stand while he cleaned up the dropped needles.

Now, he's carefully placing the elf next to the ornament, and I'm watching him from the couch.

"You love this, don't you?" I ask, the question brewing for days now.

"Hmm?" he asks, still staring at the elf. It's become less of the bane of my existence, slowly turning into a small, delicate tether holding me and my girls to Nick.

"The Christmas stuff. The magic, the tree, the elf. You love it."

"Yeah. I do. My parents weren't too big into it, and I knew I always wanted to do it for my kids. I didn't realize it would happen so soon." The laugh he lets out is self-deprecating. "And then I started working at the tree farm and . . . I don't know. Every winter, I get to see families making memories every day. Then I started to see them come back every year—their kids growing up or getting pregnant or married or whatever—and it felt like I was a part of that magic. Kind of grew from there. We added the shop and the carriage rides and the Santa meet and greets after I started getting more involved because it made sense, but also because it just . . . adds to it."

"You're basically Santa Claus," I say and can't fight a giggle as he plops down onto the couch beside me.

"I don't know if I'd go that far," he replies, then his hands go to my hips, moving me until I'm straddling him. It's not necessarily a sexual act in and of itself, more like he wants me as close as humanly possible, and again, slowly, I'm starting to accept that about him.

He's *clingy*.

I never thought I'd like that, a clingy man, someone who always wants me within arm's reach, but now I'm starting to see it as a confirmation, a consistent, low hum of a reminder that he *wants me*.

It's become a bit of a comfort.

"Oh, I would," I say, and it might be the glass of wine I had while we set the tree up, but I'm feeling warm and giggly and slightly more confident than I'm used to.

Or maybe it's just Nick.

"Hmmm." His hand moves to brush hair behind my ear again.

"You give off major Santa energy. You've got . . ." Another giggle bubbles in my chest at the thought that came to my mind, and even though I fight not to say it aloud, I can't stop it from tumbling out. "You've got *big Nick energy*." And then I burst into laughter. Nick smiles.

"Big Nick energy?"

"Yeah. You know, like Saint Nick? Santa Claus? But your name is Nick, soooo . . ." His smile grows wider, and my belly goes warmer as his hand travels from my hip and up under my shirt, brushing on the skin right above my loose sweatpants with a rough, calloused thumb.

The simple touch sends a lightning bolt of desire shooting through me and has my breath stopping.

"You know, I think that saying is a little different," he says, and his voice is rough and low now, like the lightning bolt hit him as well.

"Mmmm," I agree. My hand moves to his neck, nails scraping there gently, teasing. I don't know what comes over me when I whisper, "Can you touch me?"

He groans, the noise ratcheting up the need rapidly taking over, his forehead pressing to mine. "Are you sure?"

Instead of answering, I reach for his hand on my belly and move it, sliding it down, under my sweatpants and into my panties until his fingers are touching the short cut curls above my clit.

"Yeah," I whisper, and then his lips are on mine, taking away any other chance for conversation or requests or arguments.

But I don't need them.

Because a single, rough finger brushes over my clit and my hips buck into his hand.

"Fuck," I whisper when he breaks the kiss to look down to where his hand is in my pants, brushing over and over on my clit.

"Yeah," he agrees.

"Inside," I beg, need building and growing within me, a need I know only he can sate.

"Sugar," he says, and the word sounds like a warning.

My hand moves again, pushing his farther down until he can feel how wet I am already from a few gentle touches and kisses. "Jesus, Shae," he says, but a thick finger slides into me.

A single finger and I'm full.

"Oh, god." I buck my hips, and he starts to pull out before pushing back in, finger fucking me gently. "More," I groan, and he does too, crooking that finger inside me as his thumb moves to circle my clit.

Fuck going slow.

"Nick," I whisper, my voice barely audible. "Nick, I need . . . I need more. My room. Let's go to my room. Please."

His smile is devious, his finger slowly sliding into me and then out again, my panties tugging at my skin as he does in a delicious tease I can't handle anymore. I want more. I want everything. I want him. I want him to fuck me and make me forget any reasoning, to forget my past and my future and just live in this sliver of *present* that is Nick and me.

"No," he says. "This is enough."

"No, it's not," I moan, writhing. "I want more. I want *you*." He pushes my shirt up then kisses my belly, his lips warm and his five o'clock shadow scratching at my skin.

"This is more than enough for tonight. But maybe we'll take these off, too," he says, then his hand moves, tugging at the waistband of my sweatpants, his eyes on my face like he's . . . waiting. It clicks in a moment, of course, what he's doing. He's waiting for me to give him the go-ahead, ever the gentleman.

I nod, praying he won't make me actually *say the words* out loud as one of his hands is already in my pants.

In *me*.

He cuts me a break, smiling when I nod and using his hand to tug my sweats and underwear down. My hand reaches over, grabbing the blanket draped on the edge of the couch *just in case* I need to throw it over myself quickly.

"Fuck, Shae," he says, his voice low, his eyes locked to where one finger is moving inside of me slowly, now fully exposed to him as I kick my sweats and underwear to the floor. Even though the air is cool on my heated skin, when I shiver, it has nothing to do with that.

The finger slides out, his other hand moving to push my legs open a bit more until one leg is on the couch, the other is on the floor, and I'm *spread*. I'm open for him, exposed to his eyes only.

Being naked has never been comfortable for me. When I have had sex in the past, it was in a bed with the lights off. Even changing in front of my husband never felt comfortable, never felt natural.

But here with Nick, my pussy bare and wet and on the couch with all of the lights on, I don't feel that. I feel . . . sexy. Wanton. Desired.

I feel like *his*, and in a way, I feel like a *gift* for him.

His wet finger slides up and down my pussy, from the entrance to swollen clit, circling around it before repeating the circuit until my hips are shifting gently, trying to get more.

"God, I wanna eat this," he murmurs to himself like he's forgotten I'm in the room with him even though he's staring at my most intimate place. But then he comes back to this world, his head looking up as I look down my body at him, kneeling between my legs on the floor. "Can I eat this, Shae?"

Common sense says no.

The little voice that wants me to keep that wall between us is screaming to say no. To close my legs and tug the blanket over myself and ask him to leave.

He'd do it. I know that for sure. He'd do it in a heartbeat.

I also know unless I tell him not to, he'll come back tomorrow, continue his gentle work of scraping through my walls until I let him in.

"You're in control here, Shae. You're always in control. You tell me yes, and you tell me no, and you tell me how much. That's how this goes, baby. So, you tell me if you want me to eat your pussy. You tell me if you want me to help you put your sweats back on and sit on the couch until I have to leave. You tell me whatever it is you want." I open my mouth, and he smiles. "Unless you're telling me to take you into your room and fuck you. That, we're not doing tonight."

I pout.

He smiles.

Then he moves up my body, his rough jeans along my bare inner thighs doing wild things to my libido, and whispers against my lips,

"When I fuck you the first time, Shae, you're going to scream my name. And I wanna hear you. Our first time, you're not screaming into a pillow, yeah? That can be the second or third time."

A full fucking body shiver rips through me, this moment sexy on so, *so many counts,* I can't even think straight.

"Third time," I whisper, because that's all I can think of. He smiles before giving me a long, deep kiss, his tongue tasting me and tangling with mine before he moves back down my body.

"Yeah. Third time, I'll make you come on my cock in your bed, screaming into your pillow so we don't wake anyone up. But the first? It'll be just us." All the air leaves my lungs as, once more, his fingers move to my pussy.

"Oh," is all I can say.

He chuckles. "But for now . . ." His eyes dip back to where his finger is disappearing inside of me and he groans. "Can I make you come on my tongue?"

And really, what is a girl supposed to say to that?

So I nod with a small, shy smile.

His wide grin is much less shy.

"Fuck yes," he says, and I can't help but let my own smile widen.

That only lasts a moment because then my eyes are drifting shut, my head is tipping back, and my back is arching as his mouth closes over my clit, his tongue playing no games as he laps at me. "Oh, Jesus, fuck." I whimper, my hips moving up to get more. His free hand moves to the open thigh and he presses down gently, telling me to stay put as he sucks on my clit.

"Fuck, Nick!" I shout, his fingers moving in me, a second added, crooking just right to hit my G-spot. It's a place only I have ever found before, a spot that has my entire body shuttering. I'm already so close to the edge, and as he groans against me, my entire body tenses.

He's groaning because he *likes* this. He's groaning because, in a twisted way, he's getting pleasure from making me feel this all-consuming thing, from making me feel so fucking good. When I look down my body, my shirt pushed up to just beneath my bra, his face between my legs, his eyes open and looking up at mine with humor and lust and adoration in them, I can't help but moan.

"Oh god. Fuck." The wave is growing, ready to crest, and I'm ready to come after just a few moments, his tongue on my clit working expertly, his fingers fucking me exactly the way I need.

Who would have thought this man, this sweet, kind, caring cowboy could be such a force between my legs?

Well, I guess I knew.

I knew the second he laid eyes on me, and I think that's why I've been so damn scared. I looked at him and knew down to my depths that there was some kind of invisible string, some kind of bond between us that meant this would have always been groundbreaking, soul-shattering.

That'd I'd never be able to turn back if we crossed this line. I'd be forever changed.

"Fuck," I moan. "Next time—" I gasp as he shifts his fingers, hitting deeper, now with three fingers. "Shit, next time you eat my pussy, you do it with that *stupid fucking hat* on," I say then ignore all forces of propriety, taking over and pushing his head farther into me. He chuckles as he sucks on my clit and that's all it takes.

I fall apart, the waves crashing over and over, my body quaking, and golden heat pours through me, spreading from my belly out to my fingertips, consuming me, chasing away the dark the way only Nick seems to be able to do.

It feels like an eternity before I come back to this universe, my body quaking still.

My eyes are closed, and I'm trying to catch my breath when Nick moves, his hands brushing my ankles and tugging my sweats and underwear back up my hips gently before tossing the blanket over me. Then he tugs me into his side, letting my head rest on his chest like this is normal.

As if him eating me out on my couch and then cuddling on said couch is normal.

Except, I can still both see and feel his erection in his jeans. He's unsatisfied, unlike me.

"What about you?" I ask once words work again.

"Don't worry about it," he says, then his hand moves hair back from my face, tucking it behind my ear, and he presses a soft kiss to the top of my head.

"Nick, I can—"

"That was for you, Shae. But it was also very much for me. I've been dying to eat you out, to taste that pussy since the day you walked into my life. Let me have this."

Another bolt of lust rips through me at his words.

"Nick, but we—"

"Give me this, Shae. We've got all the time in the world. We're taking it slow. I refuse to fuck this up by rushing it because I need to know what you feel like coming around my cock."

I don't know where to focus first. The fact that we are taking it slow? That he wants to feel me coming around his cock? That we've got all the time in the world when I've been quietly worried this will all end once Christmas comes?

"Stop with the overthinking, Shae," he says. "What's on your mind?" I could say a million things, but I stick to just one, the one closest to my sex-filled brain.

"I've never done that."

"Taken it slow?" I laugh.

"No. The, uh . . . the last part. About me . . . you know . . ." I was just riding this man's face, pushing his head into my pussy while I came on his fingers and mouth, but I can't even talk about sex like an adult less than five minutes later.

"Oh. The coming on my cock part? We'll fix that sooner or later, no worries, sugar."

More heat.

More desire.

"No. Well . . . yes, but . . ." I should let it go and never admit this and stop making it weird and— "I've never come during sex." His head moves back when I look at him, like he's shocked.

"What?"

"I've never . . . ," I start and give him wide eyes, too shy to say the real thing even though minutes ago, I was completely exposed to this man.

"But . . . ," he starts, but then stops, thinks about it, and smiles. The man *fucking smiles*. "Well, I'll be honored to be the first. And the last." My eyes are wide and I contemplate an answer, something to say, but my mind is blank, be it from shock or the euphoria of my recent orgasm, I don't know. So instead, I just shake my head and smile.

We lie on the couch like that for a while, sitting in peaceful, calm silence before he speaks.

"Tomorrow is Wednesday."

"Yes," I say, sleep starting to fill my veins, the way he runs his fingers through my hair not helping at all.

"You're off."

"Mmmm," I mumble.

"Farm is closed on Wednesdays."

Some far-off part of my brain knows that from my search of Nick and his ranch, but it doesn't click.

"Okay?"

"Let me take you out."

"Take me out?"

"On a date."

"A date?"

"Yes. You know, two people doing some kind of activity, eating, enjoying company. Ideally without little girls around." I open my mouth to argue, but he stops me before I can. "Not that I don't love the girls, not that I don't want to spend all my time with them, but I like it when it's us. When I can kiss you anytime I want without you looking over your shoulder to see if they're looking." I can't argue.

I totally do that when they're around.

And I can't deny that a date with him would be amazing.

Maybe it's because of the orgasm or because I'm sleepy or because he's just finally starting to break through the last of my defenses, but either way, I say something that should terrify me.

And when it doesn't, that should be even *more* concerning.

"Stay the night," I whisper. His eyes reflect the shock pouring through me. "That way, you don't have to come back in the morning. You'll have to make an excuse why you're here so early, but . . . we can think of something," I continue. When he doesn't say anything, panic starts to creep in and I think maybe I stepped too far, too fast, that maybe he doesn't want that. Maybe he just wants a fun time. Maybe—

"Stop overthinking," he says, pushing my hair back. "I'm just trying to think what I did to earn this."

"Earn this?" I ask.

"Earn you. Your trust. Your confidence in me. It's all I want from you, Shae, and you giving it to me little by little? I must have done something really fucking great in a past life."

I don't know how to respond to that, but I don't have to.

Because then Nick is standing, putting a hand out, and pulling me up.

"I'd love to spend the night."

# THIRTY

## 12 SLEEPS UNTIL CHRISTMAS

### SHAE

Nick woke up at 5:30, before the girls, before I was even really up, rolled out of my bed, tugged his jeans back on, pressed a kiss to my forehead, and left.

Thirty minutes later, when I'm shuffling around the kitchen, trying to make coffee quietly in hopes I can get caffeine into my bloodstream before the girls wake up, he knocks quietly on the door.

He's holding two brown paper bags, one bulging and the other much smaller, and two coffees with familiar logos in his other hand.

"Bagels," he says.

He had left my place at 5:30 and drove to Harper's favorite bagel shop on a Wednesday morning.

"I bought Harp a couple of extra rainbows. She can probably take one to school, if that's okay, and you'll have breakfast for the rest of the week."

The man is a myth.

He comes at night to create Christmas magic for my daughters because I'm too tired and spread thin to do it myself, then eats me out with no expectation of me returning the favor, and *then* he wakes up before the sun and gets my kid the only food she'll willingly eat for breakfast.

I don't say words. I thank him with a kiss before we go about what has become our little routine of getting things done—I get the girls up while he toasts bagels, then he makes sure the girls' teeth are brushed while I get myself dressed for the day.

And then he helps to make sure lunches are in backpacks, laptops are charged, and homework was signed off on. He stands in the cold while I watch from the warmth of my kitchen window to see them off to school, and then he comes back inside and kisses me senseless before taking me on a date.

A *date* is heading to the ranch, making out in Nick's foyer long enough that I started to wonder if this *is* the date (not that I would be disappointed in the least) before he steps back, grabs my hand, and leads me to his couch, where he instructs me to wait for him. I scroll on my phone while he bangs around in the kitchen for ten minutes before he finally comes out with a soft-sided cooler in hand and leads me to the stables.

Then, he takes me on a ride.

Nick's body cages me, his arms along mine as he holds the reins, his lips dipping occasionally to press cool kisses to the skin of my neck.

This, too, would have been more than enough for me to happily consider this in my top three dates of all time, but then we reach a field where he lays out a big blanket for us to sit on and builds a fire, and we . . . sit.

And we talk.

And we enjoy being outside, despite the cold. In that cooler is one giant thermos of cocoa and another of coffee along with still-warm grilled cheese sandwiches and tomato soup from the store down the road, he tells me. He's no cook, apparently, but because of that, he knows all the best places to shop.

It skyrockets this date from top three to the absolute best one of my life.

Simple.

No kids.

No expectations.

No *people*.

No fanfare or one-upping or side eyes waiting for me to give some kind of grand thank you.

Just the desire to be together without the pressure of life getting in the way.

Now, we're back in the stalls, Nick putting his horse up while I stand next to Ruby's favorite, Minnie. My fingers scrape along Minnie's muzzle and she snorts, seeming disappointed. It's time for us to head back to Hudson City so we're not late to pick up the girls.

"She smells Ruby on you," Nick says. "She's mad you're not here with her."

"I'm sorry, girl," I murmur. "She's got school today. We'll bring her back soon, though, yeah?" And like the horse knows what I'm saying, she nuzzles my neck, wet lips brushing my skin and making me laugh.

"This weekend," Nick says, his hand moving to my waist, his other to the horse, patting her neck. "We'll get your girl back here this weekend, Min." The horse seems to understand him, too, and though I never understood the whole horse whispering thing, I'm wondering if Minnie and Nick have that ability.

From what I have heard, I know she and Ruby have that bond for sure.

"This weekend, huh?" I ask, turning to look at him with a smile.

"If you think you're not coming to this ranch again this weekend, you're out of your mind." My hand drops from the horse, and I lean on the wood of her stall, crossing my arms on my chest.

"Is that right?"

"Yeah. Already told Ruby we'll do another round of lessons this weekend." I shake my head at him.

"Why do I feel like you and my daughters are plotting against me?" I ask, but there's no malice or irritation there. Just a silly question. He moves closer to me, whipping his hat back and cornering me into one place.

"Oh, because we so totally are," he says with a smile. "I know you're mine. The girls know you're mine. You're the only one left to convince," he says, and my heart skips a beat.

"Nick," I whisper, the panic rising. He bends down and presses his lips to mine gently, a slow, easy caress that feels like Sunday mornings and warm nights near a fire. Kissing Nick never feels like an obligation, like a requirement for a relationship to work or the beginning of something sexual, like all of my kisses with Todd always felt.

Instead, they just feel like . . . home.

Comfort.

Warmth.

He steps again, moving back toward Minnie and keeping his eyes on the horse and not on me, like he somehow knows, like this horse, I'm easily spooked.

"Don't worry. We're taking our time, letting you get used to it. To me. To us. I've got all the time in the world, sugar."

I don't respond.

I can't.

I'm worried if I do, I'll say something stupid—either something that I'm not ready to say or something to try and scare *him* off, so instead, I move to the horse and pet her nose.

"Ruby can't stop talking about her. About brushing her. About how you guys came out here and fed her before breakfast and bedtime. She likes it, taking care of her." I pause, staring at the large, dark eye of the horse my daughter already loves before speaking. "It's only been a weekend, but it's helping, I think. Having something else to take care of, something she can talk to. They say horses are therapeutic and I kind of thought it was bullshit, but Ruby . . . she's coming back to me. My Ruby is coming back." I sigh, admitting what I've been trying to ignore. "I need to find a camp for her, somewhere she can learn to ride, maybe a summer camp."

Nick's quiet for long minutes after I admit that, but I'm so lost in my head, trying to budget and justify using that child support and figuring out how to shuttle her from Hudson City to somewhere with horses all summer, that I don't even notice.

Until he finally speaks.

"I wanna give her to Ruby," he says, his voice low.

A long moment passes before I realize what he said, before I understand what he's telling me.

"You can't do that," I say, my brow scrunched and my face confused, I'm sure. Because . . .

"I mean, I can. My horse, I'm free to give her to whoever I want."

I roll my eyes.

"Nick—"

"She was born the day you came into my life."

"What?" He reaches out, rubbing down Minnie's nose.

"Mickey went into labor, and Connor called me to tell me he was going on a date with some hot mom with kids. I was worried about him, didn't want him to do something stupid, play some woman. I remember thinking he was crazy while I was tugging my boots on, ready to go help Mickey. A few hours later, she was here and you were in my life whether we knew it or not."

I don't know how to respond.

"Kind of feels like she was always meant to be Rube's." It's sweet. It is. But still . . .

"Nicolas, you can't give a 9-year-old girl a *horse*."

"I can give my girl a horse if I want her to have it, Shae."

The world stops spinning.

*I can give my girl a horse.*

My girl.

He's calling Ruby *his girl*.

"Nick . . ." My words trail off because I don't know what to say or how to respond.

The panic starts in my feet and slowly moves into my veins, a dark mix of anxiety and nerves and *what-ifs* flowing into my bloodstream. Nick shakes his head, closing the gap between us and holding my hands between his, both like he's trying to warm them and combat the cold panic from taking over.

If anxiety is a dark venom, Nick's touch is a golden antidote, fighting it back, assuring me I'll be okay. That we'll be okay.

With his touch, I think I could overcome anything, and that might be the scariest truth of all.

"This is moving fast. Too fast for you to accept it, too fast for you not to get scared, and that's okay. Like I said, I've spent the last nine months learning about you, hearing about you, and getting to know you and your girls through Connor. So I've got the advantage here."

"This is—" I start, but he continues.

"And I am not a man who meets a woman and her girls and inserts myself into their lives. I'm not. I've been single since Connor was born, Shae, because I was waiting for you and those girls to be free to be mine."

"Nick—" Breath won't enter my lungs with his words, the world spinning like I'm lightheaded.

"That scares you, and that's fine. I told you, sugar. I'm a patient fucking man. If I have to spend the next ten years driving an hour every night just to see you guys, just to have dinner and tuck in the girls, to slowly ingratiate myself in your life, to earn that trust, I'm in. Because when it comes to you three, I'm *all in, Shae*. It makes no sense, but I am."

Finally, he stops, one hand leaving mine to brush against my cheek, his hand warm against my cool skin.

I think he'll wait for me to answer, to give a response to his declaration, but he doesn't. "Now let's go," he says. "We gotta go pick our girls up."

And when he tugs on my hand and starts to lead me toward his truck, I don't even bother to correct him, to tell him they aren't *our* girls, they're mine, and that this is too much too soon.

Because with every moment I'm around him, that's starting to feel more and more like the truth.

# THIRTY-ONE

## 12 SLEEPS UNTIL CHRISTMAS

### NICK

I drive Shae back to Hudson City and to the girls' school where we walk straight to the door where Harper gets let out right as the bell rings, then we walk to Ruby's.

"Who are those girls talking to your sister?" I ask Harper. Shae is a bit ahead as she walks to the teacher, and I can see from here Ruby is surrounded by a group of girls who are talking to her in a way that's making her body go tense, her eyes pointed directly at her shoes.

"Catherine and her friends," Harper says with disdain no 7-year-old should be comfortable with. But then again, this is sassy Harper we're talking about, so I'm not *that* surprised.

"Is that the girl that gives Ruby a hard time?" I ask, my voice lower as we get closer, remembering Shae mentioning Ruby was having issues with girls at school a while ago.

"Yup." As Shae approaches, she waves at Ruby, who instantly stands straighter, moving toward her mom like she's her saving grace. Shae turns and points to Harper and me before she smiles, and they both start walking toward us, but my eyes stay on the mean girls, all three of who are laughing and whispering to each other, now staring at Ruby's back.

"Hey, Nick," Ruby says with a small wave.

"Hey, girl. How was your day?" I wrap an arm around her, pulling her close, hoping it can offer her some kind of barrier and solace. She shrugs in response.

"I'll be right back," Shae says, tipping her head to Ruby's teacher. "I need to ask her teacher about the class party tomorrow." I nod then step back with the girls, watching as some of the mean girls walk off with their parents before going back to watching Shae, who seems to be next in line to talk to the teacher.

"I haven't seen you around before," someone says, and I break my gaze on Shae's ass that looks spectacular in a pair of simple jeans. When I turn to my left, a woman is standing there, Ruby's bully next to her.

"I'm here for Ruby and Harper," I say bluntly before looking down at the girls, trying to make it clear I have no desire to talk to this woman.

She doesn't get the hint.

"Ugh, that's so amazing," she says before putting her hands to her chest like she just saw the cutest thing ever instead of a grown-ass man standing out in the cold with two young girls. "They really could use a good influence."

That has my head snapping up, my eyes concentrating on her. She's pretty, I'll give her that, but in an expensive way I don't necessarily like. Not in the natural, effortless way Shae has. And it's also hard to miss the giant rock on her finger, especially when she moves her hand to fucking *touch my shoulder*.

I rotate my arm, angling away from her as I do, but instead of taking the hint, she steps forward.

"What do you mean by that?" I ask.

"It's just . . . you know. They don't have a father in the home, and"—she lowers her voice like she's sharing a secret—"their mother's always so busy. She works all the time from what I hear." I shake my head in faux confusion, like I don't understand the dig she's handing to Shae. That speech she gave me weeks ago replays in my mind, her telling me that no matter what she does, someone will always assume she isn't doing enough, isn't good enough for her girls.

I understood to a degree, but to another, I didn't.

Over the past few weeks, I've started to understand better, and this is just another piece in the puzzle, this mother assuming Shae isn't enough for her girls.

"I'm Molly, by the way. Head of the PTO." She gives me a wide, very fake smile and sticks her hand out for me to shake, but I just stare at it, confused.

"You know, I hear she completely cut their father out of their lives. Decided to leave him one day without warning and then worked the system to get alimony and child support. With all that money, I'm not sure why she always has other people picking those poor girls up. It's a shame. They really do need their father, you know?"

There are a lot of things I want to say to this woman.

With context, I now know this is the PTO mom who always gives Shae shit, who judges her and adds more stress to her already heavy plate, but I also know there is no universe where she'd be happy with me arguing with this bitch where everyone could see and hear.

"They're doing more than fine in the care of their mother," I say. The woman looks confused, probably lost as to why I'm not eating up her praise of me. And her *fucking hand* is still on me.

"Well, I'm just saying. A man's . . . touch is always good."

First, she's talking shit about Shae, and now, she's . . . I think she's hitting on me?

This is wrong in *so many ways,* I don't even know how to proceed, but then I look down at Ruby, who is staring at her shoes, and her bully, who is smiling like she won some kind of staring contest.

I'm done. I'm done playing nice. Shae can be the nice one in the relationship.

"This the girl that's mean to you?" I ask Ruby, tipping my chin to the woman's daughter. The girl's eyes go wide, but Ruby doesn't reply, instead looking at her boots. I look to where Shae is, trying to gauge how much time I have, but she's still waiting, her brows pinched as she looks at her phone.

"What? I—" the mother starts, but I ask again.

"Ruby, is this the girl you said is bullying you?" Finally, she nods her confirmation.

"Catherine would never—"

"Yeah, she does!" Harper says, her feistiness coming out, her hands on her hips. "I've heard it! She always makes fun of us for not having our dad around and laughs at Ruby's clothes because they aren't fancy." My stomach sinks when I think about how fucking cruel kids can be.

"I think this is—" the mom starts.

"She does," Ruby says, her voice low. "She makes fun of me and a bunch of other girls and tried to get everyone else to not talk to us." Looking at Ruby, I see the same shock I'm feeling reflected on her face, like she can't believe she said it.

"Ruby—" I start, my voice low.

But it seems something has snapped in my girl and she's done too.

"You're mean to me, but my mom always says hurt people hurt people. You're just mean to me because you're sad *your* dad isn't around. We *could* have been friends because of it, but instead, you're just *mean*. Now, I have Nick who has *horses,* and one day, I'll have a sleepover there and you will *so* not be invited because you're *mean*." Her face is red, and her chest is heaving, and the girl and her mother are both standing there in shock. When I look up, I see Shae ending her conversation with the teacher and I decide it's time to wrap up this conversation.

This can be between just the girls and me. I just *know* Shae would feel the need to apologize and make things "right." I grab Harper's backpack she dropped on the ground, slinging it over a shoulder and turning toward the mother.

"You might want to teach your kid some manners," I say.

"Excuse me?" she asks. "I don't—"

"Your daughter has been giving my girl shit for her birth father not being in her life for reasons I don't need to explain, but you're old enough to understand it probably wasn't ideal circumstances. You should try teaching her some empathy, show her how to move through this world with kindness, instead of hitting on men who are very much *not interested*."

The woman stares at me with wide eyes, her cheeks beginning to flush with embarrassment. "I, uh," she starts.

"Don't you agree?" I ask.

She doesn't answer, and I lift an eyebrow, tipping my head in her direction, waiting for a response.

Ruby tugs at my jacket and murmurs my name, but I don't look at her. Instead, I just wrap my arm around her, pulling her close, feeling her small body relax a bit, the same way her mother does when I pull her in, when I claim her as mine to take care of and she lets me take on the load she carries on her shoulders all day, every day.

"Yeah, I guess," the woman says, looking at me then the girls. I smile then squeeze Harper and Ruby.

"You guys . . . Uh, you guys ready?" Shae asks, coming over to us. "Hey, Molly. Catherine."

"We're good. Just talking to Molly about the girls."

"You're . . . talking to the head of the PTO about . . . the girls?" Shae is getting more and more confused, but I'm understanding more and more. This is the PTO mom that Shae told me didn't like her. It seems she's given that venom to her own daughter to spread to Ruby.

"Sure am. I think we've got a pretty good understanding, all of us just trying to teach our kids how to be kind." The woman doesn't speak, but she doesn't have to. "Have a great day, Molly."

# THIRTY-TWO

## 5 MONTHS EARLIER

### NICK

"Wait, so you picked her kids up?" I ask, pausing as I muck out the stalls to better concentrate on what my son is telling me.

I have hands to do this, but sometimes, I just need to feel *useful*. Some days, I feel like I'm in an office crunching numbers or reaching out to people when all I ever wanted to do was the dirty work. I wanted to care for the animals and plant the trees and tend to everything. Owning this ranch was the best choice I ever made, but sometimes, it's hard not to question if I made a mistake.

"Yeah, it's no big deal," Connor says, and I shake my head.

"So you picked her kids up from school—does that mean you're on the list?"

He sounds confused by my question. "Well, yeah." I shake my head and close my eyes with a sigh.

"And you're still trying to tell me you two are just friends?" Now Connor sighs.

"Yes, Dad. It's not like that. She gets these headaches. Migraines. She'll be out for a day. She had one yesterday and it was still lingering today. I figured I'd pick up her girls and take them to the park and dinner so she doesn't have to deal with it."

"Connor, son, I love you and I trust you, but this isn't normal. A 20-something picking up a woman's kids from school because she doesn't feel well and they aren't his—"

"It's not like that. Trust me."

"I'm just saying—"

"And I'm just saying," he says, his voice firmer. "It's not like that. You raised me to help people when they need it. I was raised by a dozen people, you and Mr. Samuels and the ranch hands and anyone who worked the farm. I had everyone and their mom picking me up from school, and you weren't fucking any of them, right? Or were you and you're speaking from experience?"

I pause because he's right. I had a lot of help when I was raising him, and from what it seems, this woman doesn't have that.

"Alright. You're right. Just . . . be careful, okay? Don't get in too deep."

# THIRTY-THREE

## 11 SLEEPS UNTIL CHRISTMAS

### SHAE

When I wake the next morning, I know I'm totally fucked.

My eyeballs throb like someone is trying to scoop them out with a grapefruit spoon, the feeling sending lightning bolts of pain into my brain, and I instantly regret waking up.

"Mom, Ruby's hogging the cereal!"

And having kids. I might regret that as well.

That's an exaggeration, but not that far. Having children during a migraine day is my absolute worst nightmare.

They happen occasionally, not as often as they used to now that I understand my triggers, but still, they happen. I can usually pinpoint it to something specific—extra stress, an exceptionally dry day, not having caffeine at the right time, red wine—but honestly, I'm in too much pain at the moment to try and narrow it down.

Before I even roll out of bed to deal with the girls, I shoot Abbie a text.

> Migraine. Any chance you can pick the girls up today and they can sleep over?

She replies nearly instantly.

> Of course! Need me to come now and get them ready?

I don't know what I did to get Abbie in my life. I definitely don't know who I was kind to in a past life to get her *and* Damien to uplift me when my life was at rock bottom, but somehow, I have them.

> I've got it. Thank you so much. Text me when you pick them up so I know there wasn't an issue?

> Of course. Let me know if I can bring you anything.

I sigh in relief, the pain not settling any but the anxiety of not having to deal with making sure they're safe easing something in me, before I roll out of bed to get the girls ready for school.

I spend most of the morning on the couch, wrapped in a blanket, while Ruby takes the lead. Again, guilt hits me, knowing she shouldn't have to do this—there should be another parent or, at the very least, a fully capable one at all times to assist her. Regardless, she helps me out, packing up the lunches I made the night before, checking her sister's backpack, and even helping to brush Harper's hair when she has a knot she can't reach in it. And once I see them off to the bus, I shuffle back into my home. I don't even have it in me to bother making it to my bed before stumbling onto the couch, turning my body to face the back of it, and closing my eyes.

I need sleep.

But first, I need to tell Nick not to come, so I grab my phone, squinting at it and swiping over to my texts.

> Hey, I'm not feeling well today. The girls are spending the night at Abbie and Damien's. I already told them the elf is staying back so they doesn't bother me, so all is good on the elf front.

He replies almost instantly.

> What do you want?

I stare at my phone, confused and unsure if it's because I can feel my heartbeat in my eyeballs and I can't read anymore or if it's because he is the most confusing man on the planet.

> What?

> I'm coming with essentials. What do you want? Soup? Ice cream? Crackers?

> Oh, that's not necessary.

> Doing it anyway.

> I'm sick, Nick, and this is your busy season.

I don't bother to clarify the *type* of sick, instead implying he also could get what I have.

> I'll be fine.

> You're not coming. I'll see you tomorrow, Nick.

I send the text and then turn my phone on do not disturb, double-checking Abbie is set to pass through in case there's an issue picking up the girls, and then I promptly fall asleep on the couch.

❄

I wake to the sound of something falling, then a quiet, murmured *fuck.* Sitting up quickly, my heart beating out of my chest, I look around, trying to find the source.

My pulse calms a bit when I see Nick in the kitchen, waving his hand in the air.

"What is going *on?*" I ask, my voice croaky from sleep. Now that I'm not worried I'm about to be murdered, my head reminds me it's not ready to function and starts to throb once more before I collapse onto the couch. I'm happy to note it *is* a bit less, though.

Progress.

That means it should be gone by the morning thankfully. But also . . .

Nick is here.

*Why the hell is Nick here?*

And the girls are *not* here. My heart races for a moment when I look at the time before it calms as I remember Abbie was supposed to pick them up. Grabbing my phone, I check for updates and see a text sent an hour ago displaying a photo of the girls smiling in the backseat of Abbie's car, having been picked up from school.

I'm so incredibly grateful that whatever god up there decided that he'd given me enough heartbreak and hardship and decided to give me Abbie and Damien. I don't think I could have survived the last year without them.

And I know from experience Abbie is being incredibly too generous, probably spoiling them rotten as she tends to do.

"Sorry, I dropped the pan on my hand," Nick says, walking over to where I am.

"Why are you here?"

"You're sick," he says then puts the back of his hand on my forehead. It feels slightly cool, a relief against the fading ache. "But you aren't warm so that's good."

"What?"

"You said you were sick. But at least you don't have a fever. Or if you did, you slept it off. You're at a normal temperature."

"How do you know my normal temperature?" I ask, confused. Nothing makes sense right now.

"I mean, you're human. So 98.6 would be the norm and all."

"Harper runs cool," I say, closing my eyes because keeping them open seems like way too much effort. I should blow my nose, too, congested from the mild cold I tend to have all winter since I had kids, but I think I'll stay stuffed up indefinitely rather than blow my nose in front of Nick.

"Good to know." His hand brushes my hair back, and I can't help but lean into the touch. It feels so fucking good, gentle, and slightly scratchy from his calloused hands.

"I'm not *sick* sick," I say. "Just a migraine."

"Mmmm, what do you need for it?" he asks.

"Nothing, really. I can usually sleep it off. I'll avoid screens for a day or two so I don't bring it back, but other than that, it's just a wait-it-out kind of thing. "

"How are you feeling now?" His voice is low and soothing.

"Better mostly. The headache is still there in the background, but I'll be okay. You didn't have to come all this way. I told you I'm fine."

"You're all alone," he says matter-of-factly.

"And?" I let my eyes close again and lean back on the couch once more. His hand continues to push my hair, moving over my forehead and down the side of my face over and over like a metronome.

"And you need someone to take care of you."

"I don't need someone to take care of me," I say, stubbornness filling my words without me intending to.

"Everyone needs someone to take care of them sometimes, sugar. Even strong women who don't want it."

"And you're the one to give it to me?"

"I'm really, really trying to be, Shae. Just waiting for you to let me." My stomach churns. I'm unsure of how to answer. I don't have to, though. Instead, he leans forward and presses his lips to my forehead. "All good, baby. Close your eyes, I'm making you dinner."

# THIRTY-FOUR

## 11 SLEEPS UNTIL CHRISTMAS

### NICK

Only the tree lights are on and Shae's head is in my lap, my fingers raking through her hair as she going in and out of consciousness, sleeping off her migraine. I spoke with her friend Abbie, made sure she got the girls easily and exchanged numbers so she wouldn't bother Shae. She let me know this is typical for Shae's migraines. They usually last a day and if she can sleep through it, she's likely not to have to suffer for more than a day.

I spent the afternoon heating the soup I bought at the store by my place and forcing her to get at least a bit of it into her system, making sure she drank enough, and researching migraines in an attempt to learn everything and anything I can in case I need to know more.

And now she's laying in my lap, humming as I play with her hair, a small smile on her lips. Her color is much better, her face less pinched in pain than it was when I got here, which is a relief.

"Do you know how to do that thing where you throw a rope and catch things?" she murmurs and I fight a laugh.

"What?"

"Like lassoing. Like they do in the cowboy movies."

"Do you watch cowboy movies often?" I ask with a laugh, and she blushes.

"No, I'm just wondering." I smile, moving her hair away from her face to watch the blush creep across her cheeks. God she's so fucking pretty, and she doesn't even realize it.

"Yeah, I can use a lasso."

"Do you ever have to tie things up?" she asks, her eyes closing. My hand pauses with her words, if only for a moment.

"What?"

"Do you tie things up? Like horses or... I don't know. Whatever it is cowboys tie up."

*I can think of something I'd be really fuckin' interested in tying up,* I think.

"I know a few knots," I say instead.

"Hmm. I wonder if I'd like that," she says, her voice going low, fading out. Her eyes close completely now and she's probably half way to sleep.

But I can't resist.

"Like what, sugar?" There's a moment where I think she's gone, lost to dreamland before she speaks.

"Being tied up. It would be interesting, you know? Not having control?"

I shift because this is absolutely not the right time to get hard.

It actually might be one of the *worst* times.

"I just wonder if I'd like it." Her breathing evens out, her eyes fluttering behind lips and she shifts a bit before she's asleep.

"Yeah, I wonder too," I whisper into her quiet townhouse.

# THIRTY-FIVE

## 10 SLEEPS UNTIL CHRISTMAS

### SHAE

The sun is warm on my face as it streams into my bedroom. I must have forgotten to close the curtains before collapsing in bed. But also . . .

The sun doesn't hit my bed until eight. I know that much from experience.

Which means my alarm didn't go off.

Which means I slept in.

Which means . . .

My eyes snap open, and I look around my room, trying to find the time or an explanation or—

"Morning," the rough voice beside me says.

Nick.

Nick is in my bed.

"I'm late," I whisper.

"How's your head?" he asks as if I didn't just speak.

"I'm *late*," I say, trying to sit up, but his hand goes to my chest, gently keeping me down.

"You're not. You're not working today. I already called Abbie.

Girls are getting dropped off at school as we speak. Everything's good. You're recovering."

"What?" I ask, confused.

"You're not doing anything today but letting me continue to take care of you," he says. A long moment passes as I think over the past 24 hours, remembering everything.

The migraine that is blissfully gone today, Abbie taking the girls, Nick coming . . .

"You took care of me," I whisper.

"As much as you would let me."

"You stayed the night," I continue.

"I sure as fuck wasn't going to leave you." Something burns in my throat.

"Can you kiss me?" I ask. Somehow, that seems like the only right answer, the only thing that makes sense. He smiles, but he doesn't kiss me.

"How's your head, sugar?"

"Better than ever. Now kiss me before I start overthinking every-thing," I confess because that's where I am, on the edge of panicking that he's here, taking care of me.

"That I can do," he says in a whisper, lying next to me in bed like he's afraid if I sit up and move, I'll feel ill again, but being as close as possible works even better for me. His lips press to mine, and instantly my hands move to his neck, pulling him closer to deepen the kiss, needing more, needing *everything*.

"Nick," I whisper against his lips, and he groans, the kiss chang-ing, Nick shifting with the same intensity and neediness. My hands move to his back as he rolls, hovering over me, holding his weight with his arms on the mattress, and I creep my hands underneath to the soft, warm skin there.

His lips move against mine, igniting a fire that's always embers, my hips moving to try and get something—anything—from him.

Because I'm ready.

I'm ready for Nick, and I need him *now*.

My hands move, tugging his shirt up until it's stuck at his shoulders, and he finally breaks the kiss.

"Shae—"

"Shirt off, Finch."

"Shae, I don't—"

Instead of arguing, I move my hands from his shirt, and even though he's hovering over me, I work to take off my mine, leaving me completely topless beneath him. His eyes move to my full breasts, the pink nipples peaked already with want and lust only he can sate, and he groans.

"Now you," I whisper, moving my hands back to his shirt, trying to tug it over his head.

"Shae, I—"

"I'm ready, Nick. I'm ready and want nothing more in this moment than to feel your skin on mine." He groans, the sound deep and pained, but he reaches behind him, grabbing the back of his tee and tugging until it's in a pile on the floor, and then I have it.

His warm skin is on mine, something that is so natural, so real, so perfect, I moan at the feel.

"Fuck, sugar," he mumbles into the skin at my neck. "Heaven."

Still, it's not enough.

My hands move to his hips, attempting to tug down the loose pants he's wearing, not entirely sure where he got sleep pants from, but considering I can feel his thick, hard cock on my belly better through these than denim, I'm forever grateful.

"Slow," he whispers, sucking beneath my ear.

"We've been doing slow for weeks. I'm ready, Nick."

"Shae—"

But I'm beating the system, slipping my hand between the layers of fabric and his warm skin, sliding down until . . . finally, his cock is in my hand, pulsing with need and excitement, even if the man himself is hesitant. I move my hand, gripping and pulling, and a moan tears from his chest despite my strange angle.

"Jesus Christ, Shae. Are you ever going to do as you're told?"

"Are you *telling*?" I ask with a smile. "Because if you want to tell me how to act, I'm more than happy to consider it." He stares at me and groans with exhaustion, but a smile plays on his lips all the same.

"You're a pain in my ass, you know?" he says, but I stroke him again, and I don't miss the way his eyelids flutter shut a bit. "Alright, my rules." Then, my wrist is in his big hand and he's moving it until it's held above my head. He smiles, grabbing the other so they're both pinned above me with one of his hands. He uses his free hand to push my pajama pants and underwear down until I can help with the rest, kicking my feet until the fabric falls to the floor.

He lets go of me, stepping back and standing before me. I don't move, keeping my hands over my head, lying on the bed and watching him. His chest rises and falls with each breath, his pants slung low on lean hips, his arms crossed on his broad chest.

"Jesus, look at you, Shae. Even more fucking beautiful than I could have dreamed," he says, looking over my naked body as I fight the urge to hide, to use my hands to cover myself.

"Are you going to even the playing field?" I ask. He looks at me confused. "Only one of us is naked, Nick." He smiles wide and boyish, like he finds this *funny*. "Come on, pants off then come back to me," I whisper, and that makes him smile, but he does as I ask, his thick cock bobbing as he frees it from his pants, and *goddammit*, the man is perfect *everywhere*.

When he kicks his pants to the side, he climbs back on the bed between my legs, and I reach for his neck to kiss him, but he has a different idea, his lips moving to my neck instead of my mouth.

He descends, trailing kisses down to my breasts, stopping to suck a nipple into his mouth. My back arches, trying to get more, to give him better access. He chuckles against the sensitive flesh, sending sparks shooting through me, all ending in my throbbing clit. My hand moves, snaking down my body with a mind of its own to touch myself to try and relieve some of the aching pressure.

"Ah, ah," he says, grabbing my wrist gently and putting it to my side. "Patience, Shae. Patience. We've waited this long; let me have my fun."

Well.

When he puts it like that . . .

He leaves my nipples, continuing to kiss my belly and down, down, down. His beard scrapes sensitive skin as he moves farther down, skipping over where I need him most and moving to my knee. His lips trail up my inner thigh, his hands moving to hold me open wide for him.

Then he stops.

"Nick," I whine, his face just inches from my pussy as he intentionally blows a stream of cool air across the heated, needy flesh.

"Patience," he says, his voice so low, I almost don't hear it. One thick finger trails along my thigh then up my center, staring at my entrance, dipping in just a bit to gather wetness and sliding up, circling my clit. My hips buck with a mind of their own, and he looks up, grinning.

"You're evil," I mumble, my hips moving gently to get *anything*. "The devil."

"Would an evil man do this?" he asks then slides a finger inside of me, crooking it perfectly as he lets his tongue slide over my swollen clit. I moan as he slides the finger out and presses it back in, the tip of his tongue circling my clit.

"Oh, fuck!" Then his tongue leaves me, a smile on his lips as he stares up my body at me. "Nick!" He just laughs, that finger inside me continuing its slow push and pull, building the heat in my belly with each scrape against my G-spot.

"Yes! An evil man would absolutely do this!" He laughs, but as he does, he lowers his head, circling his lips on my clit and sucking hard as he simultaneously slides his finger inside, pressing harder. His chuckle vibrates through me better than any toy I've ever used, and my body starts to quiver with pleasure already.

"Please," I murmur, staring down as he continues, his dark head of hair moving on me as he sucks on my clit, as he groans like he's enjoying this more than I am, his hand moving faster as he finger fucks me, pushing me higher and higher. Closer to the biggest orgasm of my life.

Except, I don't want this. I don't want to come like this. My hand moves to his head, gripping and pulling, and he looks up at me, concern on his face.

"I want to come with you inside me," I whisper, the slight embarrassment I feel with asking for what I want hidden behind need and desire and pleasure. "I don't want to come like this, Nick." He groans, a deep sound before he moves back, a slight glint of my wet on his chin, his finger still deep in me. He uses his new angle to watch, moving his finger inside again, fucking me one, twice, three times like he can't help himself, like he's enjoying this as much as I am. But then he looks up at me.

"Protection?"

"I haven't been with anyone since my last test and I have an IUD," I whisper, my pussy clenching around his fingers at the thought of him sliding into me bare, nothing between us.

"Jesus. I'm all clear, too," he says, crawling up my body. "Please tell me that means I can fuck you without a condom. Please tell me I can come inside you."

The mouth on this man might very well do me in.

"Fuck me, Nick," I whisper in confirmation, and then he's on top of me, a hand between us as he guides his thick cock into me. My eyes drift shut, my head falling to the mattress as my back arches, as he stretches me, filling me to the point where it's almost too much, stopping when it's a perfect fit, my body singing with the rightness of having him inside of me.

"Oh god, Nick. It's . . . Oh, fuck." I moan, my head thrashing from side to side. He slides out then pushes back into me, going deeper this time but no harder, the fierceness and roughness that I've come to know as *Nick* missing from the movement.

It's all the sugar-sweet side, the side of him that loves to take care of me, that puts me above his own desires and wants.

"I never knew it could be like this," he whispers into my ear. "God, fuck, Shae. You're everything. Everything. You're everything to me." He's rambling, sweet nothings spoken in the heat of the moment, but each syllable is burning itself onto my soul all the same as he slides in and out of me.

We continue like this, soft and slow and sweet, his eyes on mine as he fucks me for the first time, the pleasure building lazily, like we have all the time in the world, before it becomes too much for me.

"My clit, Nick. I need more." I breathe into his neck, and his hand reaches between us to gently touch my clit, to drive me higher, always giving me exactly what I ask for. But . . .

"Nick, I need . . ."

"I know what you need, sugar. I've got you. I'm gonna take care of you," he says, his words panted through heavy breaths.

But I think . . . I think for the first time, he *doesn't*. He doesn't know what I need because he's treating me the way he always does, with gentle passion, kindness, and adoration.

And I want the other side of him. The rough side, the side that is calloused hands and filthy words. The side that tugged my hair the very first time he made me come, who *let* me be in control but didn't *give me* the control. I'm desperate for it, for him to treat me like he can't break me. "Please, god, fuck!" I moan, unable to make the words form, to tell him what I need as his cock slides into me slowly, smoothly.

Gently.

I fucking hate it.

"I need . . ." There's a slight hesitation in his thrusts, his brows coming together just a bit as he starts to understand I might need something different. Something more.

"Tell me what you need, Shae. You're in charge of this." I groan because for the first time in well over a year, I don't *want* to be in charge.

I want to be *controlled.*

My hand moves to the back of his head, grabbing onto his hair and forcing him to look at me. He must see the franticness in my eyes, the panic, the need.

And because I'm in this state, I confess.

"I don't want to be." I moan, his eyes meeting mine once more. "I don't *want* to be. Take over, Nick. That's what I want. Fuck me. Use me. I'm yours."

# THIRTY-SIX

The world stops spinning with Shae's words. They ricochet in my mind, her blunt nails digging into the skin of my scalp, the slight pain grounding me long enough so I can process what she said.

I assumed Shae's need for control would bleed everywhere, especially when she's at her most intimate and vulnerable. I've been playing this safe, going slow and easy, but here she is, demanding the opposite.

"Shae," I whisper, looking at her. "We don't—"

"I don't want you to treat me like I'm fragile, Nick. Take over control. I don't want it," she whispers then lifts her upper body to press a kiss to my neck, her pussy tightening on my cock as she does.

I snap.

Something in that single, simple move snaps everything in me, and I slide out of her quickly.

"Nick, what—"

"Roll over. On your knees, ass to me," I say, standing at the end of the bed.

"What? I—"

My cock bobs as I take in her body, on display for me and me alone. I groan, sliding my hands from her knees up, gripping her upper thighs tightly, and tugging her to the end of the bed before splaying her wide for me, putting her feet at the edge.

"Fine, this will do," I say mostly to myself, then I take a knee until I'm face-to-face with her pussy. "Jesus fuck, Shae. Look how wet you are for me." I look up at her, propped up on her elbows to watch me, and I smile. "You want me to take control?" I ask, sliding a finger through her wet.

She's dripping.

So fucking wet, and the knowledge of it takes me closer to the edge I'm already dancing on, the edge I've been dancing on for weeks, sated only by lackluster sessions of jacking myself off in the shower, thinking of the sweet moans she makes when she comes.

If we're going to play this, if we're throwing the sweet and slow handbook out, then I need to get her to the edge. There's no way I can fuck Shae like I won her after all this time, after all this slow, beautiful torture, and last long enough for her to enjoy herself.

"I said, *do you want me to take control, Shae?*" I hold my hands to her thighs, pushing wide enough where there might be a pinch of pain, trying to figure out her limits on this spectrum.

I watch as her hands move to her knees, tugging her legs even farther, exposing herself to me.

"Yes, please," she says in the sweetest fucking voice I've ever heard, and it rips a groan from my chest. I can't help but run my tongue over her, flattening it at her entrance and circling her clit before backing away.

Standing, I tower over her as she squirms, hips moving to try and get something—anything to take her over the edge.

"Nick!"

"Do not move until I tell you, Shae," I say then take two fingers and slide them into her soaking cunt once more, feeling her clamp down. I moan alongside her at the thought of that being my cock in a moment. Her face tells me she's already close to that edge. "Be good and stay still while I . . . What did you ask me to do? Use you?" I smile as she groans, pain and pleasure mixing into her next word.

"Please," she whispers. My hand leaves her, going to grip my cock, using her wetness to lube myself as I stroke. Her eyes watch every movement with hunger as I step closer between her still spread legs and rub the head of my cock between them. "Nick!"

I need clarity before I continue, though, so with the head of my cock notched in her, I lead forward, putting a hand around her neck and pressing a kiss to her lips before speaking. "Rough? Is that what you want, Shae?" She stares for a moment, mouth slightly open, then nods. "I'll do that, but the second you want different, you tell me and we go back to sweet. I'm happy either way."

"Please," she whispers.

"You don't want it, but even when you think you don't, you have all the power, Shae. You need to know that." I press my lips to hers one last time before standing straight, putting my hands on her inner thighs to keep them wide, and sliding in all the way. We both moan as I bottom out. My eyes lock to hers.

"It's gonna go fast. Fingers to your clit, work it until you come," I say, and then I slide out and slam back in hard.

"Fuck!" she shouts. Her pussy tightens on me as she puts her fingers to her clit, working furiously as I slide out and slam in again, fucking her hard and fast. This is not the sweet, emotional connection I thought our first time together would be. I thought there was a chance that this lay beneath the surface, but I was sure it would take time and trust to get there if it ever happened.

But now that I have her? Have this? If I wasn't already sure she was mine, I'm positive I'm never letting her go now.

She was fucking made for me.

"How's it feel, sugar? Your man fucking you hard, taking over." She moans, her hips tilting to get me deeper as I push in again, and her moan turns to a scream with the new angle as she clamps around me, taking me higher.

"I'm so close," she whines, her head thrashing side to side as her hand works at her clit, my eyes unable to stop watching.

Without thinking, I reach for her wrist, pulling it to the side, and spit where her hand just was, watching her eyes go impossibly darker as I do.

"Rub that in, sugar, and then you come on my cock like a good girl, yeah?" I growl through gritted teeth as I continue to slam into her, my balls tightening as I fight coming first.

But I don't have to worry about leaving her hanging.

One, two, three circles of her clit and she comes, screaming my name, her eyes open and locked to me. One more thrust later, I slam in deep, pulsing inside of her as I fill her with my cum, forever cementing her as *mine*.

"Now what?" she asks, an arm over her eyes, chest heaving, and I can't help but laugh. I look at the time and then back to her, naked curves fully on display.

"First," I say, crawling up her body. "I'm gonna kiss you good morning, properly." I do that, and she smiles through it, a feeling so fucking beautiful and bright, I can't help but smile too. "Then I'll clean you up, and I'm gonna feed you since you barely ate anything yesterday." She starts to protest, but I kiss her again. "Then I'm gonna fuck you one, maybe two more times before we have to go get the girls."

*That,* I note, she doesn't protest.

"Then I'm driving you three back to the ranch for the weekend, where I'll quietly fuck you in my bed. I think I made a promise to you about screaming into a pillow?"

That smile grows again.

"I think I remember that, too," she says.

"So it's a deal?" I ask.

"It's a deal."

"Go, team," I whisper, and then I get on with our day.

# THIRTY-SEVEN

## 7 SLEEPS UNTIL CHRISTMAS

### NICK

Monday, I walk up the stairs, once again spotting the notice Shae hasn't mentioned to me, telling residents the move-out date is January 31$^{st}$, and I can't help but wonder what her plan is.

She mentioned in passing how she needed to find a new place a week or two ago but hasn't spoken about it since. The way things are going, if it were up to me, I'd force her and the girls to move in with me, but my Shae is much too independent and much too cautious to agree to that.

But there's one other plan tumbling in my mind, something Shae might be just a bit less hesitant to take on.

At the end of the day, I want them as close as I can get them to me.

This weekend was even better than the one before, yet another reminder of how well these three fit into my life and how well I fit into theirs. We went to the ranch Friday night after the girls got out of school and Shae brought an arsenal of supplies and bakeware, including two pizza pans and a box of brownie mix. *Pizza Friday* was a tradition Shae told me she had skipped for the past few months, too tired and stretched thin to make it happen.

So I watched as Shae and the girls made a disaster of my kitchen, giggling as they listened to music (Harper insisted on Christmas music, and her mother begrudgingly agreed, rolling her eyes at me when I smiled) and after we got the girls set up on the couch with a movie, Shae and I worked like a well-oiled machine, baking the brownies, cleaning the dinner mess, and serving up the girls.

After we put the girls to bed, we didn't even bother playing the game of *whose bed is Shae staying in*, with her walking straight to my room and dumping her overnight bag on the floor with a small, shy smile before I finally tackled her and had my way with her in my bed.

Saturday, the girls witnessed an engagement at the farm, something that happens regularly but made the girls ridiculously giddy to see. Ruby stared with hearts in her eyes, and when the groom-to-be kneeled with a bouquet of flowers and a black box, Ruby whispered in an awestruck tone, "I want flowers like that."

It reminded me of the first time I met Ruby, her telling me she loved horses and flowers, and when I was out on the ranch this morning, I couldn't stop myself from looking for a good spot for her to start a cut flower garden this spring. I spent the morning thinking of what it would take to make her a stand for the side of the road or if I could convince Shae to let me bring her to a farmer's market, make her own little booth.

But it also made me realize I've slacked on my gentlemanly duties, which is why today, I'm walking up to Shae's place, juggling three bouquets of flowers.

In my defense, two of them are mini bouquets for the girls.

Shae's is full-size, though.

That's a lie.

Hers is so fucking huge, nearly the size of my head, I almost left it at the florist when I picked up the order, knowing she'll be annoyed with how much I spent on her.

I fully anticipate her throwing a fit at me, telling me to stop, that it's too much, as if the act isn't already done, as if I wouldn't buy an entire flower shop just to see her smile.

But as seems to be the way, Shae surprises me when she opens the door for me, her mouth dropping open and her eyes going wide as she stares at the giant red and green and white bouquet.

"Oh my god," she whispers.

"Is that Nick!?" the voice I know to be Harper's asks, little feet pounding on the wood as they run to the door. "Oh my GOD!" she yells. "RUBY, COME HERE!"

Ruby's feet pad slower, if not louder, with her sassy stomps, like she's being inconvenienced by her sister calling her to see something so mundane as me coming over. But she stops when I come into view, her eyes as big as saucers.

"Oh my god!"

Yeah, I think I did okay.

I smile at all three of my girls, nodding at them. "Okay if I come in?" None of them move. "Shae, sugar?" The low words knock her out of some kind of reverie, and she shakes her head before nodding and stepping back.

"Shit, yes, sorry. I, uh . . . Come in."

"Are those for me!?" Harper asks, her eyes somehow going even wider as she takes in the light-pink mini bouquet in one of my hands, right next to a purple one.

"Sure is," I say then bend low and hand it to her. "And one for you, Rubes." Ruby just stares at my hand reaching out to her. "Ruby?" She blinks a few times, still staring at the small bouquet of flowers, before she reaches out and takes it from my hands, her eyes wide and starting to water.

Fuck.

I was wrong—I didn't do okay. I fucked this up big time somehow.

I wanted to bring Shae flowers but always want the girls involved too, so I thought it would be a good idea, especially since Ruby looked so enamored by the flowers last weekend, but . . . now I'm second-guessing this.

"Ruby, I'm sorry. I—"

"I've never gotten flowers before," she says in a whisper.

My heart sinks, and her eyes break from the flowers to look up at me.

Handing off the red one to Shae without looking at her, I bend to my knees until I'm face-to-face with Ruby. "They're just flowers, Ruby. No big deal. If you don't like them, I can—" I start, but her eyes go impossibly wider with panic.

"No!" she shouts then grabs the flowers. "I love them. Thank you."

I never thought it was possible for your heart to break and heal at the same time but here we are. It's happening as I watch this girl, who not so long ago stood in a stable and refused to talk to me at all unless it was about a horse, hold a small bouquet of flowers close to her chest like they're a prized possession.

"I've always wanted flowers," she says, her voice low, and I move a bit in my crouch, stepping closer and tucking a piece of hair behind her ear like I do for her mother.

"Yeah?" She nods.

"Last year, there was a dance. All the girls got flowers, but I . . ." She looks up at her mom but shrugs. "I didn't go. It was for girls and their dads."

My heart breaks for this girl who deserves the entire world. That's probably what has my hands reaching out, grabbing the sides of her head, and pulling her close so I can press a kiss to her forehead. It might be too much, too soon, but I need this, need to give her this.

And I need all three of them to understand my intentions.

"Next year, I take you, okay?" I ask.

Ruby smiles a thin, watery smile before she nods.

"Me too!" Harper shouts. I look to her, her smile wide, one of her lower teeth missing after it fell out on the ranch this weekend.

"Of course." I'm nervous to look at Shae, to see some kind of frustration on her face for making assumptions that I'll still be around, but instead, she's holding her bouquet, leaning against the wall, eyes watering like Ruby's, a near identical look on her face.

*Thank you,* she mouths, and I know then.

These girls are mine.

# THIRTY-EIGHT
## 6 SLEEPS UNTIL CHRISTMAS

### NICK

"Nick, Nick!" Harper says when I walk into the apartment a full two hours before the girls go to sleep, her hair flying behind her as she runs my way in the small apartment. "You're here!" As the season winds down, I can sneak out earlier, especially on weekdays. The crew can handle almost everything, and I really like having this extra time with Shae and her girls.

"Hey, Harp," I say, bending to hug her, her thin arms wrapping around my neck, and fuck, I like this. I like getting out of work and having Harper rush me with a hug. I like Ruby watching me come in from the kitchen, a shy smile on her lips. But most of all, I like Shae leaning on the hall wall, arms crossed on her chest, a smile on her face as she watches our interactions.

"We got ornaments!" Harper shouts then grabs my hand, dragging me toward the tree. "Come see, come see!" I follow her, my long strides making it so she's not dragging me along.

"Ruby got to put on the angel this year, but Mommy said I can *next* year. She's *brand new* and we got to pick her out!" Harper says once we're in front of the tree, pointing to the top.

The angel sitting there looks a bit like their mother, fair skin and light hair, and ornaments are placed all over haphazardly. There's an explosion of tinsel with a heavy concentration on the bottom half, right at Harper's height.

"I did the tinsel, though," she says proudly, and I smile. It's impossible not to when Harper is excited like this, I'm beginning to understand.

"And the ornaments?"

There's a handful of silver and red balls, generic ones you buy in big packs, and just a few that look to be sentimental.

"Well, we had to buy a bunch," Ruby says, her words measured, like she's trying not to tell the whole truth. "So we got a bunch of normal ones to fill it in, and we got to pick out our own."

"This one's mine!" Harper shouts, tugging my hand to show me an ornament of an orange kitten wrapped in lights. "Isn't it soooo cute?!" I smile.

"The cutest, Harp."

"This is the kitty I want for Christmas," she says, and without even looking to her mother, I just know she's staring at the ceiling, her lips moving in silent prayer to some unseen god.

"Well, you gotta remember, Santa and the elf can't bring real animals, you know." Her eyes go wide.

"What?"

"Well, Santa and the elves make the gifts, right?" She nods. "And you can't make a cat like you can a puzzle or a doll." She stares at me, and for a split second, I wonder if this is going to be Thanksgiving all over, if I'm going to face the wrath of her mother for crossing some line I didn't know existed. I look to Shae quickly with wide eyes and she's . . . smiling.

It's a *you can handle this one, big guy* kind of smile.

She's relishing in my panic.

But it's unnecessary when Harper nods like I make all the sense in the world.

"Got it. So I gotta ask you and mom for it?" It takes everything in me not to smile since that would be a confirmation to Harper. But the idea of her saying *you and mom* as if we're already a team in her eyes fills me with warmth.

"We'll see, Harp. We'll see."

It's not a yes, but it's not a no, and that's all she needs to beam.

"I picked out this one," Ruby says, her voice lower and nervous. "It looks like Minnie." She gently touches the brown horse ornament, a wreath around its neck.

"It does. Just like her," I say.

Ruby smiles and I return it.

"And Mom?" I ask, looking around the tree, trying to find Shae's pick.

"This one!" Harper says, nearly shouting and pointing to a yellow bird. She explains, but she doesn't have to. I know—I've been looking at them my entire life. "It's a finch!"

My eyes move to Shae, whose cheeks are flushed red, rolling her lips into her mouth.

"Girls, go make sure your room is cleaned up before dinner, okay?" she says, purposely not looking my way as I turn fully toward the kitchen.

"But Mom, Nick just—" Ruby starts, and even though it warms me, I know my job is to help, not make things worse.

"And I'm not going anywhere. Listen to your mom, Ruby," I say, giving her a look with wide eyes and a small smile. She looks like she's about to argue further before looking at me and nodding like we have some kind of silent agreement I can't quite remember. Shae tries to step away once the girls are down the hall, to turn back to the stove and ignore me, but before she can, I grab her wrist, pulling her into me with a smile.

"A finch, huh?" I ask. She fights a smile of her own and rolls her eyes.

"It was just a pretty bird. Harper liked it." I shake my head at her lie, my nose brushing hers as she tips her head back and I tip mine down.

"Sure it was. You don't have to admit you got a finch bird for me, sugar."

"I didn't," she says, standing her ground. I tighten the arm on her waist, pulling her farther into me, until our lips are brushing.

"Lie to yourself all you want, Shae. I'll play along. But you and I both know you got that bird because of me."

And she doesn't even bother to argue before I kiss her.

"Do you guys have other ornaments?" We just ended a marathon make-out session after the girls went to bed and she's lying on the couch, her head in my lap, some fluffy, straight-to-cable holiday movie on the screen.

"We did," she says in a murmur. "The rest are at Todd's house."

I should have known since she told me she took only the essentials, leaving even those stockings she had to remake for the girls.

"You know, I can—" I start because I *would*. I should.

If she even seems slightly on board, I will. I'll go down to that fuckwad's house and get whatever shit she wants, whatever memories he's keeping from her, and she won't even have to look at him.

"No. It's fine, really. I don't . . . It sounds weird, but I don't want them. I gathered a few things when I started to understand I'd be leaving, so the really important ones . . . they're there." Her head tips to the tree where after dinner, the girls showed me the ornaments they each got when they were born. "But this is our fresh start. Everything else is . . . tainted."

A fresh start.

I like that for her, for her girls. And I really like being able to be around to witness her rebuilding.

"I'm honored to be a part of your fresh start, Shae," I whisper. Silence fills the room before I tiptoe into the next conversation I need to have with her. "Speaking of fresh starts, any news on a new place?"

She groans, and not in the fun, sexy way.

"That good, huh?" She sits up, leaning back on the couch next to me, and stares at the ceiling.

"Everything in the area either has a far-out waiting list, is in a neighborhood I'm not fond of, or costs way, way too much. I'm kind of hitting a wall. But I lined a few up to look at tomorrow, so we'll see."

"Lined up a few what?"

"Apartment viewings."

"Apartments." The word tastes sour in my mouth.

"I need to be out of here by January 31$^{st}$. There's nothing in Hudson City within my price range with two bedrooms, so I need to look around a bit. I'm taking off tomorrow to do it."

"Your boss is cool with that?"

She laughs. "I think Abbie and Damien would be mad if I *didn't* take the day off. They're the most supportive people on this planet. They're actually super pissed I won't take any kind of help to get a nicer place."

Well, at least I know I'm not the only one she refuses help from; it's a strange comfort. My mind works on what she's telling me then flips quickly through my calendar to figure out what my plans are tomorrow before I say, "I'll come with you." Her head moves back in confusion as she stares at me.

"Uh, no, that's not necessary." There's a little laugh in her voice, like she finds the idea ridiculous.

"Yes, I will."

"No, Nick, you won't."

"Why not?"

She stares at me, trying to think up some kind of excuse, I'm sure, for why I shouldn't go. She lands on, "Because you already do enough for us. You don't have to traipse around, looking for places with me, too." I shake my head and turn my body to face hers before sliding a hand up her neck and into her hair.

"You don't get it yet, but you will." Her voice is low and throaty when she answers.

"Get what?"

"I'd traipse around the entire world with you if you let me." She rolls her eyes and shakes her head like I'm exaggerating, like I'm telling her what I think she wants to hear, but if I were telling her what I thought she wanted to hear, I'd be playing it much, *much cooler*. I'd be telling her we're casual, that I don't care. I sure as fuck wouldn't be worried about her running around to apartment viewings on her own.

"But what I won't do is let you wander around the city into neighborhoods you don't know and apartment complexes you're not familiar with when I have off anyway and can go with you."

"Nick—"

"Call it a date."

"That's a pretty shitty date," she says under her breath, and it makes me smile.

"After, I'll bring you back here and fuck you until you can't see straight before we pick up your girls, okay? How's that for a date?" She glares at me but can't hide the fire in her eyes at my words. I smile.

"I'll be here at nine tomorrow." She shakes her head and smiles but doesn't argue.

# THIRTY-NINE

## 5 SLEEPS UNTIL CHRISTMAS

### NICK

We go from apartment to apartment, Shae in my truck as I drive her around Hudson City and a few surrounding towns, and each option gets worse and worse. At the first apartment, the front door doesn't latch and there's no one standing at the security desk, meaning just about anyone can come in no matter what. At the second one, the would-be-neighbor stands in the hall the entire time we're checking the place out, staring and documenting every curve on Shae's body, despite the fucking death glares I give the old man. In the third option, I count at least three fire hazards and four items that would fail a safety inspection.

There is no way she's living in *any* of these.

The plan in my mind formulates, building and churning as I try and figure out how to convince her to see things my way, how to let Shae keep her power and her distance without scaring her off.

We're in my truck on my way to the girls' pretentious private school when I finally break.

"Don't like this for you." Her face turns to look at me, but I keep staring out the window.

"What?"

"I don't like this. You finding shitty places to stay, having to choose between one with no security and one with creepy fucking neighbors."

"That's the reality of life, Nick. Not all of us have a huge ranch and land and a business."

I win against the desire to tell her she *could* have that.

*Too soon, Finch. You're walking on thin ice with her. The wrong move will scare her off,* I tell myself.

Instead, I ask, "Are you committed to living in Hudson City?"

She tips her head from left to right as I pull onto the road her townhouse is on. It's a nicer area of the city, and I'm pretty sure she got incredibly lucky with this place, as it should have been *well* out of her budget. I wonder if Damien Martinez had anything to do with it, and if he did, does she know about it?

Maybe I should talk to the mysterious man and see if we can work together behind the scenes to get her into a safer place without sacrificing her independence.

"Yes and no. I don't actually love Hudson City, but the girls' school is here."

"And you want them to stay here?" She laughs and shakes her head.

"Honestly? No. The kids are all assholes and the girls don't really like it there, but it is much better than public schools in this area and I don't foot the bill. A year ago, I figured adding another change to their lives wouldn't be best, so . . . here we are."

This time, I can't fight the urge.

"Schools in Cherrystone are really good," I say.

"Are you suggesting I look for places in Cherrystone?" she asks, and when I finally move from looking at the road to her, she's picking at her nails, avoiding looking at me.

"I would definitely not be mad if you were closer. If I could come to help out when you have headaches or pick up the girls on nights you have to work late. If I could drive less than an hour to have dinner with my girls."

"Your girls?" she asks, skipping over the rest. I reach over, grabbing one of her hands to stop her from picking and squeezing.

"You know you three are my girls, Shae."

"Nick, I—" I moved too quick, got too close to her fears, and she's about to put that fuckin' wall up.

"I know it's too much and you're not ready for that, sugar. I get it. But I *am*. I'll wait until you are, but I'm just trying to say if you lived in Cherrystone, a small town with good schools and a lot slower living than Hudson City, I wouldn't be mad about it."

"I don't . . . ," she starts, then she stops, looking out her window as I enter the parking area of her place. "I don't know what to say when you say shit like that, Nick."

*Progress*, I think. This is progress, right? Her admitting this has to be progress. I put my truck into park outside her place and step out, walking to her side where I open the door and tug her out, then press her to the side of my Ford.

"That's okay," I say. "You don't have to say anything at all. Just let me help you. Let me take care of you. That's all I want."

"I don't want you to—" she starts.

"It's okay to let people take care of you, Shae. To help. It doesn't mean you're losing your power, doesn't mean you're not strong. And it sure as fuck doesn't make me like you any less."

"Are you saying you like me?" she asks, her voice breathy, and I can't help but laugh and shake my head. My hat tips a bit as I bend to press my lips to her forehead.

"Don't play stupid, Shae." My head moves until my lips are at her neck, kissing her there. "Now, let me show you just how good I can take care of you," I whisper against her skin.

"Nick," she whispers, her breath coming out in a cold puff of air, but her hand goes to my neck to keep me there.

"We can either go out to lunch and then pick up the girls or we can skip lunch, I can take you inside, fuck you good, and we can have a big dinner."

There is a minor hesitation, but not long enough for her to actually have thought out her options, already having made her mind up before she speaks. "My keys are in my bag," she whispers.

I laugh, lean into the passenger seat to grab her bag and the keys that are right on top before lifting her, smiling as she squeals and wraps her legs around my waist, and take her into her apartment to show her just how well I can take care of my girl.

# FORTY

## 5 SLEEPS UNTIL CHRISTMAS

"So, what are your Christmas plans?" Nick asks, his fingers sliding through my hair as we watch some movie on TV that I'm barely paying attention to.

It's strange to think that not long ago, my nights were spent playing catch-up, burning the wick at both ends to keep this house afloat before crashing in bed. Now, Nick helps take on some of the workload every night he's here, meaning I have time and energy to just . . . be.

"Nothing much," I say, my eyes now locked to the TV as if I *do* find it interesting.

My mind has been tiptoeing around the issue of December 25<sup>th</sup> for a while now for multiple reasons, and as it creeps closer without either of us bringing it up, my worries bubble up.

What happens after?

Will we see Nick on Christmas?

Will he still come over at night to hang out with me, with us?

"What about you?" I ask instead, keeping it casual.

*Don't be needy, Shae. Don't be clingy. Don't assume—*

"Well, I was hoping I could convince you three to spend it at the ranch."

Silence.

Silence fills my little living room. The only thing heard is the woman on the Christmas movie we're watching feverishly telling her assistant she's too busy to go work at the family's bakery for the holidays. (We all know how *that* story ends.)

"Shae?" Nick asks, tipping my chin to look up at him.

"Hmm?"

"I said I was hoping you and the girls would spend Christmas at my place." I'm not completely sure how to respond, so I go with my normal instinct of deflecting.

"Nick, you don't have to do that. We don't—"

"Never did I think I *have* to do anything, Shae," he says, then he's moving me so I'm sitting up, so his hands are on either side of my face, forcing me to look at him even when I want to look away, to pick at my nails, to pluck the loose thread on my tee shirt.

"I didn't *have* to come here every night for a stupid elf. I didn't *have* to make a room at my place so your girls feel safe and welcome. I didn't *have* to start planning where Ruby can plant flowers at the ranch next spring or how I can convince you to let me give Harper one of the kittens that was born in the barn. I don't *have* to be falling madly for you, but here we are. I'm doing all of these things because I *want to*. I'm doing them because I want excuses to see you, to spend time with you. I'm doing it because I like you, Shae. I like you and I like Ruby and I like Harper. I need you to understand that and to let go of this anxiety that I'm not in this for the long haul. I'm here, Shae. I'm yours."

My heart races with his words, words that, if we're being honest, I'll probably have to hear again when the voices in my mind tell me there's no reason for this perfect man to be here with me, but for now, it's enough.

It's enough to tame the nerves, to quiet those voices, and to make my belly feel like a million butterflies have taken flight.

"So, I'm gonna ask you again, sugar. What are your plans for Christmas?" I fight the watering of my eyes, but I can't hide how my hands are shaking. Because this is real.

This is Nick and me and the girls starting something *real*.

Something good.

My Christmas miracle.

"And by that, what I mean is will you and the girls spend the holiday at my place?" My chin wobbles but I force myself to answer.

"I need to make the girls snowman pancakes for breakfast," I say, my voice cracking as I do. "It's a tradition." His smile could light up the entire room.

"Well, we can't break tradition, can we? We'll go shopping for what we need on . . ." He pauses, letting me fill in.

"Girls have a half day Friday. I can pack everything up and go right from there," I whisper through the still present lump in my throat.

He leans forward and presses his lips to mine, soft and sweet. "We'll go shopping when you get there, do pizza and movie night."

"Go team," I whisper. Then he kisses me again and again, each getting less sweet and more fiery until we're a tangle of limbs on my couch.

# FORTY-ONE

## 4 SLEEPS UNTIL CHRISTMAS

It's 7:30 and I'm getting the girls ready after dinner while Nick does the dishes when there's a knock on my front door. Confused, I stand from where I was sitting on the floor and reading a book.

"Let me go check that. I'll be right back," I say. Both girls are exhausted, already on the edge of sleep when I walk out, and I wonder if I can skip the bedtime story tonight and get to sitting on the couch with Nick even sooner. Nights cuddling after the girls go to bed have quickly become some of my favorite, whether we're actually watching a show or just letting it play low in the background while we make out like teens.

It's glorious.

The knock comes again, and I've never realized a knock can sound annoyed. This time, I'm walking past Nick, who is drying off his hands.

"Who's that?" he asks, moving toward the door as I do. I shrug, my phone with the video doorbell app on the couch, long forgotten.

"Probably a neighbor," I say, thinking about the time one of my neighbors *literally* asked for a cup of sugar or the dozen or so times I've had to go move my car because the parking area behind our townhouse is chaotic and as hard as I try, it's not uncommon to get backed in.

Nick moves quicker to get to the door before me.

"Nick, what—" But he's moving an arm out in front of me as he reaches for the doorknob with the other hand.

"Who the fuck are you?" a voice asks.

And my happy, safe snow globe world comes crashing down.

# FORTY-TWO

## 4 SLEEPS UNTIL CHRISTMAS

### NICK

A man is standing in the doorway of Shae's house, towering over her, and when I look to her quickly, she's shrinking right in front of me.

*Shrinking.*

My gorgeous, beautiful, strong Shae is *shrinking* and before I even ask, I know the answer of who this man is.

"What are you doing here?" she asks, her voice low and soft.

"You've been ignoring my calls. I figured I'd come talk to you face-to-face."

I think back to our first real date at the ranch, her getting a text and telling me he'd been reaching out recently. I didn't push, haven't asked since, hoping if there's an issue, she'd let me know.

But now, there is definitely an issue.

"That's because you're supposed to go through my attorney, Todd. I—" Venom is in his words when he cuts her off and it makes my hands curl into fists on instinct. Instinct to protect Shae.

"I'm not going through your fucking asshole attorney."

This is Todd, Shae's ex-husband.

The girls' dad.

The abuser.

And, from what I'm understanding, the man who has *continued* to contact Shae. We can deal with that later, talk about her not telling me really fucking important shit like her ex is harassing her. But right now, I need to protect Shae, protect her girls.

Protect what's mine.

# FORTY-THREE
## 4 SLEEPS UNTIL CHRISTMAS

"Is this him?" Todd asks, crossing his arms on his chest.

"What?" Nothing makes sense right now, not him standing across from me, not him looking so fucking angry, nothing.

"I said, *is this him?* The guys who's picking up *my daughters* with you from school?" Cold rushes into my veins with his words.

How does Todd know *anyone* picked up the girls with me? I haven't answered any call, text, or email from him since I accidentally picked up on Thanksgiving, much less given him information about who I'm spending my time with.

"What are you talking about, Todd?" I ask, my voice calm despite the panic and rage bubbling in my veins.

"You've got some man picking up *our daughters* with you. I'm asking if this is him. He's walking out of your place like he fucking owns it. Is this the man you're being a whore with?"

My mind races, trying to put pieces together.

My ex knows about Nick.

My ex thinks Nick has no place in my life.

My ex called me a whore.

My mind tries to process, to prioritize these facts.

*How does he know about Nick?*

"How do you know anything about me?"

"You think I pay for that fucking school out of the goodness of my heart, Sharon? Jesus fucking Christ, I didn't think you were *that* idiotic.?"

"You've been keeping tabs on me? What the fuck? Me and the girls? We're *none of your business*." I take a moment to think, to run through the people at the stupid prep school my girls are *absolutely* not attending for much longer, trying to figure out who possibly could be giving Todd information about us. Really, it could be anyone, since he picked out the school and he pays for it, but—

The car door opens and a heeled foot slides out, a lithe woman following, and it all makes a bit more sense.

Molly *fucking* McGee.

It all begins to click.

She's hated me since Ruby started going to school in *kindergarten*, despite my best efforts to try and play nice, to make friends when I had none. I think about what Nick told me about her hitting on him, about her saying it's a shame the girls don't have a man in their lives, about the fact her daughter bullies my kid and . . . it all makes sense.

"Todd is your fiancé?" I ask, and there's no venom in the words. If anything, it's pity.

I *pity* this woman. She's staring at me like she won some kind of competition I didn't realize we were in, but really, she's the one losing. I got free.

"I've known Todd since high school," she says with a smug look. "We were always meant to be together. It just took a little longer than anticipated." She looks at him with a smile and reaches for his hand as if to prove some kind of point, to rub salt in a nonexistent wound.

I don't miss how he swats it away or the deadly glare she gives me when he does.

"The high school girlfriend you told me about," I say, remembering years and years ago when we talked about our dating history and he told me about his girlfriend from when he was a teen. The one he broke up with before college.

Before he met me.

She had to have known who I was, knew from the beginning and held that anger and that hatred tightly. She hated me so much, she let it trickle to her own child, to mine.

"That's why you hate me so much," I say with new understanding and irritation. "You hate me, at your grown ass age, because your high school boyfriend *married me?*"

"He was always supposed to be mine, you know. We took a break while we were at school and when he came back home, we were going to be together. You stole him from me."

She sounds *utterly delusional.*

"Jesus Christ, you psycho. You can have him! Good luck!" Her smile lessens a bit, as if maybe she's confused as to why this isn't making me upset, why I'm not angry *at* her.

But truly, I can't be mad at a woman who is so wrapped up in the delusion of Todd that she's been pining after him since high school, that she hated me so much, it leaked to his children by turning into her daughter bullying my kids.

I'm sad for her.

Because I've been there. I convinced myself he was a good man, that we were meant to be, that his outbursts were because he was stressed or he worked too hard for our family. And eventually, I got out—I got away from him and I found peace and happiness and I found *Nick,* and she'll never have *that*: Nick Finch coming in, changing her world for the better. And that?

That's one of the saddest things I've heard in some time.

Before I can say anything more, though, Nick speaks to Todd.

"So you start fucking some woman at your daughters' school, give her a big rock, and use her to keep an eye on your ex-wife and the daughters you abandoned?" Nick asks, because while I'm not angry, it seems *he* is. Todd doesn't respond to the accusation, instead pushing the blame to me as he tends to do.

"I didn't abandon them. I was cut out of their lives. I—"

"Because of choices you made, because of changes you *didn't* make. I'd call that abandoning," he says.

"You have no idea—"

"I know enough. I know that I have been here every day since November, helping the girls, earning their trust, undoing the damage *you* did. I've been here while Shae was sick and when Ruby had nightmares and not once—not *once* have I seen you. I haven't even heard your name muttered."

"I don't know why you're even here. This is a personal matter."

"Yeah, and Shae and those girls are *my fucking people.*" He pauses, waiting for Todd to say something, but he doesn't. That alone is so very telling. "You know, that's the difference between a man like you and a man like me. Nothing—and I mean *nothing*—could keep me from Shae and those girls. Hell or high water, I'd follow them, treat them right, make sure they were always safe, always loved. That's what a real man does. You?" He shakes his head. "You think you're a man, but you're just a child, throwing a fit every time you don't get your way, regardless of who you hurt along the way." Nick wraps his arm around my waist, and Todd's eyes flare with anger.

It seems Nick finally found the tipping point—touching what Todd sees as "his toy."

I guess that's what I always was: his toy to play with, to show off, to treat however he saw fit. And now that someone else is playing with it, he wants it back.

"Get the fuck away from my wife. This is a family matter," he says, stepping forward.

"Your wife?" Molly says, anger sparking, her hand reaching out to grab his arm, but he swats it away once more.

That anger turns into something else. Frustration or hurt or indignation, I'm not completely sure.

It's then I wonder if maybe I'm wrong.

Maybe she will get away. Maybe this will be her wake-up call before she's in too deep.

My own wake-up call—a different one. One filled with love and understanding and kindness—comes when Nick speaks and with his words and his actions, all hesitance I've felt over the past few weeks about him being mine, being *ours*, vanish, leaving me with a sweet warmth that is so unexpected in the cold presence of my ex.

# FORTY-FOUR

## 4 SLEEPS UNTIL CHRISTMAS

### NICK

I'm so fucking over this jackass and the woman he clearly manipulated and used to continue his hold on Shae and the girls long after they were out of his life.

*My wife.*

Those two words on that man's lips make me fucking twitchy.

I didn't miss the hurt in Molly's eyes when he said it, masked by anger, or the way Shae's body tightened with his declaration.

But acknowledging any of it is letting him win.

"She's not your wife and this is not your family," I say, moving so Shae is behind me. "And I'm done with you getting some kind of sick joy by intimidating her. Shae, go inside. Make sure the girls are in their rooms, call the police, then text Damien."

"Nick—" I start because I don't want him out here alone.

"Shae, go do what I said, sugar. I've got this."

"Nick, I—"

"Now." My voice is firm, no room for argument, and she knows it. She feels it.

And she accepts it when her hand loosens from mine and the door behind me opens then clicks closed.

Then it's me and this fuckwad who threw away the three most amazing women on this planet but, even now, wants to rule them, and another woman he's manipulated and gaslit to believe he's worth anything more than a passing glance.

"Look, man, I don't know what kind of bullshit she's spun, but—" He tries the *man to man, aren't women crazy* shit, but that won't fly with me.

"I'm not your man and I'm not the *kind* of man you fuck with. What I do know is you put your hands on Shae and she left you before you did the same to those girls." He opens his mouth to argue and I see a quick flash—almost imperceptible—of shock on Molly's face, but I don't slow. "And before that, you spent years hurting her with words, with your control. You wore her down until she didn't know who she was and then once you were gone, she built up a wall ten feet high to keep herself and those girls safe. I've spent time—lots of it, time I would spend over and over and over again, I should note— trying to get her to trust me, and I'm not going to let you come in and fuck that up."

"You have no right—"

"Neither do you. Fortunately for me, the right to be in her life was given to me by Shae. You can't say the same."

"The fuck—" The door opens once more and her small hand touches my lower back before her soft voice speaks.

"They should be here in a few seconds. An officer was already nearby," Shae tells me. "Damien wants a report filed."

"Good. The girls?"

"Asleep, I think," she says.

"This is ridiculous," Todd says with irritation, but just then, a police car pulls up. Shae's shoulders relax instantly.

"We were told there was a disturbance?" an officer says, stepping out of his car.

"This man is harassing his ex-wife. We'd like to file a report," I say.

"No need, officers, I'm on my way out," Todd says, like this was a minor inconvenience. The officer walking toward us pauses, looking to me, then Todd, then Nick who looks like he wants to murder my ex in cold blood, to Molly who looks not nearly as smug as she did a few minutes ago, then back to me.

"Absolutely not," I say before anyone else can speak. "We need a record of him coming here, of him harassing Shae."

"I don't think that's necessary," Todd says, suddenly taking on a good ol' boys demeanor. He slides into it like a second skin and for a moment, I can see who Shae thought she was getting, who Molly is defending.

"I disagree," I say.

"What's going on?" the officer asks.

"I'm just coming to a building I own, officers," Todd says with a small smile, a bomb he's been holding onto tightly falling from his grip. Shae's hand tightens in mine.

*A building I own.*

The words echo as I try and grasp onto them, to understand.

"What?" Shae asks, her voice alarmingly small.

"What the fuck does that mean?" I ask.

"You've gotten notices, right, Sharon?" The name sounds wrong even though I know it's her full name. In this man's voice, it sounds like a dig, a painful reminder of a past life. "The building was sold. You're to vacate by January 31st."

*No fucking way.*

"I'm the new owner," he says, his sick smile widening.

"Jesus fucking Christ," I murmur.

"So, I'm not trespassing, you see, officers. I'm simply checking in on my property."

"But he's not," I say, forcing my mind to clear, to process and move forward. Shae's hand has gone limp in mine, but I don't let go. "He came to harass his ex-wife."

"This is your ex-wife?" the officer asks.

"Technically, yes." Like a divorce is just a technicality. This fucking guy.

"But you own this place?" The officer is trying to put pieces together, same as we are.

"Call Damien," I say to Shae, eyes locked on Todd.

"What?"

"Call Damien. Ask what we should do."

"Nick, I don't—" I watch her process all of the arguments—probably something about it not being a big deal, not wanting to bother him, not wanting to be a burden—and with pride, I watch them all fail. "Okay," she says then dips back inside while the officer tries to understand what's happening.

It's a long hour later, after we talked with Damien, who ensured we get a police report, and the police decided that, for the time being at least, Todd had to leave and come back with some kind of proof he owns the building, since the address on Shae's license stated she lived here and his did not.

By then, the girls are fast asleep and I can't help but wonder if they heard anything at all or if we dodged that bullet. Either way, they're going to need to wake up in a few minutes.

The idea that had been formulating all day today comes to a head, becoming something more concrete, something more necessary.

"Pack your stuff," I say, tipping my chin to Shae after I lock the door of the townhouse.

"What?" she asks, that determination and stubbornness kicking in as she crosses her arms on her chest.

"I said, pack your things. Clothes for a few days, whatever gifts and shit for the girls."

"I don't—" Her brow is furrowed and in her eyes, it's clear she's ready to fight, but I don't have it in me.

I lay it all out on the table. I grab her face between my hands and speak low.

"You're going to get clothes for a couple of days, grab all of the gifts for the girls, and we're going to pack them into my truck. Then you're going to wake the girls up and tell them we're going on an adventure. Tomorrow's a half day, so they won't miss much. Then you'll spend Christmas with me at the ranch. You were going to anyway."

She opens her mouth, ready to argue even though she has to know it *makes sense,* even though they were planning to come tomorrow afternoon, but I cut her off.

"I don't trust him, not until we have something concrete in place. I don't like that he owns this place, don't like that he's been keeping tabs on you. I don't feel like you're safe. I know you like to be in charge and this is scary and the opposite of that, but I'm hoping you'll give me this. That you'll gift me this peace of mind, the gift of knowing you're safe, under my roof."

She stares at me for long heartbeats, and I can see it on her face, her trying to separate and organize all of her emotions before she finally speaks.

"Okay, Nick," she whispers.

# FORTY-FIVE

## 3 SLEEPS UNTIL CHRISTMAS

### SHAE

Nick presses his lips to my forehead early in the morning, the sun not even up, and even though *morning person* has never and will never be a part of my personality, I can't help but smile.

We got to the ranch late last night after packing everything we needed for a few days into my car. We also stealthily packed up all of the gifts for the girls into Nick's truck without them seeing.

*It's a fun sleepover!* I told the girls. *We're going to have Christmas at the ranch!*

Harper was instantly excited and rambling about seeing the barn cats every day, about being able to say *Merry Christmas!* to them and the chickens and sleeping in her room at the ranch and being at the *center* of Christmas magic.

But, of course, Ruby had heard Todd at the door.

She heard Nick whispering to me as I tried to keep it together and saw the red-and-blue lights as the police took my statement at Damien's request. He's filing a last-minute restraining order and is wildly mad at me for not telling him about the prior contact attempts Todd has made, but both Damien and Nick assured me this was the end.

Because even though we've had no contact with him as per our agreement in almost a year, Todd has been dating a woman at the girl's school seemingly with the sole intent of keeping tabs on us. It's why for the last year, Ruby's had a hard time with Catherine and why her mother always gave me dirty looks. I always thought it was because she was just a fucking bitch, but it turns out it's because her fiancé, my ex-husband, would never stop asking her questions about me and it made her hate me *and* my children.

All that to say, in the new year, I will be widening my search for a new place since I have no tie to Hudson City anymore. The girls will keep going to that school until I can transfer them to a new school system, but there's no way we're keeping *any* potential tie to Todd.

"Morning," he whispers as my eyes flutter open. "I have chores to do. You go back to sleep. Just wanted to say goodbye."

"One more minute," I murmur, my arms reaching out from under the covers to wrap around his neck. He chuckles.

"I wish I could stay. I have a few things to do though."

"Mmm," I mumble again but don't let go. He laughs, the feel rumbling through me. Even though it's lingering, I don't give into the guilt of lying in his bed while he goes off and does work. I think that in and of itself is progress.

"Girls have gifts from the elf today," he says into my hair, and my eyes open to glare at him.

"Nick," I start, about to give him shit for spending *more* money on my girls. It seems it's all he does.

"So do you. Don't open yours in front of them though, okay?"

That has me waking up a bit more, releasing him and sitting up, pulling the blanket with me to cover my naked body.

"What?"

His smiles wide.

"Wait until you're alone. We'll play tonight."

"What does that mean? Play?" His smile goes impossibly wider.

"Gotta go, sugarplum," he says.

"I hate that name," I grumble as he leaves the bed.

"You're a terrible liar, Shae," he whispers then bends to kiss me once more before reaching for his jeans. Once he's dressed, he moves, grabbing my hand and pressing it to his lips. "Go back to sleep, baby."

And then he's gone, and even though the bed is a bit colder without him, I sleep well in the warmth of him.

The girls are jumping off the walls with excitement at the idea of starting winter break early *and* spending the holiday here at the ranch. When they wake up, I roll out of Nick's bed, throw on some comfy clothes, and go see them in their room here. They zoom past me with the seeming confirmation that it's an appropriate time to be awake, shouting when they find the elf on the kitchen table, sitting with a small stack of gifts. They're even more excited when they find another new set of pajamas, the fancy (read: too expensive for kids who will grow out of them in a month) kind with buttons and lacy edging, and a set of little crafts to keep them busy this morning while I sip coffee and attempt to wake up.

They, of course, bug me, begging me to open the third box with my name on it, but despite him telling me while half asleep, I refuse.

But once they're preoccupied, I sneak back to Nick's room and tear open the wrapping to find . . .

Rope.

Rope?

At least, it looks like rope. It's black and cottony, smooth and a bit stretchy.

I take a photo and send it to Nick.

> What is this?

He replies near instantly.

> Rope.

I sigh. He's such a fucking *man* sometimes.

> Yeah, I got that. Why is there rope in a box for me? And why couldn't I open it in front of the girls?

> Didn't want you to have to explain that I'm going to use it tonight to tie you to my bed and have my way with you.

Heat suffuses my body, rolling through me in waves. My mouth drops open and images flit through my mind, daydreams I've ignored coming to the front of my consciousness.

> What?

> We'll talk tonight, sugar.

> Nick.

> Nick!

> Don't ruin the surprise, Shae. Tonight.

And I don't have it in me to keep bugging him or to ruin his surprise, so I slide the box into an empty drawer and go into the kitchen to make cookies with the girls.

# FORTY-SIX

## 3 SLEEPS UNTIL CHRISTMAS

"So about this . . . rope," I say later that night, after the girls are asleep at Nick's place. I've been distracted all day, barely able to focus as I sat on the couch and watched Christmas movies with them, finished the crafts the elf left, and inevitably cleaned up Nick's place a bit.

I was even more distracted when Nick got back after a day of doing God knows what, kissing me as if he didn't leave a package that was burning a hole in my mind all day before going off to shower. And I stayed distracted through dinner and movies and the bedtime routine.

And now we're here, in Nick's room, the soft fabric in my hands.

"So this . . . is rope," he says, grabbing it from my hands. "You mentioned it last week, when you weren't feeling well."

"Oh my god," I say, embarrassment filling me. I remembered that, but I was in a weird fugue state and sure it was all in my head. A dream.

And now he's holding rope to . . .

"No, no," he says, grabbing my hands. "No. We don't do that here. Shae, when you said you wanted to know if you'd like to be *fucking tied up,* I had to fight going hard right then and there. So no, we're not doing the embarrassed thing. Shit like this? It doesn't work if you're embarrassed."

I roll my lips into my mouth, contemplating thoughts and ideas and responses, but instead, I go with something very different.

"So, how does it work? The whole . . . tying me up thing." He smiles wide then walks over to where I'm sitting on the bed.

"There's a lot of things we can do with it. A lot of different ways I can use this on you." His fingers are warm as they grab my wrist. "I could tie your forearms to your thighs, like this." His fingers hold my wrists gently to my knees and he smiles.

"Hmm." My breathing is already getting heavy.

He's taking any semblance of control.

*I give it willingly.*

I remember the first time with him, when I begged him to take over, to use me after he tried sweet and gentle when I wanted *anything but.*

"Could tie your hands behind your back or to your feet." Images and options flit through my mind, google searches I inevitably made once I found the rope in that box, once my mind started to spin, thinking of what he might be planning with it.

"But I think this time—"

"This time?" I ask, interrupting. His smile, like a wolf who just found his next meal, makes me clench in anticipation.

"This goes the way I think it will, sugar, we'll be doing this a lot."

"Oh," I say. I can barely get a breath into my lungs, nerves and anticipation and desire burning in my veins. He sits next to me, his face going soft and serious.

"But if you don't, that's fine too, Shae. No big. This is all about playing, experimenting. Seeing what you like, what I like, what we like together."

*What we like together.*

I like the sound of that so much more than I would ever have thought. He moves then, standing between my spread legs as I sit on the edge of his bed, holding my hands in his and staring at me, clearly intent on me understanding what he has to say.

"But before I do anything, I need you to know I'm not *taking* control from you. You're giving it to me." I furrow my brows tighter, wholly confused on the difference.

"Isn't that the same thing?" I ask, and he shakes his head.

"No. It's very, very different and I need you to know that from the start. This? This is a gift for me. You're gifting me with your *trust* and I take that incredibly seriously. You say stop, control goes back to you. There's a pair of scissors on the bedside to cut you free quickly if you need it, if it's too much, if something doesn't feel right. You—"

"You don't need to give me the whole speech, Nick." I say, dying to get this moving, my chest rising and falling rapidly.

"I do," he says, pushing my hair back. "I do. That's how this works. This is not . . . This is not playtime, fun experimentation, shits and giggles. You are my priority. Your safety? Mentally, physically? It comes before *anything*. This is serious to me and I need you to know I'm taking it seriously. Because I . . ." He lets the rope slide between his fingers. "I do like this. I like this and I would very much like to do this with you."

My stomach flips with nerves and excitement.

"Oh," I say, a blush creeping over my cheeks. "So you've . . ."

"I've tied a woman up and fucked her before, yes. You spend a good chunk of your life tying knots, you get ideas. I got ideas, and I did my research, and I learned I like it. But if you don't? That's cool too." He smiles that boyish smile I could easily fall for. "There's a whole world we could explore. I just want to explore it with you. But right now . . ." He pauses, his face going serious. "Right now, I'm trying to gauge if you want *this*." He lifts the ropes again and I stare at it, weighing my options.

I don't have to, though. Not really.

"I want to . . . I want to try," I whisper, and he groans against my lips.

"You're perfect, you know that?" And then he's on the bed next to me, his hands going to my face and pulling me in for a long, sweet kiss that turns into something else quickly. It's reverence and adoration and heat and need all wrapped in one, and as each second ticks by, with each movement of his lips tasting mine, his hands explore my body, building heat.

It doesn't take long before I'm on fire, burning with need to feel him, to touch him.

As always, he knows what I need. Slowly, he begins to peel off my clothes, starting with the pajama shirt I have on, unbuttoning it with more restraint than I could muster with my shaky hands, his rough fingers grazing smooth skin as he pushes it off my shoulders, quickly followed by my bra.

"Beautiful," he whispers, and I shiver as he dips, taking a nipple into his mouth like he can't help himself.

"Nick," I whisper.

"Patience," he tells me, his hand sliding down to my hips, taking my pajama pants off. He presses one sweet kiss to my hip before gently pressing me to the bed, telling me to lie there without words.

And then he's grabbing my present.

Carefully, he ties one end of the rope around my wrist before securing it on his sturdy bed frame, the rustic wood I admired when I first came here. He does it with precision and care, caressingly skin before tying, tugging to make sure it's secure, peppering kisses across my naked body throughout.

A peaceful, caring contrast to how my brain told me this all should feel.

When he's done, when my hands are secured, he steps back to take in his handiwork, satisfaction clear on his face.

I tug on one wrist, then the other. "This is way cooler than a lasso," I say with a laugh, then I try to cover my face, embarrassed, only to remember I *can't*. Instantly, a ripple of heat rips through me at the realization. "That was stupid. Ignore I said that." I laugh.

"No, I agree. This?" He plucks at the rope I've pulled tight. "Much cooler than a lasso. You know, I've tied a lot of knots over the years for work. This, though? This is my favorite." He runs a rough finger up my side, almost tickling me as he goes from my hip to my ribs to my breasts, pinching one without warning. My back arches and a small moan leaves my lips. Again, I tug at my hand to grab him, to touch him, but I *can't*.

It's intoxicating.

Already, I'm understanding the incredible level of control Nick has over this situation, the power I've given him.

I've *trusted* him with.

Heat pools in my core when I thinking just how he's going to use it.

"There are a lot of things I want to do with you like this." He walks around the bed, crawling up between my legs, still fully clothed, a contrast to my nudity. "But this is absolutely first."

Again without warning, he spreads my legs with one hand and slides a finger inside me with the other before bending and covering my clit with his mouth, sucking hard. I shout at the sudden heat, at the intense pleasure cracking through me as he scrapes his teeth over my somehow—already sensitive clit, as he crooks his fingers.

It's a tidal wave of sensation that rips through me, but just as quickly, he pulls back, the pressure of his mouth on me barely even there.

I need more.

I move to hold his head to my pussy, to take what he's denying me, and I'm reminded it's not an option, my hand stopping short. Lightening shoots through me at the reminder, the loss of the control I typically hold so tightly, and his eyes look up to me, a wolfish smile on his lips.

"You're mine, Shae. You get what I give you," he says then presses a kiss to the crease of my thigh.

"Nick," I moan.

"I know." He presses another kiss to the other side. "But you have to be patient." His finger slides into me, then out, and I hold my breath, waiting for more. *Praying* for more. "God, you are a wet little thing, aren't you?" he asks, mostly to himself it seems, because when he takes that wet finger and rubs my clit, I can't speak, can't answer or argue or barter, all syllables and letters and vowels falling from my mind.

He continues to play with me, changing from a light graze to a rough press, circling my clit then sliding inside of me, fucking me gently with two fingers. He watches, fascinated, eyes clicking from my pussy to my wrists to my face, but my eyes are locked on him, staring down my body, watching him work.

"I could do this all fuckin' night, Shae. Play with you. Tease you, listen to you moan and whimper. Intoxicating. And you can't do a thing about it, can you?" One of those pained whimpers falls from my lips, my hips bucking toward him. "How are you doing, sugarplum?"

I can't see the smile I know is on his lips with those words. I don't answer though, his fingers wreaking havoc on my clit finally just enough to start to drag me up, up, up—

He stops.

"How are you doing, Shae?" His voice has gone serious and I realize this is a check in, not a taunt.

"Good, great if you'd make me come." I groan, hips bucking to try and reach his fingers.

"Eventually. In the meantime, you lie there and look pretty while I play with you." There's a laugh in his voice, and if I could, I think there's a chance I'd slap him. But then his fingers return and he's, fingering me the way he knows I like, that I need, before moving to my clit, a torturous circuit.

"What about this?" he asks, his thumb dipping into my pussy then out and down. He presses it against my asshole. "Have you ever had anything here?" The digit presses again, not entering, a tease, and I moan.

"No," I whisper, but my mind is *screaming* for him to be the first, to have him push me off that edge.

"Hmm," he mumbles, the pressure lessening then returning. A pulsing touch that has me moaning his name.

"Do it," I whisper, shocked by my own brashness. He moans with the words I don't think he expected and slowly, torturously slowly, he presses in, his thumb slowly entering me. It feels nothing like I thought, none of the pain or discomfort, but, instead, a burning heat flowing through my body. As his other hand rubs gently at my clit, I find that elusive orgasm building quicker, my hips moving to get his thumb farther into me. I need it. I want it.

I'd take more, if I thought he'd give it to me.

"Here's what we're gonna do," he says, his thumb moving slowly, almost gently rocking in my ass. My body is on fire, pleasure and the edge of discomfort mixing, every nerve ending over-sensitized with the need to come, with the lack of control, with *Nick*. "I'm gonna fuck your ass with my thumb and I'm going to eat your wet pussy while I've got my pretty girl all tied up and at my mercy. You're going to beg me to let you come and I will . . . eventually."

"Nick," I moan, his thumb sliding out then back in, my eyes drifting closed as he fills me.

He smiles.

It's a wicked fucking smile.

"And when you think you've had enough, I'm going to make you come on my face. Then I'm going to fuck you. I'm going to use you, Shae." He nips at my inner thigh and I moan. "I'm going to use you for my pleasure. You'll come too, but I'll decide when." He kisses that bite mark. "And how." He kisses the crease between my thigh and my pussy. "Does that work?" He kisses my belly. "Answer me."

"Y-y-yes," I hiss out, his thumb moving, his breath grazing my clit as he speaks right above me.

"Good girl."

And then his mouth is over my clit, sucking hard, and I scream. Pleasure tears through me, a ball of molten lava growing in my belly, twisting in on itself and growing with each scrape of his beard against my inner thighs, each press of his thumb into my ass, making me feel unbearably full as he slides two fingers of his free hand into my cunt.

"Jesus, Nick, oh god!" I moan, my head moving from side to side, and I know this is what he meant when he said to tell him if it was too much. It's not the lack of control, not the power exchange, but the fucking *teasing*. The way I'm unable to even the playing field and drive him wild with my own touch, the way I can't move his hand or his head to get him where I want, where I need. The way when his head moves up, wet lips grinning at me, I can't take my hand and press him down, can't make myself come.

It's overwhelming.

Overwhelming in the *best way possible,* but overwhelming all the same.

And when I think I might implode, when the pleasure comes tinged in pain from the lack of orgasm, I finally moan his name. "Nick," I say, the words rough and ragged. "Nick, please. God, I need to come."

He lifts his head again, staring at me, taking me in, reading me. "You want out?" he asks, his fingers stilling in me. I shake my head.

"I just want to come." I moan. "I *need* to."

He smiles, and I panic for a moment, but then his smile turns into a look of determination and his head drops.

His mouth latches onto my clit, sucking hard as one hand fingers my ass, the other in my pussy, and his eyes look up at me over my body.

It feels like permission.

I take it as such and my body arches, one leg hooking over his back as I scream his name, coming harder than I ever thought was possible.

"Fuck, fuck, fuck, fuck," I mumble and scream, one orgasm rolling into a second, even more intense one as he continues to eat me before, after what seems like an eternity, he stops.

My body is still on fire, and it only ratchets up when he stands and starts to undress himself, cleaning his hands on the tee he slips off before stepping out of his loose sweatpants.

"I'm gonna fuck you now, okay?" he says as he stands before me, his breathing heavy, his cock bobbing before him, the tip wet with precum the thumb that wasn't in my ass is expertly rubbing in. I glare at him in a haze. As if I would say no. As if I'm not dying to have him inside of me, not already back on the edge he just pushed me off of.

"God, you look really fucking pretty like this," he says, kneeling between my spread legs and taking me in like we have all the time in the world. "Next time, though, you're on your belly, hands tied behind your back." His hand moves, brushing my hair back as he likes to do then putting his thumb, wet with precum, into my mouth. "Maybe I'll fuck your face before I fuck this pretty pussy." I take his offering, licking and sucking, dying to give him a shred of the pleasure he's given me. "That way you can suck me off, all tied up and at my mercy." I moan around his finger. "Yeah, something tells me you'd like that."

He takes his hand back, moving until he's kneeling before me on the bed, all broad shoulders and lean hips and too fucking handsome for his own good.

For *my* own good, if we're being honest.

It moves in a blur, the next minute. His hand is on his cock, pumping as he looks at me, as he rubs the head against me, and I can't stop my eyes from looking at his face. I'm in a trance he put me in, one only he can break, and slowly, so fucking slowly, painfully slowly, he slides inside of me.

One inch in, half an inch out, a tease that goes on for decades and centuries, a torture I need to stop and never want to end. And when he slides all the way in, he stops and stares at me.

I'm breathing heavy, every few breaths coming out in a moan as I tighten around him, his hand moving up and down my side then up to my hands, fingers gently touching at the ties at my wrists.

"Good?" he whispers.

He'd stop.

He'd stop and pull out and go to sleep, cock hard and body unfulfilled if I asked him to. He'd do anything for me.

"Perfect," I whisper.

He groans, the sound low and loud, and I can feel it to my bones as he slides out slowly then slides back in. I'm sensitive from the way he made me come just minutes—or was it hours?—before, but that adds to it in a way.

So does the way my hands move, straps tightening once more as I try and touch him, to touch his face, to grab his ass, to make him move faster.

With each unconscious jerk of my arms, he pushes in deeper, his voice filling the room despite how quiet it is.

"Perfect," he says. My hands jerk, he thrusts in again, and my body convulses. "Perfect." Tug, thrust, quake. "*Perfect.*"

Then, between each perfect thrust, between each soul-changing slide of his body against mine, there's a kiss.

To a nipple, to my neck. To my forehead, my nose. Each kiss, each thrust, each word adds to it, adds to the pleasure overcoming my body until I'm shaking with the need to come, with the need for him to *let* me come.

But I wait.

This is his show.

This is his body.

I am his.

I know in the depths of my soul, he's going to get me there when it's time, that he'll take care of me.

Finally, he leans forward until his hands are on either side of my head, our faces just inches away from each other.

"This. This is what I wanted. Not your control, Shae, but your trust." His words, gravelly and raw and full of emotion, rocket through me, hotter than any dirty talk. My pussy clamps around him as he slides in and out of me at a fevered pace, the angle making everything so fucking tight, his thick cock sliding against sensitive nerves, my entire body short-circuiting as he locks his big blue eyes on mine.

"Thank you for giving it to me," he says through a groan, and that's it.

That's what has my body igniting, has my back arching, has a silent moan tearing through me, my mouth open as I come and come and come around him. My body continues convulsing as he slams in deep once more, filling me completely before his body goes limp on top of mine.

We lie like that until we both catch our breaths, until he slides out and I mewl at the loss. Nick shoots me a small smile over his shoulder before disappearing in the bathroom. He reappears with a washcloth and cleans me gently before he unties me, helping me stand and walking me to the bathroom before carrying me back to his bed and holding me all night.

He might think my trust was a gift for him, but him teaching me how to give it was the real gift.

# FORTY-SEVEN

## 2 SLEEPS UNTIL CHRISTMAS

Nick's morning scruff scratches my neck as his lips press there, waking me up, and I sigh.

I'm quickly getting too used to this, too obsessed with waking up in Nick's bed, in Nick's arms, and feeling him pressing kisses to my skin.

It definitely beats an alarm clock, that's for sure.

It seems a lifetime of waking up before the sun to get the animals ready for the day means Nick's internal alarm has *no concept* of sleeping in.

I hum a sound of contentment as his lips move down, over my bare shoulder, and he pushes my wild bed hair aside, and I wonder if we'll have time for a quickie this morning. Last night was spectacular, and my body aches in the best way, but that doesn't mean I'm not up for . . . more.

Until my thoughts come crashing in and I realize we went *right* to sleep after cleaning up last night, which means . . .

"The fucking elf," I whisper, hearing the girls giggling in the room down the hall.

"What?" Nick asks, his lips on my collarbone now, but I can't bask in the beauty of that because of my *arch fucking nemesis*. I push him off, sitting up while holding the blanket to my chest.

"The stupid fucking elf. You didn't move it last night, right?" He groans and rolls to his back.

"No, I was kind of preoccupied." His smile is wide, and I smack him on the shoulder. "Can't we ignore it?"

"We're in this predicament because of *you*, mister. You better get your ass up and move it. The girls are up."

"Are they?" He tugs my arm until I'm on my back again, and I fight the urge to snuggle into the warm, cozy blankets.

"Yeah, I can hear them giggling with each other. Probably scheming to sneak out and find that stupid fucking elf." He tries to listen for them nearly across the house and clearly fails.

"How do you know?"

"I can hear them a mile away. It's a mother's curse." He smiles, rolls over until he's hovering over me, and presses his lips to mine again.

"Alright, sugarplum." I roll my eyes, but it's halfhearted. "Here's the plan. I get pants on, run to move him. You go to the girls, distract them. Teamwork makes the dream work and all that. Deal?" He presses his lips to mine again and warmth fills my belly at the ease of this.

This is what I thought it would be, back when I was young and delusional and marrying a man so very wrong for me.

"Deal," I whisper, the lump in my throat aching. He moves to stand but must somehow see it, see the ache in my eyes.

"Go team," he whispers then finally rolls out of the bed, grabs a pair of sweats, and tugs them up, leaving them riding low on his hips. God, he's fucking delicious. He smiles a wicked smile when he sees me staring before pointing at me, then toward where girls' room is, tipping his head in a *come on* kind of move. I groan, standing and pulling on his shirt he hasn't put back on.

That wicked, wicked smile grows.

Jesus.

Illegal. He should be illegal.

"Go team," I whisper after tugging my panties up, the tee covering my ass and then some. It's fine either way. I'll just be going to the girls and then coming right back. He wraps an arm around my waist, tugging me close and pressing his lips to my head.

"Like being on your team, sugar," he whispers, and then we both go on to play this new game.

# FORTY-EIGHT

## 1 SLEEP UNTIL CHRISTMAS

On Christmas Eve morning, the bed is cold, Nick having left early once more to go do *I don't know*, kissing me gently before telling me to go back to sleep. It isn't until I'm sipping coffee at Nick's kitchen table, the girls eating rainbow bagels Nick got at *some* point, that I open my phone and scan my emails.

One in particular piques my interest and makes me sit up straighter.

The subject line reads: *Necessary apologies.*

The sender is Molly McGee.

My hands shake as I stare at it, confusion and intrigue mixing in my stomach as I tap the message to open it and begin reading.

Dear Shae,

I've tried writing this a few times since the other day, but each time, I couldn't for the life of me figure out how to start it, so I'm going to start with the most important part: I am so incredibly sorry for how I've treated you in the past.

A lot of things have become blatantly clear to

me in the past few days and I feel like, in a way, despite how horribly I treated you, you saved me from a future I know you've unfortunately already experienced, and for that, I'm unbearably grateful.

While it doesn't excuse how I've acted, I would like to give you an explanation. Todd was my high school sweetheart and my first everything. I was so deeply in love with him, and when we went away to college, he insisted on going on a break. I was heartbroken but accepted, and when I found out you two had met and were marrying, I was so hurt. He had spun stories to me of a future and in my young, naive eyes, you were stealing that from me.

A few years ago, he was picking the girls up from school and we saw each other and reconnected. I heard so many stories, Shae, and he was *so convincing*. He told me about how manipulative you were, how your marriage was in trouble, and I was in a vulnerable place and so fucking stupid that I fell for it.

When you separated and divorced, the story became larger, him telling me you were actively keeping him from his children, that *you* were abusive to *him*, that you were a narcissist and that the courts took your side in things. I thought I was in love, and whoever did Todd wrong was now my enemy.

I hated you, Shae, for, what I thought was taking Todd's children away from him and for turning everyone and everything he knew away from him. And before that, I hated you because you had what I thought was supposed to be mine. And that hatred grew as more and more, you became the only thing he would talk about.

Over the past year, he would ask about you incessantly, about your daughters, and I'll admit, it made me resent you. It's no excuse, but I was so lost in him, so manipulated and blinded by him, that I believed him, and when he asked me to keep him updated on you, I did.

The other night, the veil fell and I saw everything for what it was. I saw how much I was being manipulated, how Todd had been using me to continue his control on you without either of us knowing. I feel so incredibly stupid, and while I know it's not an excuse, I wonder if maybe you, of all people, would understand the hoops I forced myself to jump through to make myself believe him.

All of this to say, I am so incredibly sorry. I wish there were more I could do to tell you just how sorry I am.

Anything you need, please, let me know. I have over a year's worth of documentation of him asking me to keep an eye on you and your daughters, of him asking me questions about you and the lies he tried to spread. I'm happy to send them to your lawyer if needed.

I know this is no excuse for my behavior, but I was told a much different story than what I'm learning to be reality. I would love to get together, have coffee, and apologize to you face-to-face. Catherine also owes Ruby an apology.

Merry Christmas, Shae.

-Molly McGee

"What's wrong?" A voice from behind me asks, pulling me out of the fog of reading Molly's email a third time. "Shae, sugar, what's wrong?" I look over and Nick is kneeling before me, grabbing my hands, his face one of concern. I look to the kitchen table to see the girls staring at me with confusion and concern, and then I feel it.

Tears.

Tears are running down my cheeks from this letter and the peace it's brought me.

I look to Nick, another source of unexpected peace, and hand him my phone before giving the girls a weak smile. "All good, finish your breakfast," I say. They look to me then Nick before slowly returning to their food. Nick reads while I think.

I've spent years thinking I was an idiot for falling for Todd's narcissistic bullshit, but in a way, this is confirmation that he is good at what he does, at manipulating things and confusing them until you fall for his bullshit, the vicious cycle pulling you deeper and deeper into his control with each argument.

In a way, this is a gift. An unexpected gift from an unexpected ally.

"I still don't fucking like her," Nick says, handing me my phone back.

"I've been her," I say. "In a way, she just gave me closure I didn't realize I needed. It . . ." I pause, trying to figure out how to explain. "I thought I was just naive and stupid all this time. That I should have seen him for who he was from the beginning, but everything in this letter?" I point to my phone. "It's the same. It's not that I was stupid. It's that he's really good at what he does."

"And you're crying because . . ." Nick's voice is low and hesitant. "Because she gave you that confirmation?" I nod then use a napkin to wipe my cheeks. "I still don't like her."

I laugh, a smile taking over my face.

The smile feels free and so do I. Like a giant weight was lifted from my shoulders, one that's been there for years.

"You don't have to. I don't know if I do, but I know that I understand her." I sigh then stand, Nick doing the same. "Are you in for a bit? I have a call to make."

"I came in because I'm done for the day." I reach up and wipe at a splotch of dried white paint on his cheek. "Go. Make your call." He leans forward and presses his lips to mine before I grab my phone and walk toward Nick's room.

"Hey, Molly?" I ask into my phone when she answers. "It's Shae. Do you have a minute to talk?"

# FORTY-NINE

## 1 SLEEP UNTIL CHRISTMAS

"Are they sleeping?" I ask as Shae walks back into the living room, the tree (and the ornaments the girls brought from their place) shining bright in the dim lights.

She sat on the phone for over an hour with Molly, talking about Todd and the ways he manipulated both of them and making plans to meet up in the new year. Then she sent the email to Damien along with more information she was given.

Shae called the email a gift and while I don't necessarily like the woman, even I can be grateful for the additional firepower behind the restraining order Damien Martinez will be filing.

But now, it's time for the magic to start.

She nods. "Ruby's snoring., Harper is all twisted in her sheets. Neither of them even flinched when I went in."

"So we're in the clear?" She smiles and opens up the hall closet where I put all of the things she brought from her place.

"Yup," she says, then she starts grabbing boxes and putting them under the tree. According to Shae, the way they do Christmas is only one gift and their stocking is from Santa—the rest is from their mother or family or friends or each other. Two medium-sized gifts are wrapped in what Shae called *Santa paper,* and all of the stocking fillers are in the same wrapping. The rest are either in pink for Harper or purple for Ruby. *This way I don't have to worry about tags,* she told me as I watched her wrap the other night at her place.

"Where should I put these?" she asks, lifting the two stockings she made for the girls. I know they were the bane of her existence, but they came out beautiful, and the girls are going to be excited to see them.

"If you want them hung, I've got stocking holders. But if they're gonna be heavy..." My eyes dip to the shopping bags filled with small, wrapped gifts, and I smile. "Maybe just lay them on the couch." She checks her options and weighs the bag with her hand before deciding on the couch.

She told me last week her worst habit is buying gifts for the girls randomly while she's out and then having to buy more to even it out so one daughter doesn't have more than the other. When I asked her why she didn't just return things or save them for another time, she just shrugged.

"They're good girls," she said. "They deserve the world. I can't give them the world, but I can give them a good Christmas. This year, I can afford it, so I'm going for it." It made sense to me. I remember some Christmases, Connor would get more gifts than any one kid should, and others, when things were tighter, he wouldn't. I remember the joy of watching his face every time, and I can't argue with her.

I watch her slowly go through the gifts, sorting them into piles for Harper and Ruby's stockings before moving to my room, opening the closet I rarely use, and grabbing a stack of gifts. The wrapping is much worse than Shae's precision, but it's the thought that counts, or whatever. As I walk with them in hand towards the living room, placing them under the tree, her hands pause, and she *glares* at me.

"What is that, Nicolas?" she asks, venom in her voice. I pretend not to know what she's saying, furrowing my brow as I walk back toward my room.

"Don't know what you mean," I say, then leave to grab the next stack.

Okay, so I also went overboard, spending my downtime scrolling on websites and *adding to cart* liberally anytime I saw something the girls or Shae might like even a *little bit*.

"Nicolas!" she says when I walk to the tree with my second stack. I set it down and look at her with a smile.

"Sharon."

"Ew, don't call me that. I much prefer *sugarplum*."

"That's because you love being called sugarplum."

"I absolutely do not," she lies, and I just smile. "Please tell me that's it."

"Don't want to start this holiday on lies, babe."

"Nicolas!" I walk back towards the room I came from. "Nick!"

"You set up the girls' stockings. I'll worry about my shit." I walk back toward her and grab her face in my hands, pressing my lips to hers gently. "I want you three to have the world. A little Christmas shopping won't break my bank, baby, but it will make my fuckin' day to watch the girls squeal as they open gifts, top watch you smile as you do."

"But I don't—" The guilt in her eyes finishes her sentence for me.

"I have everything I need. Now go fill the girl's stockings," I say, then press my lips to hers and walk off. When I return with the last of my shit in hand, she's setting up one of the crochet stockings, pink, so it's Harper's, Ruby's already sitting there, little wrapped gifts spilling out.

"Looks good," I say, then move to the end of the couch, pulling out what I need and beginning my own stocking stuffing.

Silence is behind me, and I try to ignore it before she finally breaks.

"What is that, Nick?"

"What is what?" I ask, even though I know exactly what she means.

"What you're holding?"

It's red and yarn and horribly ugly, but...

"Your stocking."

She doesn't speak, and I continue doing what I am doing, putting little trinkets and candy and junk she probably doesn't need or want into the disastrous stocking I made her before finishing and turning to look at her.

"What?" I ask like I have no idea why she's looking at me.

"You said..." She clears her throat, her face a mask of so many emotions, I couldn't read them all if I had the time before she tries again. "You said it was my stocking?" Her eyes move from my face to my hands to the stocking propped on a pillow behind me.

"Yeah," I say, then stand, moving boxes around under the tree, hiding the gifts Shae got them from Santa, along with a few gifts I want them all to open last.

"Nick," she says, and I turn to her. Her green eyes are wide and shining and shit. That wasn't the plan. "Did you . . . Did you make that?"

"I mean, I sure as hell didn't pay for that ugly thing."

"It's not ugly," she defends. Both of us look at the hideous red stocking, holes and pulled threads, thinner spots and thicker, and the top half that's a different shade of red because I couldn't' remember the type I got the first time. "It's beautiful."

"It's hideous, Shae."

"You made it." Finally, I sit next to her.

"Yeah. I made it."

"For me."

"Knew the girls were getting theirs. You should have one too."

She stares at me for long, long minutes, breathing, thinking, processing, and I let her.

I give her space to think through everything, but I do it holding her hand, so small in mine, so soft compared to my work-roughened ones.

Finally, she speaks.

"I wish I met you first," she whispers.

"What?"

"I wish I had met you first, that you were the girls' father. That I could give you everything without all of my . . . baggage. That you were here first." I shake my head and use a thumb to brush under her eye where a tear has fallen.

"I don't," I reply, and she furrows her brow, confused.

"What?" I hold her face inches from mine and tell her the truth.

"I don't wish you met me first. If you did, you wouldn't be the woman I'm falling for. The girls wouldn't be here. We wouldn't be us. I'm glad I met you when I did. I'm sorry you had to go through hell to get here, wish that never happened, but you met me when you were ready for me," I say. Her eyes start to water, and when one tear falls, I quickly brush it aside with a thumb. "None of that."

"You can't be this sweet and not expect me to cry, Nicolas Finch," she says with a sniffle.

"I guess I'll have to make an exception for happy tears then, Shae. But only happy tears from, here on out," I say.

"Okay. Only happy tears."

Her smile is watery, but her words mean everything.

They mean there is a here on out.

And I'll fight to make them all happy.

# FIFTY

"OH my GOD!" a voice shouts from down the hall before the sun is even up.

I groan.

"HE CAME!" another shouts, and I know we've got approximately thirty seconds before the girls come rampaging in here.

"Morning," Nick says, his voice gruff and hot.

No one should sound that hot this early in the morning.

His hand moves, grabbing my chin and tugging my face out of his chest, so I look at him. He leans in, pressing his lips gently to mine.

"It's too early," I grumble.

"It's Christmas," he whispers.

"MOM! SANTA CAME!" Harper shouts, her feet pounding on wood floors, coming toward Nick's room.

"Merry Christmas, sugar," Nick whispers. Heat fills me. Heat and joy and happiness and everything good as his lips press against mine again, soft and sweet, and it's then I finally figure it out.

Christmas magic.

That's what his kisses feel like. He's a mix of childlike joy and happiness and cheer. Kissing Nick is that feeling when you wake up too early on Christmas morning, half nervous, half excited, and tiptoe to see the tree and, and the feeling that takes over when you see *Santa came!*

That's what kissing Nicolas Finch is like.

"Here's the plan," he says, my face in his hands. "You sit with the girls and, they open stockings. I'll make coffee. Once the stockings are done, we make snowman pancakes, and we eat breakfast. Then, the girls go crazy with the presents. Sound good?"

I stare at him. Confusion and surprise are taking over quickly, and I don't know the right way to combat it.

"I . . ."

"Does that work, sugar? We've got maybe thirty seconds before they break this door down." I keep staring at him, my brain not functioning, and it has nothing to do with the early hour.

It's fully because I've never had this.

*Never.*

Never had someone helping with the kids' stuff, divvying it up so we could give them the absolute best while still enjoying the day. I've never had someone who looked at me and told me which parts I would take on and how we'd juggle it together.

This is *my* Christmas gift. I don't care if there's an entire house under the tree, if there's a million dollars or a new car or diamonds. I'd trade them all to keep this.

"That works," I whisper.

The doorknob jiggles, the girls entrance foiled by a simple lock. Shaking my head, I laugh. "I guess it's time."

"Go team," he whispers, kisses me, and then rolls out of the bed to go about our plan.

Hours later, Nick hands the girls each a small box before throwing an identical one to me. Everything else is opened, a mess of wrapping paper and packaging and ribbons covering the floor of Nick's living room.

It's been a joy to watch the magic at play and to do it without worrying about following with a bag to collect trash or having to worry about getting to some party by noon.

Just a holiday morning with my little family and Nick.

"This is just something small. Something we can add onto in the future," Nick says, sitting next to me as the girls get started on their wrapping paper.

"Add onto?" I ask, shaking the small box.

"Open it up, sugar," he says with a roll of his eyes. As I gently undo the thick wrapping paper, the girls are already down to cardboard boxes.

"A bracelet!" Ruby shouts, and when I look at her, she's holding a thin silver chain, small charms hanging off.

"Me too!" Harper says.

I give Nick a look of *what did you do?* before I start opening up the box. He moves to Harper, who is struggling to put hers on, and I see it's a bracelet with three charms and space for plenty more.

There's a key charm, a horse, and a house. Obviously, the horse is Ruby, but . . .

"What is this?" I ask, touching the key charm.

"Get your shoes on, girls," he says, tipping his chin.

"What?" I ask, confused, but the girls are already standing, eager for one last surprise.

"Get your shoes on, Shae. I have something to show you."

"Close your eyes," he says in my ear as we step off the walkway in front of the house, and despite the chill that runs down my spine, I grumble.

"This sounds incredibly unsafe."

"I like it!" Harper says with a giggle. She and Ruby are both blindfolded and sitting on a sleigh Nick is tugging across the freshly fallen snow.

A white Christmas.

Finch magic, I'm calling it.

"Me too!"

"Hush, you two," I say, but I do as he asks, closing my eyes as he grabs my arm, guiding me I don't know where.

"Step," Nick says, slowing me down, and I follow his instruction, lifting my foot and stepping onto a hard step. "There's three." I follow his instructions, desperate to open my eyes when a door creaks open, but I don't. If he wants some kind of grand surprise, I'll give it to him.

"Stand here, don't open," he says, and then he's talking to the girls, lifting one and standing her next to me before getting the other.

"I'm so excited!" Harper says, and I can't help but smile.

"Okay," Nick says, his voice strangely shaky. "Now, I'm gonna preface this with a few things. One, no expectations. This wasn't some grand, difficult process so I don't want to hear it. Two, we can talk about the details another time, but not now." His words have me nervous and completely unsure of what he's talking about.

"Nick, you're scaring me."

"And three, you're not allowed to be scared," he says, a smile in his voice.

"You're an ass," I say, rolling my closed eyes.

"Mom said a bad word!"

"It's not a bad word if it's the truth," I grumble.

"God, sugar, can you please just trust in this for three seconds?" he says with a laugh, and I don't have a choice but to smile as well. "Alright, open your eyes, girls," he says, his voice low. When I do, I'm confused. I look to Nick, who is gently removing the blindfolds from the girls, before I begin looking around the small space.

There's what I assume is an unfurnished living room attached to a small but cute kitchen. There's a small table, nicked and dented but solid wood and in good condition, with four matching chairs. The living room walls are painted a comforting, buttery yellow, and the floors are a gorgeous dark wood. Just like the table, the floors are old and scuffed, like they've been there for decades, but not in a broken-down way. In a well-loved way.

"What . . . What is this?" I ask, confused. The girls look just as confused as I am, and I start to move, walking slowly, like I might bump into some kind of invisible wall. Nick's hand slides into mine, squeezing once before moving to guide me along to a small hallway with two doors. He cracks one open then reaches in to turn on a light. Inside, there are light-purple walls and a bunk bed. A small circle rug of various purples and pinks sits in the center, and when I dip my head in, there's a huge doll house with a bow on it.

"OH MY GOD!" Harper yells, running into the room and racing toward the dollhouse. "Is this mine? Please say it's mine!" she begs, and Nick laughs.

"It's yours, pumpkin."

*It's yours, pumpkin.*

The words, so fucking simple, so filled with adoration and kindness, slide through me.,

He leans against the doorframe, my hand in his still, and tips his chin toward a box wrapped in pretty purple paper with a big silver bow on top. "That one's yours," he says, and Ruby races there, ripping it off.

"Oh," she says when there's a small toy horse in the box. "It's a toy." Her voice is so clearly disappointed, that mom mode kicks in.

"Ruby Jane," I say in warning.

"There's a note beneath it, Rubygirl." She grabs a light-purple envelope and opens it, and then she's holding a small slip of paper, what looks like a photo falling to the ground., She stares at it, her little brow furrowing before reading it aloud.

"This one is yours?" she reads, her voice skeptical and confused.

"On the floor," he says, tipping his chin to the fallen and seemingly forgotten photo.

Nothing is making sense.

Absolutely nothing.

A purple room in a small house, a dollhouse for Harper, a . . . I don't know for Ruby.

None of it makes sense.

The charm bracelet on my wrist feels heavy.

A house.

A horse.

A . . . key.

The world swirls.

"WHAT?" Ruby shouts, waving a photo in the air. "She's mine?!"

"She's yours."

"Minnie's *mine!?*"

Oh my fucking god, he's insane.

He's out of his goddamn mind.

"Please tell me you did not buy a 9-year-old a fucking horse," I say under my breath, and his laugh fills the room.

"I didn't buy a 9-year-old a horse. I gifted her a horse I already had."

"It's a *horse,* Nicolas! I can barely keep the *girls* alive!"

"Oh my god, can we go see her? Can I feed her? Can I *ride her!?*" Ruby is oblivious to my mental breakdown, of course.

"Can't ride her for a while still, Rubes. She's not old enough. But you can learn on Mickey and take care of Min until then." Ruby jumps and squeals. "We'll go see her in a bit. Go play with Harp," he says, tipping his chin toward where Harper is lost in playing with the dollhouse nearly taller than she is.

"Wanna see your room?" he asks, his voice low.

"My . . . room?"

"This is your new place, Shae. If you want it."

"My . . . new place." The panic starts to build. My mind went there, of course, but I didn't actually think . . .

"Before you lose your goddamn mind, no, I barely spent anything on it. It already existed on the property. I haven't used it because I thought Conor would want it. He wants to live in the city, so it's just sitting here. This was my place, where I lived when Connor was born." The panic starts to crest because I can't accept this. I can't. It's a *goddamn house*, and—

"Before you ask, not because I want it or need it, yes, you can pay rent. I know there's no world where you'd accept this as a gift."

"I can't take this, Nick," I whisper, looking around the living room with new eyes, seeing where my couch would fit, where I'd put a television. Thinking about where Nick and I would sit after putting the girls to bed.

"You're not. I'm giving it."

"Nick—"

"You're being kicked out of your place, Shae. You can work from wherever, and neither of you three is in love with that school. Public schools in Cherrystone are great. You refuse to ask Damien for help or for a raise, and you won't touch the money Todd gives you. What are your options, sugar?"

I stand there staring at him. I had moved this topic to my *after-the-holidays* list, the freak-out churning and waiting for December 26th to come to fruition.

"This is too—"

"It's not. It's selfish." I laugh at him.

"Selfish! You don't even know what that word means, Nick. This is . . . This is too much."

He pulls me into him, moving us farther away from the room the girls are in and into the hall. "It's selfish because I don't want to drive an hour twice a day to see you. It's selfish because I want you close, want the girls close. It's selfish because the girls will have to move schools. It's selfish because it's farther from your friends and you'll have to work from home more. Which, I talked to Abbie and she said it's totally fine. She actually said she's been trying to get you to stop coming in so much, but we can talk about that another time."

"You talked to Abbie?"

"Of course I did. And Damien. I needed to obliterate any

concerns ahead of time. I also looked into how to transfer the girls. It's not hard, mostly paperwork."

"I don't understand. This is . . . This is too much. We are too new. You're going to—" He stops me before I can continue.

"I've been trying to tell you all along I want to take care of you. Fuck, we all do, but you won't let us. I just forced myself on you."

"No shit," I murmur, and he laughs.

"I want you close, Shae. I want the girls close. I want to be there if you get sick or if Rubes has a nightmare. I want to help you continue to dig out from that shield of not wanting to accept help." He pushes my hair back and I look at the small hallway, picturing the girls' school pictures hanging there. "It's mostly for me. Something happens, that's an hour it takes me to get to you. An hour too long. And here?" He points to the door, to the windows, indicating not just this little cottage but Cherrystone and Finch Farm. "Nothing gets to you here. Only one road in and out of the ranch. No one gets here without me knowing. You're safe here. I know you're safe here."

"I'm not charity," I say. "I'm paying rent." It's an acceptance of sorts, but really, who am I to say no? He's right. This place is perfect. The Cherrystone schools are known statewide to be some of the best, and here, we have a small place of our own. No noisy neighbors, no worrying about traffic or neighborhoods.

Ruby would be close to Minnie and the horses, could probably start lessons without me having to find a horse camp and sell a few organs to send her. Harper could go play with the barn cats every single day, and . . . we'd all be close to Nick.

Because even though it makes no sense, Nick is right. Somehow, us finding each other was some kind of Christmas miracle, a reward for the shit I've been through, lived through over the years.

"Yeah," he whispers. "You can pay rent." His smile is wide and warm. "If it means you're agreeing to move in, you can pay rent." I shake my head because even now, a part of me knows there's a *but* to that statement that I won't find out about until long after I've moved in.

"Mom, we *have* to stay here. I need to be close to Minnie!" Ruby says, stepping into the hall, still in her pajamas.

"I LOVE IT HERE," Harper says, even though all she's really seen of this place is a toy dollhouse.

"Can we live here? Please, Mom?" Ruby asks, her eyes wide.

I look at her.

I look at her sister.

I look at Nick, whose arm is still wrapped around my waist, a hopeful smile on his face.

I have no choice, really. So I smile.

"Yeah. We'll move here," I say with a laugh.

And then Nick grabs me, kissing me in front of the girls, who giggle and cheer, and all I can think about is how ridiculously grateful I am for that *stupid freaking elf*.

# EPILOGUE

"What are we doing?" Ruby asks, her arms crossed on her chest with a preteen attitude as we walk toward the barn. Everything with Ruby has become a pissing match, who can out attitude the other. It's normal, a desire for control while her hormones are running amuck, but it's driving her mother to the edge.

She'll always be my girl, but I swear to God, some days she's testing me. Today seems to be one of the more argumentative days, but this can't wait so I'll have to deal with it. I need to talk to the girls, and I need their help.

"Drop the attitude, Rubes." Her jaw goes tight and I smile. "You know I raised Connor, right? He was a little shit when he was your age."

"Ha ha, Nick said shit," Harper says. I turn to give her a look and fight the smile when her eyes go wide.

"What are we doing here? Ashley wants to FaceTime." I did *not* have to deal with preteen Connor wanting to FaceTime friends, though. That's a new hurdle.

"You'll have to talk to your friends later. I have a question for you both." I tip my chin to their horses. "Get on and we'll talk."

✳

"You know I love you guys, right?" I ask, and the girls look at each other, having some kind of silent sister conversation I'm not privy to, before Harper answers.

"We know, Nick." There's a quiet hesitation in her words.

"And you know I love your mom."

"Duh," Ruby says with her now-signature eyeroll.

"So, when you love someone—"

"Oh my god, is Mom pregnant?" Ruby asks, and I nearly choke on air.

"What?"

"Is she pregnant? Gianna's mom is pregnant and she told me they had this long talk with her before—" I cut her off to nip this in the bud before it's an issue I am not equipped to handle.

"NO," I say firmly. "Your mom is not pregnant. You two and Connor are more than enough for us." I watch her shoulders visibly relax and make a mental note to talk to Shae about that, about her reaction. "As I was trying to say, when you love someone, you want to spend forever with them."

"OH MY GOD!" Harper shouts, bouncing up and down in her saddle as birds frantically fly from a nearby tree.

"Jesus, Harp, chill," her sister says.

"I can't. Mom's gonna get married!" she shouts with excitement, and Ruby freezes then looks to me. I should have known there was no chance for a dignified conversation about this. I've spent the last three months planning and practicing, trying to figure out the best way to bring it up to the girls, and this was the best I could come up with.

It's been three years of year-round magic. Shae and her girls melted into my life, into life at the ranch so easily, it's like it was always meant to be. The girls transferred schools and by January, one of the barn kittens found her way into Harper's room permanently, so now we have Ginger the cat roaming the halls of our house.

The girls' first spring at Finch Farm, we found a small plot for

Ruby to plant her cut flower garden and Shae started working with me a bit, helping turn some of her ideas for more consistent income at the ranch into a reality, and now she works here nearly full-time, doing work for the nonprofit on the side.

"Are you guys getting married?!" Ruby asks, her voice squeaky.

My god.

These two are too much.

"I mean, I'm thinking about it. That's part of why I brought you two out here. I wanted to see what you think about it." The girls look to each other again, that telepathic conversation rolling once more before Harper turns to me.

"You both are basically married anyway."

"Why do you say that?" Harper starts ticking items off on her fingers.

"You sleep in the same bed every night. You live together."

This is true.

The mother-in-law cottage lasted about nine months of Shae paying rent, rent that went into a trust for the girls, before I broke her down and convinced her to move into the farmhouse with me. And before that, there were very few nights I didn't spend in her bed or they weren't having sleepovers at the farmhouse.

"And you kiss *all the time*," Ruby adds.

"It's so gross," Harper says.

"And you are always looking at her with gooey eyes."

"Okay, so, yes, I would like to ask your mother to marry me," I say before they start completely veering off course. This isn't going even near to how I thought it would.

"What's this?" Harper asks.

We've reached the same field I took their mother to on our first actual date. The same blanket is laid out but this time, the cooler is full of junk food and sandwiches I bought from the deli down the road. Italian for Ruby and the special for Harper, who now has the palate of a food critic, always open to trying new things.

"A picnic. Come on." I hop off my horse then move to Harper to help her down while her sister slides off Minnie with grace, as if she were born on a horse.

That much is still very much the same: Ruby's love for horses, the way they healed her, and her bond with Minnie.

We settle onto the blanket and I hand out food and drinks before Ruby speaks, crossing her arms on her chest and giving me the stink eye.

"So, you want to marry Mom."

"I do," I say, my gut for some reason nervous now, as if I'm speaking with a protective father instead of a 12-year-old. My mind flits to 10, 20 years down the road when some asshole boy is sitting in front of me, asking to marry Ruby, and nausea rolls through me.

Actually, let's pack that one away for another time.

"I do, but I need your help proposing." Harper claps with glee.

"Oh my *god!* This is going to be so fun! I have ideas."

*Of course* she does.

If Abbie Martinez had a mini version of herself, it would be Harper, hands down.

"Before we do any kind of planning, though, I wanted to talk to you two first."

"Why?" Ruby asks. "It's not like we'd say no or anything. You're . . . You're Nick." She says it like that explains everything, and I guess, to her, it does.

"Because I wouldn't just be marrying your mother." Silence takes over and Harper moves her fingers to the silver bracelet at her wrist, where there are now a dozen or so charms. I give them a new one for holidays and birthdays, something that means something just to us. Ruby has a flower and an equestrian helmet, Harper has a cat charm for Ginger, and Shae has . . . Well, Shae has a little lasso charm, and yes, she smacked me when she opened it right before asking me to fasten it on.

"I'd be marrying you two, of course. You're a package deal."

"Oh," Ruby says.

Butterflies float in my stomach because I'm unsure of what that *oh* means.

"Would you be open to that? To joining my family?"

"So Connor would be . . ." Harper looks at me, trying to figure it out.

"Your stepbrother."

"And you would be . . . ?" Ruby asks, touching on where I am bringing all of this, my true intention on this little picnic. I set down my sandwich and lean forward, grabbing each of their hands.

"In a perfect world, I'd be your dad, girls."

A bird chirps but no one speaks.

Both girls' near identical eyes are locked on me at once, both looking more and more like their mother by the day.

"Before I ask your mom to take my name, I want to ask you two." The silence continues and no one shouts at me, so I continue on. "You both are the most amazing girls in the entire world. I've been so damn lucky to get to know you, watch you grow, to get the opportunity to love you, to, I hope, earn your trust. *Your* love. But I want more."

"More?" Harper asks. Ruby doesn't speak, just stares at me as she bites her lip.

"I want to try and adopt you two. I know . . . I know your biological father isn't around." Harper's lip quivers and I squeeze her hand tighter.

No one talks about him, Todd not deserving the justice of mentioning him, but sometimes he hangs around like a ghost, haunting their memories. Every time I see that far-off look in their eyes, I know it's him, coming in and tainting their minds.

"I'd like to give you my name. So you'll be mine for real. You're already mine in my mind. If anything happened with your mom and me, to our relationship, you'd still be mine forever. You can't get rid of me." I swallow around a lump in my throat.

God, I practiced this so many times.

It should have been easy.

"I want you to be Harper Finch. And you"—I shift my eyes to Ruby—"to be Ruby Finch."

I don't tell them I want that because I don't want that man to have any hold on them at all. I don't tell them I want them to have my name for legal reasons or to make school pickups and doctor visits easier.

I tell them the truth.

"I want you to be mine, girls."

They don't speak for a bit, but then Ruby does.

"Forever?" she asks, and her voice cracks as she does, her eyes watering.

*Goddammit.*

I pull both of them to me, tugging hard until they're both in my lap, faces to my chest as Ruby starts to cry into my shirt.

*God fucking dammit.*

"Forever, Rubes. I want to be your dad forever. And you too, Harp."

They cry for a few minutes and I let my hands move through their hair slowly, letting them get it out, their emotions and their worries and anything else lingering, until finally, Harper sits up, followed by Ruby. Both have red eyes but both also have small smiles on their lips, which I think is a good thing.

They look to each other, that bond that's always been there almost tangible, before Ruby nods.

"Okay. Yes. We'd like you to adopt us."

"And to marry Mom," Harper finishes.

"Good," I whisper, because that's all that will work. I'll save my own emotions for a rainy day, when no one is around and I can thank whatever being put these women into my life. Whatever being made Shae date my fucking son, him invite her to Thanksgiving, and then me shove my foot in my mouth and have to make it up to her.

I need to make a shrine for that godforsaken elf.

"But only if we get to plan the proposal," Harper says with a wicked gleam in her eye. I shake my head with a small laugh, pulling them both in once more to press kisses to the tops of their heads.

"Alright, we'll be team *get Mom to say yes.*"

Ruby smiles at me. "Go team."

# WANT MORE HOLIDAY FUN?

Check out Damien and Abbie's story, Tis the Season for Revenge, my Legally Blonde inspired holiday revenge romance!

Abbie Keller thought that Richard Bartholemew Benson the Third would be her forever. In their four years of dating, she never doubted that she wouldn't end up with his grandmother's engagement ring on her finger. Sure, she had to change a few things about herself to fit that mold, like dying her hair, dressing more conservatively, and finding golf enjoyable (honestly the most difficult of the changes), but she was sure that at the end of it all, it would be worth it.

That is, until he leaves her crying outside her apartment wearing a Halloween costume, having broken it off with her because she's *just not serious enough*. She was just fun, he tells her - and now that Richard has becoming a partner at his law firm in his sights, he needs to focus on work.

So she does what every girl does when she's broken up with: she calls her friends, gets drunk, dyes her hair, and formulates her plan for revenge. It just so happens that the universe supports her efforts and gives her the perfect match to prove to her ex that he made a huge mistake: his boss.

Abbie starts dating the founding partner of Richard's law firm, Damien Martinez, with one thing in mind: convincing him to invite her to the huge annual Christmas party as his date.

But when the relationship starts to become something more than casual dating and Abbie sees that the tough New York lawyer has a soft side, will she be able to follow through with her plan of deceit?

**Read it here!**

# ACKNOWLEDGMENTS

A year ago, I bemoaned how writing acknowledgments felt uncomfortable and now, they're one of my favorite things to write. Funny how that works. But I am an incredibly codependent person, and wouldn't even get back the idea stage of any book if it wasn't for my literal *team* (who am I, with a freaking TEAM of people helping me?!) of incredible humans who help get me to the finish line.

And I want—no, *need* you all to know how amazing all of these people are.

Thank you always Alex, the person who has pushed me from the beginning, who knew how big my dreams were before I was even brave enough to whisper them, who pushes me to do things that scare me. I love you infinitely. I'm honored to be yours, to write a bit of you in all of my main characters.

Next: Ryan, Owen, and Ella. Thank you for teaching me how to be a mom so I can write one. Also, close this damn book.

Thank you to the world's best cover designer, Madi, the Jack to my Taylor. I can't believe it's only been a year since I found you and I'm forever grateful I sent you a panicked voice memo on Thanksgiving.

To Shaye, thank you for pushing me when I want to stand still and for yelling at me when I get stuck in my own head. I'll look forward to your, "I told you so," when things go crazy.

Lindsey, thank you for being there from the start. Last year we manifested my book being at a Barnes and Noble and this year you're giving me watery eyes at a *barnes and Noble signing*. (Also please stop giving me those eyes, they make me cry.) I wouldn't be here without you.

Thank you to Rae who makes sure I'm running smoothly and without having mental breakdowns. Thank you for gentle reminders when I forget something for the millionth time and for sending me chaotic texts freaking out about Noah Kahan and mommy issues.

Thank you Norma for taking my typo filled mess and adding a million commas and being kind when you confirm that my nerves are warranted but we can fix it.

Thank you to Emily, who leaves the most hilarious notes in my documents and always makes sure I'm up to date with all of the hip lingo. Thank you for coworking and listening to me work through plots.

Thank you to Lo for always doing the most when I send you the most chaotic drafts and for never getting mad when I turn my DND on and disappear from the universe.

To Rae, thank you for making sure all of the spicy parts make sense and for fan grilling over Noah and Taylor mash ups with me.

Thank you to my ARC team, the true stars of any hint of success this book will receive. You accept my crazy stories, read them, and share them with the world. I can't thank you enough.

Thank you to Booktok - yes, the whole damn thing - because without you, this would all be a pipe dream. Thank you for enduring my cringeworthy videos, finding gems, liking and sharing and reading my books. It makes me cry if I think too long about how much you have changed my life.

But most of all: thank YOU, dear reader. This past year has changed my life in ways I can't even explain, and it's all because of you. Thank you, thank you, thank you from the bottom of my heart.

I love you all to the moon and to Saturn.

# ABOUT THE AUTHOR

Morgan is a born and raised Jersey girl, living there with her two boys, toddler daughter, and mechanic husband. She's addicted to iced espresso, barbeque chips, and Starburst jellybeans. She usually has headphones on, listening to some spicy audiobook or Taylor Swift. There is rarely an in between.

Writing has been her calling for as long as she can remember. There's a framed 'page one' of a book she wrote at seven hanging in her childhood home to prove the point. Her entire life she's crafted stories in her mind, begging to be released but it wasn't until recently she finally gave them the reigns.

I'm so grateful you've agreed to take this journey with me.

Stay up to date via TikTok and Instagram

Stay up to date with future stories, get sneak peeks and bonus chapters by joining the Reader Group on Facebook!

# WANT THE CHANCE TO WIN KINDLE STICKERS AND SIGNED COPIES?

Leave an honest review on Amazon or Goodreads and send the link to reviewteam@authormorganelizabeth.com and you'll be entered to win a signed copy of one of Morgan Elizabeth's books and a pack of bookish stickers!

Each email is an entry (you can send one email with your Goodreads review and another with your Kindle review for two entries per book) and two winners will be chosen at the beginning of each month!

## ALSO BY MORGAN ELIZABETH

**The Springbrook Hills Series**

The Distraction

The Protector

The Substitution

The Connection

The Playlist

**Season of Revenge Series:**

Tis the Season for Revenge

Cruel Summer

The Fall of Bradley Reed

Book 4, Coming March '24

**The Ocean View Series**

The Ex Files

Walking Red Flag

Bittersweet

**The Mastermind Duet**

Ivory Tower

Diamond Fortress

Printed in Great Britain
by Amazon